searching for redemption

redwood coast rescue
book four

Tonya Burrows

part one
monster

"If you don't deal with your demons, they will deal with you,
and it's gonna hurt."
- Nikki Sixx

chapter
one

SOMETHING WAS DEAD NEARBY.

If not completely dead, then nearly there, judging by the condors circling in the pale, icy blue sky overhead.

Shane Trevisano shielded his eyes and watched the scavengers for a moment. Yeah, they were waiting for something to draw its last breath, meaning easy prey was close by. This winter had been rough on his supplies and he needed a successful hunt. The snowline had dropped farther down the mountain than ever before and the snow had stayed around later than usual. It was the end of March and there were still no signs of thaw. Good for the environment—lots of snow equaled lots of water equaled less chance of another wildfire in the summer—but bad for the dumbass who didn't prepare for a long, hard winter.

He picked up his pace, keeping one eye on the sky, judging from the condors' circles that he might find his prey down by the creek he used for water. As he crested a hill, he spotted the animal lying in the snow. It was smaller than he'd hoped, but still better than nothing. He raised his rifle to peer through the scope—

Fuck.

A fucking dog.

What was a dog doing all the way up here on the mountain?

Shane shouldered his rifle and skidded down the hill to study the half-frozen creature. Its ribs were visible as it heaved, and it was clearly malnourished and dehydrated. Its matted tan fur was dirty, caked with snow, and its body visibly shook from the cold. He glanced around, looking for the dog's owner even though he'd know if another human was anywhere nearby. He was as attuned to the danger of humans as he was any other predator up here, because he could always count on a cougar to act like a cougar, but humans? They were volatile, unpredictable, and terrifying.

If there was a human nearby, he'd hear them. Smell them. Sense their presence.

But he was blissfully alone, high on Mt. Humboldt, where the weather was less like a Northern California spring and more like winter in the Arctic Circle. Just him and the mutt and the condors, still circling, undaunted by his appearance next to their upcoming meal.

The dog gave a faint wag of its tail and tried to stand when it spotted him approaching. Shane paused several yards away, but the dog never gained its feet. It collapsed back into the snow with a soft, exhausted huff.

At a loss, Shane knelt down and studied it. He couldn't leave it here to freeze. That just seemed wrong, especially when it stared at him with those sad, pleading eyes. But he couldn't take it back to his cabin, either. He wasn't a dog person. He didn't know how to take care of them and, even if he did, he couldn't spare the supplies. He was running out of food himself, and his hunt today had turned up nothing but one measly squirrel.

He sighed and looked up at the white sky, hoping for some

kind of guidance. Not that the big guy upstairs had ever done much for him in the past.

The condors continued to circle.

He returned his attention to the dog, watched it struggle to breathe, then straightened and turned away. It was as good as dead already, so no point in wasting his time or energy trying to save it. He'd just let Mother Nature do what she did best. Circle of life and all that shit.

He made it two steps away when he heard it try to stand again. And, again, it fell into the snow with a soft thwump.

He stopped moving and shut his eyes.

Hadn't someone once said that same thing about him? He distinctly remembered the medic telling his teammates that he wouldn't survive his injuries, so there was no use trying. They could only give him morphine to ease his transition to the afterlife and move on to the other injured SEALs who still had a chance.

The scar tissue on face was thick and unyielding under his balaclava. He couldn't say surviving had been in his best interest. He'd be doing the dog a favor if he left it here to fall asleep and never wake up. Freezing to death was a much gentler end than the explosion that had nearly killed him eight years ago.

He took another step.

The dog gave a weak whimper.

It wanted to survive.

Fuck.

With a heavy sigh, he trudged back to the animal and scooped it up into his arms. The dog was light for its size, severely underweight. How long it had been since it had eaten? How long had it been wandering in this snowy wasteland looking for food?

It had a dirty pink collar around its skinny neck, but no tag, so it must belong to someone. Why wasn't its owner looking for it?

He trudged through the snow, the dog's head resting on his shoulder. His cabin was a mile away, but it felt like an eternity as he struggled through the drifts. It was slow going, even with his snowshoes, and the dog was growing colder by the second, shivering against his chest.

No. He would not lose the animal now.

He picked up his pace.

Finally, he made it back and kicked open the door. Since he never left the fire going while he was out hunting, it was cold inside. He set the dog down on his bed and started a fire in the wood stove with quick, practiced motions. Within minutes, heat filled the tiny space. He pulled off his wet clothes, hanging them by the stove to dry.

He looked at the dog. It watched him with exhausted brown eyes. He needed to feed it, but what did dogs even eat? Other than dog food, which he didn't have on hand. He rifled through his meager supplies and found a can of beans that had been sitting at the back of his pantry for who knew how long.

Could dogs eat beans?

No idea, but he supposed it was better than nothing.

He heated them up and mashed them into a bowl, adding some water to make a kind of soup. The dog lapped it up eagerly, its tail twitching across the blankets, then nosed the bowl when the concoction was gone.

Now what?

Shane grabbed a strip of venison jerky from his dwindling stash and offered that. The dog sniffed it, then took a dainty, gentle bite.

"You're a real lady, aren't ya?"

Man, his voice sounded rough, even to his own ears. When was the last time he'd spoken out loud? He had always been a solitary man, an introvert who preferred his own company to others, even before his life went to hell. Now, he was perfectly happy as a hermit.

Well, "happy" was a stretch. He couldn't remember the last time he felt anything close to happiness. Or sadness. Or anger. Or... anything. He just existed. He breathed. He hunted. He ate. He focused on the task of survival until he fell into an exhausted heap and slept. Then he did it all again. And he didn't need or want a companion for any of it.

He would take the dog off the mountain, he decided. That meant going to town—and he fucking hated going there—but it couldn't be helped. If tomorrow's hunt was like today's, he'd be completely out of food within the week, even if he rationed. He had to make a supply run, and the dog needed more care than he could give it.

The dog seemed to read his mind, snuggling up against his leg as if to say, *"I'm not leaving you now."*

Shane sighed and rubbed his eyes. Going into town was exhausting, both physically and mentally, but it was the only way to ensure the animal's survival. And for reasons he couldn't begin to name, it was important to him that this dog survived.

He gathered his things and packed up his ATV, hooking up the little cargo trailer he used to haul firewood and bigger game. It wasn't much—just a rusting steel box on wheels— but he tried to make a soft nest out of his sleeping bag before he carried the dog out.

The ride down the mountain was treacherous on a good day, but today the snowflakes hit like pebbles and the wind flayed any exposed skin, almost as if Murder Mountain didn't want to let them go.

Shane huddled deeper into his jacket and ducked his head against the wind.

Where the fuck was spring?

Finally, he broke past the snowline. The trees thickened, the air warmed, and the snow changed to a driving rain that was like needles on his exposed skin. It was still cold, but much milder than on the mountain.

He glanced back at the dog, surprised to find it awake and its head up. Snow crusted its muzzle and eyebrows. It had a stubborn, determined look in its eyes.

Yes, this animal wanted to live.

The ATV's wheels found the path leading to town, and more signs of civilization started popping up along the way. Unease twisted Shane's stomach into knots. It had been years since he had ventured into civilization, and the thought of interacting with other humans made him queasy. The last time he'd spoken to anyone other than himself was...

Hell, he couldn't even remember.

Two summers ago? When those two girls went missing and the sheriff and his snarky friend came up looking for them. His mountain had been crawling with searchers and he'd hated it, so he'd found the girls himself and pointed them in the right direction.

It was so much louder down here. Deafening. He couldn't even describe how, because it wasn't like there was a busy highway or city nearby. He just felt the increased presence of other humans like an itch under his skin, a static buzzing sound inside his head. Sweat broke out along his spine and he tightened his grip on the ATV's handles.

He could do this. He'd been a fucking SEAL, capable of sneaking into enemy territory without notice. He could go into this small, rural town without losing his mind. It was just another mission, like the countless operational strategies he had formulated in the field.

Objective: Safeguard dog's welfare and secure essential provisions.

Opposition: Local law enforcement. Possibly local civilians.

Infiltration: Drop the dog at the nearest vet clinic and travel to the grocery store.

Extraction: Secure provisions to last the rest of this godforsaken winter.

Exfiltration: Get the hell out of town and back to the safety of his mountain.

His teammates used to call smooth, straightforward, unchallenging missions a "milk run." But this was a literal milk run.

He *could* handle this.

As he guided the ATV out of the forest and onto a paved road, he felt like an outsider. The people in Steam Valley always looked at him with suspicion, their eyes lingering on his patchy, scruffy beard and the disfiguring scars twisting his face into something from a nightmare. He couldn't blame them. Even he didn't like to see himself.

He looked like a monster.

He *was* a monster.

There was a dog rescue right at the base of the mountain and he recalled they had a vet clinic, so he adjusted course and steered toward it, passing through the blackened scar left by last summer's fire. The rescue seemed like a safer option than the vet clinic in town. He didn't know how to deal with people anymore, and wanted to limit his contact as much as possible.

When he finally pulled into the parking lot, his hands were shaking. The rescue was bigger than he remembered, with multiple buildings and several cars in the lot despite the late hour. One of those vehicles belonged to the sheriff, who always looked at him with something between pity and suspicion.

Fuck.

Maybe he should go somewhere else...

He glanced back at the dog. It was still curled up in his

sleeping bag, but it was shivering, and now too weak to even lift its head. It whined softly.

The animal needed help now.

He took a deep breath and got off the ATV, scooping the dog into his arms. The rain was coming down harder now, soaking through his clothes and making the trek across the parking lot even more miserable. He thought he felt the eyes of people on him, their curiosity prickling at his skin, but he didn't actually see anyone around.

Hello, paranoia, my old friend.

It was his one constant companion.

Shane shouldered into the clinic, the little bell on the door jangling loudly as he entered. A bolt of panic zinged through his system. He wanted to run. He wanted to go back to the safety of his cabin, the familiarity of the mountain. The dog whimpered, and he realized he'd tightened his hold on it. He forced himself to loosen his grip.

Relax.

It was a fucking bell.

The vet's lobby looked like something out of a cartoon, with cheerful artwork and colorful paw prints painted on the walls. It was all bright and new, the smell of paint still fresh in the air.

Nothing here was going to hurt him.

Gritting his teeth, he stepped farther inside.

A woman in a white coat appeared from a back room with a tablet in hand and looked up in surprise. She was curvy, with long dark hair pulled back into a ponytail and pale skin that went paler at the sight of him. She took a step back, her hand involuntarily coming up to cover her sharp gasp. A wedding ring glinted on her finger in the too-bright overhead lights.

"I have a dog," he said, his voice sounding like gravel to his own ears. "It's sick. It needs help."

The woman hesitated, her gaze darting between Shane and

the dog in his arms. The wariness in her eyes, the way she held herself back as if afraid he might lash out at any moment, was a look he was all too familiar with, one he had seen countless times before.

But then she seemed to shake herself, her gaze softening as she focused all of her attention on the dog. She gestured to a door behind her. "Bring her back here. I'll see what I can do."

Shane nodded and followed. The room they entered was spacious, with gleaming white countertops and shiny tools lined up neatly on a tray.

"Here." The woman motioned for him to lay the dog on the stainless steel table she folded down from the wall. She set her tablet aside and placed a hand on the dog's head, stroking it gently. "Oh, you poor baby. Let me take a look at you, okay?"

Shane stepped back and watched as the vet approached with a stethoscope and began the exam. She murmured soft words to the dog as she worked, her hands gentle and sure. Then she looked up at him. He saw the shock in her eyes again, the flicker of revulsion before she hid it behind a professional facade.

Just once, he wished someone would look at him without fear and disgust.

"What happened?" she asked, all business.

He took a deep breath, trying to steady his nerves. "I found it on the mountain."

"Her," the vet said. "She's a female. Young. I'd say only about a year old, but it looks like it's been a rough year. Despite all that, she's very sweet. Good-tempered."

He preferred to keep calling the dog "it." He didn't want to know if it was abused or what its temperament was like. He didn't want to know more about it than he needed to. He just wanted to tell this woman what he knew and get the hell out of here.

"Think someone—" His voice cracked. He'd said more words in the last five minutes than he had in years. He cleared his throat and tried again. "Someone left it to die."

The vet sighed and stroked a hand over the dog's head. "It was very good of you to bring her here. Did you want to keep her, or are you surrendering her to the rescue?"

"I'm not keeping her." He strode to the door. He didn't know why he'd stayed this long. He'd done what he'd come here to do, so there was no point in sticking around, torturing himself with the vet's horrified stare and the claustrophobic walls and buzzing, too bright lights.

"We'll take good care of her," the vet said to his back.

He paused with his hand on the doorknob. He couldn't seem to turn it. "Will she—" The word "die" stuck in this throat.

"No," the vet said softly, understanding his question without further elaboration. "She won't die. Not on my watch."

"Good." He walked out, ignoring the dog's sad whine echoing off the walls behind him.

chapter
two

RUN.

It was the only thought in Alexis Summers' head, playing on a loop.

Run and live.

But her body ached from weeks of abuse and her stomach was an empty pit, gnawing on itself in hunger. He'd fed her only enough to keep her alive for his games, but not enough to keep her strong. He didn't want a fair fight. He wanted a scared, weak plaything.

And, yes, she was terrified. Yes, she was weak. But he'd underestimated her sheer stubbornness, and she knew their chase was getting as old for him as it was for her. He was losing his temper, and angry people made mistakes. So she just had to keep going. Keep staying a step ahead of him. Keep running and living until—

What?

She didn't know.

The toe of her oversized boot snagged on a rotten log hidden in the snow and she stumbled, falling hard to her knees. She gritted her teeth as pain shot up her leg.

No, she couldn't keep going like this, couldn't keep

running forever. She needed to think. Needed a plan. Needed just one goddamn second to breathe.

Choking back a sob, she sank behind the thick trunk of a downed tree and curled her knees to her chest, despite the pain. Straight ahead of her was a tree, twisted and blackened, split in half by lightning. She stared at that tree like it could give her all the answers to the universe and strained her ears for any sign of him.

The forest was silent.

Or... no.

Was that a footfall?

A boot crunching in the snow?

She looked over her shoulder, her heart pounding so hard in her chest she couldn't hear anything else. She couldn't see him. Couldn't hear him. But he was still following her. He would not let her survive, just like all the other women he'd tortured and killed. She had to keep moving, had to find some-where to hide.

The snow softened into a slushy rain, chilling her to the bone as it penetrated the oversized, bloodstained parka he'd given her before turning her loose from his bunker. She'd noticed the stains when he gave it to her and told her to dress, but now she noticed the holes as the cold seeped through them.

Bullet holes.

Oh, God.

Other women had worn this parka and died in these woods at his hands.

So many others.

And he wanted her to be the next.

She couldn't sit here any longer.

Another crunch in the snow.

Closer.

An unmistakable footfall.

He wasn't being quiet now. He wanted her to know he was right behind her.

Alexis pushed to her feet and stumbled forward on shaking legs, each step a new torture as her knee protested. She could feel it swelling. Before much longer, she wouldn't be able to bend it.

She didn't know how far she'd come, but the trees were getting thicker, the snow deeper. She was heading away from town, further up the mountain. It didn't make sense. She should go downhill.

Out of the snow.

Off of the dormant volcano the locals had dubbed Murder Mountain for the many bodies that turned up on its slopes.

But the small town nestled between the mountain's base and the wild, rocky coast was miles away. Miles of rough, dangerous terrain with thick, dark forests of gigantic trees, abrupt cliffs and all manner of four-legged predators. The snow felt somehow safer. At least with the snow, she could hear if anything approached.

Maybe there was a hunting cabin out here somewhere? Somewhere she could hide until he gave up?

No, he'd know where all the cabins are. And he'd know she'd be looking for a place to hide. He knew these woods, and she didn't. He'd find her if she tried to hide. Of that, she had no doubt.

She ran faster, her breath coming in ragged gasps as she tried to stay ahead of him. Suddenly, two shots shattered the pristine air, and she froze in terror, waiting for the blackness of death. It didn't come. He'd missed, but she swore she still tasted the metal of the bullets. She turned to keep running and then the pain hit, ripping white-hot trails through her chest and upper leg. She gasped and stumbled, slamming into a tree trunk while shock coursed through her veins. Everything became cold, wet glass, like her blood had frozen in her veins, like frostbite, like she was looking at the world through a window of ice.

He had found her.

Footsteps.

The crunch of snow beneath a heavy foot.

Coming fast now.

She pushed away from the tree and staggered. The metallic tang of blood was hot on her tongue. She choked as it filled her mouth and drizzled down her throat.

His chuckle carried on the wind.

The fucker was enjoying himself.

Alexis tried to keep moving, tried to run, but her body wouldn't cooperate. Her leg buckled underneath her, and she collapsed to the ground. The snow soaked through her clothes, and she shivered uncontrollably. She was so cold that she couldn't feel her fingers anymore. She tried to push herself up, but her arms gave out, and she fell flat on her face.

The footsteps came closer and closer until they stopped right beside her. She heard him laugh, heard him breathe heavily.

"Looks like you're not so tough after all. I was hoping for a challenge, but you're just like all the others."

She tried to speak, but all that came out was a gurgle of blood. She could barely keep her eyes open, barely keep herself conscious. She knew that this was it, that she was going to die here in the snow. She was going to be another name on his list of victims. But she refused to go out without a fight. Summoning all the strength she had left, she raised her hand and tried to reach for something—anything—to defend herself.

The man laughed again.

She grabbed a handful of snow and hurled it at his face. It hit him square in the eyes, and he took a stunned step backward. Alexis seized the opportunity and pulled herself up, using the tree trunk as support. She was swaying on her feet. The world spun, but she staggered forward. He grabbed her, his arms clamping around her in a twisted, lover-like embrace. Bile surged in her throat and she brought her knee up, nailing him in the groin.

The man grunted in pain, doubling over, and Alexis took off running once more, clutching her side, ignoring the fresh, hot blood soaking through her glove and the spikes of agony that shot through her leg with every hobbling step. The woods loomed before her, dark pillars of redwoods dusted with snow, stretching into a steel gray sky. Somewhere behind the thick veil of clouds, the sun was setting.

Nightfall.

She had to find shelter.

If she didn't get out of this freezing rain, she would die of hypothermia before she bled out.

Alexis stumbled forward, boots slipping on the carpet of dead needle-like leaves under the muddy snow. Her vision swam in and out of focus. The trees seemed to close in around her in a dizzying spiral. She blinked hard, clenching her jaw until her teeth hurt.

Stay awake.

Keep moving.

In the distance, a dim light peeked through the forest. Her heart leapt. Shelter. She lurched toward the light, emerging into a small clearing.

An old cabin sat in the center, its weathered logs moss-covered and rotting. But it had a roof, and walls, and maybe, just maybe, something she could use to bandage her wounds. And something she could use to fight, to defend herself. If she was really lucky, maybe there would even be a radio to call the stern-faced sheriff for help.

With the last of her strength, Alexis dragged herself to the front door of the cabin. Her fingers fumbled with the rusty padlock. It wasn't locked, thank God, but it still took several tries to pop it open and slide it from the hinged plate holding the door closed. She was shaking and sweating from the effort by the time it dropped from her hand.

The door creaked open. She stumbled inside, collapsing to the floor as darkness closed in around her. The lingering warmth of a recently doused fire was the last thing she sensed before everything went black.

chapter
three

IF HELL WAS REAL, it had to be a grocery store.

Fluorescent lights overhead buzzed like thousands of angry bees, casting an unnatural glow over the neatly arranged shelves and colorful produce. Shoppers—so many, too many, why were there so many people?—moved up and down the aisles, their chatter creating an indistinguishable hum under the tinny country music filtering in through speakers in the ceiling.

Registers beeped.

Bags rustled.

Shopping carts clattered.

All of it was a dissonant symphony that made Shane's teeth hurt, and each new note threatened to unravel the thin strands of his composure. He was a raw, exposed nerve and stood frozen just inside the door for a moment, his heart pounding like the heavy thud of boots on concrete. His breath came in shallow, panicked gasps and his chest tightened until he wasn't sure his heart had room to beat. His gaze darted around, scanning for any potential threats, any signs of danger lurking in the rows of cereal and pasta and canned goods.

Dammit, it was a grocery store, not a battlefield. There was nothing to fear here.

He clenched and unclenched his fists, grounding himself in the sensation of his own too-tight skin. His shopping list crumpled in his hand and he focused on it. The paper was a lifeline, a tether to reality that guided him away from the edge of panic. He needed supplies if he was going to survive until winter loosened her unforgiving hold on his mountain.

He could do this.

He grabbed a cart and charged ahead, focused on the mission.

Supplies.

Survival.

As he moved through the store, the sights and sounds intensified. The smell of baked goods mingled with the sharp tang of cleaning chemicals, assaulting his senses. The overhead speakers crackled to life with a muffled announcement. Cereal boxes stared at him with their bright, exaggerated smiles, grotesque in their cheerfulness. The blaring colors of advertisements clashed with his memories of muted desert landscapes and shadowy hideouts and dangerous nighttime missions.

Navigating through the crowded aisles, he avoided making eye contact with any of the shoppers, their wide-eyed faces blurring together in a collective horrified stare as he hurried by them. His grip on the cart was so tight his knuckles turned white. He tried to read the list and scan the shelves for the items he needed, but he was drowning in a sea of sensory overload and couldn't focus. He longed for the silence of the mountains, but his beloved mountain would kill him before spring if he didn't complete this mission.

Supplies.

Survival.

It was all that mattered.

He found himself in the canned food section. The rows of

neatly stacked cans were a comfort, a reminder of the order he had once known before the chaos of war had taken over his life. He reached out to grab a can of beans when he heard a soft voice behind him.

"Excuse me, sir?"

He turned to see a woman standing a few feet away. She was pretty, in a soft way, with long brown hair and muted bluish eyes that sparkled with kindness. But as he faced her, he watched that sparkle change to horror, the kindness to revulsion.

His scars.

He usually covered his face when he came to town, but his balaclava had been soaked and icy from the ride off the mountain, so he'd removed it at the vet's. How could he have forgotten? He knew better than to show his face in public.

"What do you want?" The question came out of him in an animalistic growl.

The woman sucked in a sharp breath like she meant to scream and he flinched back, covering his face with both hands. It had been a long time since he had seen himself in a mirror, but he knew how bad it was. His patchy beard. His missing eyebrows. His sunken, uneven eyes and contorted nose and melted earlobes. The shiny ropes of puckered scar tissue that twisted his once-handsome features into a grotesque network of ridges and valleys in mottled reds and pale, waxy whites. He was a parody of Freddy Krueger. The original nightmare fuel. A monster.

"Sorry," he mumbled, but it was too late.

The woman backed away quickly, disappearing around the end of the aisle. On the floor where she'd stood moments ago, he saw his list. He must have dropped it in his haste to get this trip over with. He snapped it up—but fuck the list. He couldn't stay here for a second longer. He swept three shelves of canned goods into his cart and pulled a crumpled wad of money from his pocket. He didn't know if it was enough or too much, but he didn't care. He would not stand there and wait for a frightened teenage cashier to ring him up. He set the money on one of the empty shelves and marched out with his cart.

Nobody stopped him.

But the sheriff's Tahoe rolled up as he was loading his ATV.

Ash Rawlings somehow always found him, and he resented the man for it. Why couldn't they all just leave him alone?

Tonight, Ash wore a dark green rain slicker with the word "sheriff" emblazoned in reflective yellow across the back, but the hood was down and the rain plastered his reddish-brown hair to his head as he climbed out of the truck. There was a big black dog in the passenger seat, and it eyed Shane with suspicion through the window.

"Hi, Shane," Ash said in a carefully modulated tone as he approached. "What are you doing in town?"

The sheriff always spoke to him like he was a bomb and one wrong word would light his fuse. Which, honestly, wasn't far from the truth.

He gritted his teeth and put the last of the canned goods in the cargo trailer. "Supplies."

"Supplies for what?"

Anger flashed hot and white through him, and his vision tunneled. "Survival," he spat and faced the sheriff. "What the hell do you think I'm doing? I'm not here for a fucking vacation."

Ash held up his hands in a placating gesture. He wore a wedding band on his left ring finger, which, like the dog, was new since the last time Shane had seen the man. For half a second, he considered asking about it.

A normal friend would ask about it.

In his past life, he would've asked. Maybe he would've even made a ball-and-chain joke. He used to be good at jokes. At one time, his teammates had considered him a funny guy and his BUD/S instructors had dubbed him "Joker" because he'd relied on humor to get him through the grueling training.

But now he wasn't funny.

And didn't care enough about the ring to ask.

Ash wasn't a friend.

He didn't need or want friends.

"Okay, that's fine," Ash said, still in that tone, like he was talking to a crazy person. "But you have to pay for what you take, Shane. You know this."

"I paid."

"Leaving money on a shelf after scaring the other shoppers is not how it works."

He didn't have the energy for this. He wanted to get back to his cabin and forget this day had ever happened. "I didn't mean to scare anyone. I just needed to get out of there."

"I know," Ash said gently and slid a step closer. "I get it. But you have to understand, people don't know you like I do. They don't know what you've been through. They see a stranger with scars dressed in furs, and it scares them."

Guilt twisted his stomach into a knot. When he was up on the mountain, it was easy to forget the looks of fear and disgust he received from strangers. The rocks and trees and animals didn't care what he looked like. Up there, he was just another part of the landscape. Part of the environment. But here in town, he was the monster in the woods that parents warned their kids about.

"Listen, I'll talk to the store manager," Ash continued. "We can come up with a delivery solution for when you need supplies that will work for everyone. But you have to try to be more... approachable when you come to town, okay? And follow the law. Don't force me to arrest you."

Shane lifted a shoulder and shoved the now-empty cart aside. "Not a problem. I'm never coming back here."

"You should," Ash said. "I know people—wounded veterans like you—who can help you cope with whatever—"

"I don't need your help."

The sheriff shook his head. He seemed almost... sad. "Yes, you do, Shane. We both know you've lost too much weight this winter. You're practically a skeleton right now. You're starving to death."

"Just a long winter. Wildfire last year scared away the game. They'll come back this summer."

"And what if they don't?"

When Shane didn't answer, Ash sighed heavily and dragged a hand over his neat beard. "You can't keep living like this, off the grid, alone. It's not good for you, physically or mentally."

He grunted, threw a leg over the seat of his ATV, and started the engine. Ash was wrong. The town, with all its noise and people and judgement, wasn't good for him. The mountain was where he belonged.

"Shane, wait," Ash called after him as he pulled away, but he didn't stop.

He revved the engine, and the tires kicked up water as he sped down the street. The rain had turned into a drizzle, and the clouds hung low over the mountains. He shouldn't have let his guard down, but he'd been so focused on his mission that he had forgotten how people looked at him. He had forgotten how it felt to be a monster.

He pushed the ATV harder, relishing the wind combing through his hair and the icy rain splattering his face. He had to get back to his cabin before nightfall. He had to put this day behind him and focus on surviving the next. And the next. And the next...

The thought was exhausting.

Fatigue seeped into his bones as he continued on the rocky path up the mountain. His ATV bounced and jolted over the rough terrain, and he gripped the handlebars tighter. He tried to focus on the road ahead, but his mind kept drifting back to the grocery store and the confrontation with Ash.

What if the game didn't return?

He couldn't keep living like this, but he didn't see any other options. He couldn't remove the scars and forget the memories that haunted him every day. He couldn't erase the past and he couldn't stand the present. He was dangerous and wasn't wholly sane. Removing himself from society was the safest bet. And if he starved to death...

Well, that was probably the best outcome for everyone.

Why was he struggling so hard to survive anyway?

As he neared his cabin, he slowed down and the roar of the engine faded to a low grumble. The rain had changed back into snow, and a heavy silence enveloped the forest. He stopped the ATV in front of his storage shed on the hill behind his cabin and climbed off, stretching his stiff muscles. He grabbed his rifle in one hand and unhooked the cargo trailer with the other. The canned food rattled as he dragged it with him toward the cabin, parking it in front of his porch. He reached into his pocket for the key—

The padlock lay on the weathered wood of his porch.

The door was open.

All of his senses fired to red alert.

Someone was here.

In his home.

His sanctuary.

Alexis resurfaced sometime later—minutes, hours? She had no idea. And she didn't know where she was or how she'd gotten there. She was flat on her stomach on a hard floor, her cheek pressed against the cold wood. She was shivering.

So cold.

Just like back there.

Trapped again.

In the dark.

And the cold.

Waiting for the monster to—

Panic flared hot in her chest and she tried to push herself upright on arms that felt like jelly.

The cabin was small and rustic, a single room with a lofted bed, a wood stove, and a tiny kitchenette. Through the windows, she saw thick trees crowding close, their branches laden with snow. An unnatural silence hung over the woods, muffling the world in cottony white.

A twig snapped nearby.

Everything stopped—her breath, her heart—as she strained to listen.

Silence.

Probably just a branch giving way under the snow.

But then came a rustle, the soft crunch of footsteps. Her breath caught in her throat. She wasn't alone.

He was still out there.

She cast about for a weapon, anything to defend herself. But the cabin was bare, not even a knife in the kitchen drawer. The footsteps were getting closer, a dark shape moving through the trees.

Hunting her.

Panic rose in her chest and strangled her. She was trapped, wounded and unarmed, her only escape blocked by him. She had nowhere to run, no way to call for help. No one would find her body until spring. If they found her at all.

The shape emerged from the woods, big and furry, lumbering through the deep snow, dragging something behind it. For a moment, her hopes lifted— it was only a bear looking for food after a long hibernation. It couldn't be human.

Then she saw the rifle in its hand and her blood turned to ice. Not a bear. It was a man in a fur coat, his face hidden behind a black mask.

The Shadow Stalker.

Alexis scrambled back as he approached the cabin. She cowered against the wall and clutched at her wounded side as agony seared through her with every panicked gasp. She had to escape, had to find a way out before it was too late, but her limbs were heavy and numb, her head spinning from blood loss. She feared she didn't have the strength left to stand, let alone run.

Nowhere left to hide.

Her investigation would end here, cut short by the very killer she had sought to expose. There was nothing left for her but the icy grip of fear and the knowledge that the Shadow Stalker would show no mercy. All she could do was wait for the crack of the rifle, the bite of another bullet tearing into her flesh.

The cabin walls seemed to close in around her as she huddled deeper into the corner. She thought of her dog waiting for her, abandoned at the motel, never knowing what became of her owner. Thought of her sister, who had worried for her safety when she decided to return to California, and of the local sheriff warning her that the Shadow Stalker was too dangerous to pursue. She should have listened to both of them.

A floorboard groaned on the porch.

The door creaked open.

Alexis squeezed her eyes shut, bracing for the gunshot, but

it didn't come. The killer was toying with her now, drawing out her suffering. Letting her anticipation of death become a torment all its own.

Dammit, no.

Her final moments would not be her cowering in fear.

She dragged herself upright and staggered to her feet. As the door opened, she straightened her spine and faced her killer.

chapter
four

SHANE CREPT into the cabin and was met with an eerie silence, underscored by the faint creaking from the floorboards under his feet. The air was still and heavy, and he smelled something metallic under the musty scent of the cabin's old wood.

Blood.

His gaze darted around, searching for any signs of an intruder. He didn't want to give whoever it was the chance to make a move first. He raised his rifle and stepped farther into the room, then froze.

There, in the corner.

Movement.

Shane's breath caught in his throat as a figure unfolded from the shadows. For a moment, all he saw was the threat. A tango he had to neutralize before it killed him. He raised his rifle and pressed his finger to the trigger, but then the shadow took shape and he blinked in surprise.

A... woman?

She swayed on unsteady feet, her blond hair a wild tangle around her head, her cheekbones sharp points in her pale, too-thin face. The winter camouflage jacket she wore swallowed her whole and was bloodstained in several places. Some spots were obviously old, dried brown, but others were a bright red, and he watched the stain at her shoulder spread before his eyes. She was bleeding. That was the metallic smell in the air. Fresh blood.

Her eyes were glassy and resigned as she stared at him. "You win."

"What?" He forced the word out of his constricted throat, and it grated against the air.

"I'm done fighting." She gestured toward his weapon. "Just do it already."

"What?" he said again. He had no idea who this woman was, or where she came from, but she was desperate, and desperate people were more dangerous than any predator on this mountain. He took a tentative step toward her, rifle still in hand, barrel aimed for a kill shot. "Who are you?"

"I'm done playing your games," she whispered.

"What the hell are you talking about?"

"Just do it. I'm tired."

Shane took another step toward her. "Who are you?"

The woman didn't respond. She stared at his gun, waiting for him to make his move. There was a wild look in her eyes. Something wasn't right and all of his internal alarms blared a warning.

"I said, who the fuck are you!?"

She didn't flinch back. Instead, she leaped toward him, attacking with a ferocity he hadn't been expecting. Even wounded, she was fast. She went for his gun, and got a hold of it in his moment of surprise, but he was still faster and stronger. In one fluid movement, he grabbed her arm and yanked the gun from her grasp, throwing it aside. He pulled the knife he always kept at his belt and lunged toward her—

And suddenly he wasn't in his cabin on a cold early spring night. He was somewhere hot and dry, and he had sand in places where no man should have sand. The woman wasn't a woman anymore, but an enemy combatant with a scarf wrapped around his head. Gunfire filled the air with a staccato rat-a-tat-tat, and he ducked, rolled away from it, and came up swinging his knife. He caught the man across the throat, blood spraying from the gash in his neck.

Tango neutralized.

The man fell to the ground with a thud, the sound of a heavy body hitting the ground echoing in Shane's ears. He turned around, and another man was standing there with murder in his eyes. He didn't wait for the next attack. He lunged toward the second man, knife raised to strike.

The man screamed.

High and shrill and terrified.

Not a man.

Shane froze and blinked as everything shifted again. He wasn't in a scorching desert country fighting an unwinnable war. He hadn't been there in a very long time. He was home. In his cabin. On his mountain. Safe.

Shane dropped the knife and stared down at his trembling hands. His knuckles were torn and raw. Sweat coated his neck. He looked at the man in front of him and watched him transform back into a woman. A wounded woman, splayed out at his feet, bleeding.

Had he done this to her?

"Fuck." Heart still pounding, adrenaline making his hands shake, he crouched down beside the fallen woman. She was shivering, but he wasn't sure if it was from the cold or fear or pain. He pulled off his fur coat and carefully wrapped it around her shoulders, helping her to sit up against the wall. "I'm sorry. Jesus. I'm so sorry."

This was why he stayed on his mountain. This was why he couldn't be around people. He couldn't trust himself not to hurt them.

Her eyes rolled back, and her head lolled, and everything else seemed to fall away.

"Wait. Wait, stay with me."

Her eyes opened and stared at him with desperation and pain. "So cold," she whispered.

"Okay. I'll get you some blankets. Hang on."

Shane stood and climbed the ladder up to his loft. He found his heaviest blanket, made from the hide of the bear he'd killed as it ransacked his storage shed last fall, and hurried back to the woman's side. Her eyes were closed. Was she still breathing? He was terrified that if he turned his back for even a second, she'd slip away and he'd have to deal with the weight of another death on his shoulders. He couldn't let that happen. Not again.

He removed his wet coat from her and draped the dry bear pelt over her instead, tucking it around her shivering form. She was still breathing, her chest rising and falling in shallow breaths, but she wouldn't be for much longer if he didn't stop the blood.

Shane hesitated for a moment, unsure of what to do. He hadn't dealt with wounds like this since he left the Navy. He closed his eyes, took a deep breath, and then opened them again. He pulled off his gloves and then reached out and parted the blanket, his fingers trembling as he unzipped her jacket.

It wasn't a knife wound. He hadn't hurt her during his flashback, after all.

She'd been shot twice—once in the upper chest and once in the thigh. He couldn't see where the first bullet had entered, but he could feel where it had exited on her upper back. Her warm blood coated his probing fingers. He swallowed hard and then retrieved the first aid kit he kept well-stocked. He fumbled through the supplies until he found what he was looking for: gauze, tape, and a tourniquet.

He tried to remember his training, tried to remember the steps to take, but his mind was a jumbled mess. He didn't know her name, didn't know how she'd gotten here or why she'd been bleeding on his cabin floor. The only thing he did know: he needed to stop the bleeding, and fast.

He took a deep breath and shook out his hands to steady them. He couldn't afford to slip up now. He applied the tourniquet to her leg, then moved on to the hole in her chest. He lifted her listless form against his chest to press a wad of gauze against the exit wound, applying pressure until the bleeding slowed.

The woman groaned in pain. Her eyes flickered open, a shocking green against her pale face. For a moment, he got lost in their depths, mesmerized by the dark emerald color. He'd never seen eyes quite like hers before. There was something soothing about the color, like his forest on a late spring day when the rains let up and the fog cleared and everything was bright and soft and clean.

"It's all right. You're safe," he said, doing his best to keep his voice gentle. It felt awkward. He'd had no gentleness in his life, even before he went to war. His dad had been soft-hearted and kind, but his mom was a cold, hard woman who loved crushing them both with her cruelness. Whatever bit of gentleness he'd had left in him after growing up under their turbulent roof had been stripped away by the SEALs. But he had to try. This woman was scared and in pain and needed reassurance.

"Shh. I'm here and you're safe now."

Somehow, despite his awkwardness, his words seemed to comfort her. Her eyelids fluttered, and she drifted into unconsciousness.

Shane laid her down and searched for the entrance wound. He found it a few moments later, just under her right breast. He cleaned it as best he could before covering it in gauze.

She didn't move.

He stayed with her, his gaze locked on her face, until he was sure that she was stable. Then he stood up, his head spinning.

And in a flash, he was back in Afghanistan, back in the desert, surrounded by enemies. He could feel the heat radiating off the sand, his lips and mouth dry from the harsh air...

No.

He closed his eyes. He didn't belong there anymore. He was here, in his cabin, on his mountain.

Focus on the here and now.

chapter
five

ELLIE SUMMERS WAS JUST STEPPING out of the shower when her cell phone rang.

Oh, shit. Where had she set her glasses? She couldn't see a damn thing without them. She groped around on the bathroom vanity until she found them, then tripped over her own feet while trying to get to the hotel room's desk, where she'd left the phone to charge. She slid her glasses onto her face and squinted at the screen.

Sheriff Rawlings.

Her stomach flipped, and her knees turned to gelatin. She sank down on the end of the bed, her thumb hovering over the answer icon.

If she answered, would she hear the news she'd been dreading for over a month?

With each passing day, the hope of seeing her sister alive again dwindled. Lexi had disappeared from the parking lot of this same motel, in front of this same room, so when Ellie arrived in town she purposely requested to stay here, hoping to find something that the police missed in their initial sweep —maybe a clue Lexi left behind that only she'd be able to decipher, like when they used to play detective games as kids.

There was nothing. It was just a motel room, a little ragged around the edges but charming in an old school Americana road trip kind of way.

And she was wasting time. She had to answer the phone. If the sheriff was about to tell her Alexis was dead, she didn't want to hear the news in a voicemail.

She took a deep breath and slid her thumb over the answer icon. "Hello?"

"Ellie, it's Sheriff Rawlings," the gruff voice on the other end of the line said and her palm started to sweat. She gripped the phone tighter to keep it from sliding out of her hand.

"Is she alive? Please, tell me fast."

"We haven't found her yet. I'm sorry if I frightened you." His voice was still gruff—always was—but he softened it, and his next words were almost gentle. "But we have found something. A dog matching the description of your sister's was dropped off at a local vet's office."

"You found Clue?"

"We think so. If you could come to the vet's and confirm the dog belongs to Alexis, it might give us a lead."

"What vet?"

"Dr. Sasha Scott. She's at Redwood Coast Rescue."

Ellie had spent the last month driving all over the town of Steam Valley and the surrounding mountains, and knew exactly where the rescue was. She also knew it was owned by Sheriff Rawlings' twin sister, Anna.

"I'll be there in ten minutes." She hung up the phone and quickly slipped into jeans and a hoodie. She grabbed her keys and headed out the door, not bothering to comb her wet hair. It would be a disaster when it dried, and she'd definitely have to shower again later to tame the unruly curls.

The parking lot of the rescue was surprisingly full. She spotted the Lost County Sheriff's SUV and pulled into a space close to it.

Redwood Coast Rescue was a series of buildings laid out in a sunburst pattern, connected by walkways and fenced dog yards. A map by the parking lot told her the building right in front belonged to the vet and, as she pulled open the door, she noticed a man running a border collie through an agility course off to her left. Beyond them was a nice two-story blue house with a wide back deck overlooking the rescue. It all looked new, and she figured the black burn scar running down the side of the mountain had something to do with that.

Distracted, she didn't notice the man in front of her until she bumped into him.

"Whoa." He reached out and caught her before she could fall on her face and break her glasses for the gazillionth time.

"Oh, God. I'm sorry." She straightened away from him and adjusted her slipping glasses, then about swallowed her tongue.

The man was gorgeous.

All California surfer good looks, with sandy blond hair and a mischievous glint in his light brown eyes. He wore a suit, but had thrown his jacket over one arm, and rolled the sleeves of his shirt up to show off muscular forearms. His tie hung loosely around his neck.

She was suddenly very aware of her disheveled appearance. He looked rumpled in a stylish I've-been-working-all-day kind of way. She looked homeless, and she resisted the urge to run a hand over her wild, frizzing hair.

"Are you okay?" he asked, still holding onto her arm.

Ellie felt her cheeks heat as she realized she'd been staring. "I'm fine, thank you. Sorry for bumping into you. I was distracted. I'm always distracted. My sister says I'm like—" She broke off and forced herself to close her mouth before she went off on a nervous ramble. "Uh, well, anyway. I'm sorry."

"No problem." He gave her a smile that made her heart skip a beat. "Can I help you with something?"

"I'm actually looking for Dr. Scott. Sheriff Rawlings called me here to come identify a dog."

"Ah, you must be Ellie. They're waiting in back for you. I'm Callum Holden. Cal." He held out his hand.

She hesitated for a second before taking it, surprised by the jolt of electricity that shot through her fingertips when they touched. "Ellie. Uh, just Ellie. No nickname. I mean, sometimes friends call me Elle. And my sister calls me Ellie Mae when she's annoyed with me, but—"

Oh, God. Why was she introducing herself again? He already knew her name. He'd said it.

Close your mouth and stop babbling.

She released his hand and told herself not to blush. "Nice to meet you, Cal. Are you a client here?"

"More like they're my clients." He lifted his briefcase. "I represent the rescue and had some paperwork for them to fill out. And I needed to talk to the sheriff."

"Represent?"

"I'm a lawyer."

"Oh." Ridiculous that news should disappoint her, but she hated lawyers. In her experience, they were all massive jackasses.

Not that Cal seemed like a jackass. But did any jackass ever seem like one at first? And not that she should even be looking for a man right now. She had more important things to worry about than Cal's dimples or his career choice.

Dammit, Ellie. Stay on task.

Cal waved a hand. "Come on. I'll walk you back."

She followed him down a narrow hallway decorated with animal-themed paintings and photographs. The scent of disinfectant and wet dog filled her nose, and she tried her best not to sneeze.

As they turned a corner, she saw Sheriff Rawlings leaning

against a counter while a curvy, dark-haired woman examined a skinny dog on a stainless steel table.

The dog's tail thunked weakly when Ellie stepped into the room.

"Ellie," the sheriff said when he saw her and pushed away from the counter. "Glad you could make it. This is Dr. Scott."

"Sasha," the vet corrected automatically. "Nobody calls me Dr. Scott, Ash. You know that."

The sheriff shrugged. "Not everyone is comfortable with first names right off the bat. I was being polite."

Sasha snorted. "You polite? Okay."

"You spend too much time with your husband," Sheriff Rawlings muttered. "His sarcasm is rubbing off on you."

Sasha said something else sarcastic in reply, but Ellie was only half listening to their banter. Her gaze fastened on the dog and tears flooded her eyes. When the sheriff called her, she hadn't really believed the dog was Lexi's. How could it be Clue after all this time?

But that scruffy, skinny mutt was definitely the puppy Alexis had rescued from their local animal shelter in Chicago last Christmas. Lexi had fallen in love with that shaggy fur and those big brown eyes and brought her home on Christmas Eve. They'd spent the entire evening drinking wine, playing with the silly pup, and trying to come up with a good name. Ellie had suggested Clue after their favorite board game as kids and it stuck.

"It's Clue." She stepped forward on shaky legs and held out a hand.

Clue gave her fingers a lick. The dog wore a cone around her neck and her front leg had been shaved where the IV was taped.

Ellie could count every single one of her ribs.

The tears she'd been holding back slipped out as she

wrapped her arms around the dog. "Oh my God, Clue girl. What happened to you?"

Sasha set a gentle hand on her shoulder. "She'll be okay. She was starving and dehydrated, but she's a tough girl. She's already made enormous improvements in the last twenty-four hours since she was brought in."

"What happened to her?"

"We think she either escaped from Alexis's motel room or was possibly let out by whoever took your sister," Sheriff Rawlings said. "She wandered into the woods and got lost. It's very easy to do around here, especially for a young dog not familiar with the area."

"She could've been looking for Alexis," Sasha suggested. "Anna says she has the drive for search and rescue. And the stubbornness."

"Also possible," the sheriff agreed. "Either way, a local man found her on the mountain and brought her in."

"She got lucky," Sasha said. "Much longer, and she might not have made it. I'd like to keep her at least through the weekend for monitoring and IV fluids, but if she keeps improving, I'd feel comfortable letting her go home with you on Monday."

Ellie nodded. "Who brought her in? I'd like to thank him for finding her."

Sasha and Sheriff Rawlings shared an uncomfortable glance before the sheriff tilted his head toward the door, where Cal still stood. "Let's talk. Sash, you mind if we use your office?"

"No, not at all." She must have noticed Ellie's hesitation to leave, because she added, "Go ahead, Ellie. I'll take care of this sweet girl."

"She's in good hands," Cal added from the doorway. "The best."

Ellie reluctantly let go of Clue and followed the men out

of the room. As they walked down the hallway, unease twisted her stomach into knots. Her sister wouldn't abandon Clue to starve. She just wouldn't.

Sasha's office was cozy, with a shiny wood desk and a large window that looked out onto the dog yards. The man and border collie were still out there. She watched him throw a tennis ball, and the dog zoomed after it in a black and white blur.

"Sit down, Ellie," the sheriff said, gesturing to one of the chairs in front of the desk. "We have some things we need to talk about."

Ellie obeyed, perching on the edge of the seat. She felt like a character in a bad crime drama, waiting for the police to tell her that her loved one was dead.

God. Alexis couldn't be dead. The world needed her. Ellie needed her.

She choked back a sob and sucked in a calming breath before lifting her gaze to the sheriff's. "What is it?"

"Cal has some information," the sheriff said.

Ellie's gaze snapped to him. She'd assumed he was only here on rescue business, but she should've realized there was more to his presence. If he'd been here just for some paperwork, he wouldn't have stuck around after their meeting in the lobby.

She narrowed her eyes at him. "What kind of information?"

Cal cleared his throat and lowered himself into the chair next to hers. "A client, who will remain anonymous, contacted me—"

The sheriff crossed his arms over his chest and grumbled his disapproval.

Cal ignored him. "My client claims to have information about your sister's location. They said they saw Alexis at a cabin in the woods, being held by the same man who brought Clue in yesterday."

Her sister was alive. Held captive. But alive.

A wave of relief washed over her, but anger quickly replaced it. How long had the bastard been holding Alexis there? What was being done to her?

"Who is he? Did anyone see his face?" Ellie demanded, her voice shaking with emotion as she popped to her feet. "Where's the cabin? We need to go there and get her!"

The sheriff made a calming motion with his hands. "Ellie, please sit down. I know the man who brought Clue in, and I have serious doubts about the veracity of this anonymous source's claims."

She sank back into her seat. "You know him?"

"His name is Shane Trevisano. He lives off-the-grid up on the mountain. He's... different, and that scares a lot of the folks around here, but he's only a danger to himself. He wouldn't hurt Alexis."

"Ash," Cal said with an exasperated sigh. "I know you have a soft spot for him, but you can't know that for sure. He's a severely disturbed man. Zak told me he shot at you guys once."

"Shot at. He didn't hit us and he would've if he wanted to. It was a warning, nothing more."

"Every time he comes into town, he rips up the grocery store and frightens people—"

"I'm not disagreeing with you about his mental state," Sheriff Rawlings rose his voice and spoke over Cal. "He absolutely needs help, and I've spoken to him about his options. But I'm telling you, he can't stand people— physically, mentally, he cannot be around them. All he wants is to be left alone. There's no way he would kidnap a woman from her hotel in the middle of town and keep her locked away in his cabin for over a month. He just wouldn't."

Ellie had heard enough. She stood up abruptly, her fists clenched at her sides. "I don't care what you think he's capable of or not. If he has my sister, we need to find him and stop him before he hurts her. And if you won't help, I'll go talk to him myself."

"Jesus," the sheriff muttered and rubbed a hand over his beard. "You're just like your sister, rushing headlong into things you don't understand."

Cal placed a hand on her shoulder, his touch gentle. "Ash is right. You can't go charging up the mountain by yourself. It's still winter up there and the weather is volatile even on a good day. We need a plan."

She shook his hand off. "I don't need a plan. I need my sister. I won't just sit around and wait for this Shane guy to get sick of her and kill her and dump her body somewhere. I've already gone through all of that with one sister and I refuse to lose the only one I have left. I'm going to bring Alexis home, no matter what."

The sheriff let out a heavy sigh. "Ellie, please. Let's just take a step back and think about this rationally."

But Ellie was done thinking rationally. She'd been doing that for weeks now, trying to piece together clues and follow leads that led to dead ends. Now, she had a lead, and she would not let it slip away.

"I'm not waiting," she said. "I'm going up there, with or without your help. So either you can come with me and help me find my sister, or you can stay here and twiddle your thumbs while I do it myself."

Cal stood up slowly, his expression pensive. "I'll go with you."

Sheriff Rawlings looked like he wanted to argue, but then he relented with a soft growl of frustration. "Fine. But we're going to do this safely and strategically. We'll head up to the mountain tomorrow morning, with backup and search dogs. I will approach Shane's cabin alone. I don't want to spook him into doing something he'll regret."

Ellie nodded. Finally, a solid lead. Finally, they were taking action.

And with any luck, tomorrow she'd have her sister back.

"Thank you," she said, her voice breaking with emotion. "Thank you so much."

chapter
six

FOR A MOMENT, Alexis couldn't remember where she was or how she got there. Panic rose in her chest as she blinked at her strange surroundings. Rough wooden walls, wood floor, dim light filtering through a grimy window. An old cot beneath her, a soft fur blanket pulled up to her chin.

Memories flooded back in a rush—the chase through the forest, a cabin, the dark figure emerging from the shadows, then...

Nothing.

Her stomach flipped, and she struggled to sit up. How did she get here? Who brought her to this place?

The cabin's door creaked open.

A man stood in the doorway, tall and powerfully built, his shoulders heavy with furs like an ancient viking. He regarded her with a stoic expression, shadows dancing across the white, gray, and dark green streaks painted on his face. Dark hair, scruffy beard. Winter camouflage pants and a hunting rifle clutched in his hands.

It was him. The Shadow Stalker.

A wave of terror washed over Alexis as she scrambled back

against the wall, clutching the blanket to her chest like a shield. "Why are you doing this to me?"

The man took a slow step forward, his gloved hands raised to show he meant her no harm. "Easy now. I won't hurt you." His voice was deep and gruff. "I found you in my cabin. You've been shot. I tried to patch you up."

Alexis didn't believe that for a second. She knew, with a bone-deep certainty, that this was the man who had been holding her captive for weeks, but she couldn't figure out his game now. Why put her in a cabin and pretend to be her friend? Why not throw her back into the bunker where she would be at his complete mercy again?

Just more mind games. A new level of torment.

She glanced around the cabin, searching for an escape route. The single window was small and high up, impossible to climb through. The only exit was the door the man was blocking.

Trapped.

She was so fucking sick of being trapped.

The man took another step forward. "There's no need to be afraid." His gaze flickered to the hunting rifle still in his hand, and he slowly set it against the wall. "See? I won't hurt you."

Yeah, right.

She didn't dare relax her guard. She watched his every move like a hawk, coiled to lunge for the rifle if he made a wrong move. Her heart pounded wildly in her chest, fight-or-flight instincts screaming at her to get the hell away from this man.

"What do you want?" Her voice shook despite her best efforts to stay calm. She clutched the blanket tighter, suddenly aware of how weak she was. Her shoulder and leg screamed with every slight movement. She felt both cold and hot at the same time, and sweat dripped down the back of her neck. It had been a long time since she last had a fever, but she was sure she was burning up with one now.

"Who are you?" The man's gaze drilled into her, dark and intense, as he countered her question with his own.

She hesitated. What was she supposed to tell him? That she was investigating his victims? But he already knew that. It was why he'd kidnapped her in the first place, wasn't it? He already knew her name. She was sure of it. But if she wanted to stay alive, she needed to play along with this sick game of his until she found an opportunity to escape.

"My name is Alexis. What's yours?"

He studied her for a long moment. She struggled not to squirm under his scrutiny.

After what seemed like an eternity, he gave a curt nod. "Shane."

Her stomach heaved, and she had to swallow hard to send the surge of fear-laced bile back down her throat. If he was willing to tell her his name, that meant he wasn't planning for her to leave here alive.

"Why are you on my mountain?" His voice was rusty, like he didn't use it often enough. "Who shot you?"

He was asking questions he already knew the answers to. Did he think this was funny? Was he amused, like a cat playing with a mouse before he killed it? She tried to gage his expression through the layers of paint, but he might as well be wearing a mask for how much emotion he showed. And there was something... wrong about his face. Like it had been broken apart and reassembled with slightly different instructions.

"I—I—got lost. I don't know who shot me. I don't remember." Maybe if he thought she had no memory, he'd consider letting her go.

"You should be more careful. These woods are dangerous, especially for a woman alone." His gaze flickered to the hunting rifle again. "You're lucky I found you before something else did."

A chill ran down Alexis's spine at the implication in his words.

Shane was dangerous.

A predator.

Alexis eyed the door of the cabin, wondering if she could make a run for it while Shane wasn't looking. But then what? She was miles from anywhere, with no food, shelter, or supplies. She had a bullet in her leg and another in her chest. As terrifying as her current situation was, she wouldn't last long out in these woods alone.

She was stuck here until she could figure out a way to escape safely. Which meant she needed to keep Shane from suspecting she was on to him.

"Thank you," she said, forcing a smile. "I can only imagine what would have happened if you hadn't found me."

Shane's expression still gave nothing away, but his eyes remained wary. "I don't like visitors. How did you find me?"

Alexis scrambled for an explanation, cursing herself for not anticipating that question. "I-I just saw a trail on one of the hiking maps and thought I'd check it out. But I lost my way pretty quickly, and the weather turned and—well." She gave a self-deprecating laugh, hoping it sounded genuine. "Clearly I'm not much of an outdoorswoman."

Shane grunted, turning away to add another log to the fire in the stove. Sparks crackled and popped as he poked at the glowing embers, and Alexis found herself mesmerized by the dancing flames. It was a welcome distraction from her churning thoughts, and the warmth was soothing after being cold for so long.

"The weather's turning nasty again," Shane said. "You'll have to stay here until it passes."

Okay. While being stuck here longer with him was far

from ideal, it would give her more time to heal. And while she was healing, she could gather evidence. She knew his name now and where he lived. If she could find something to prove Shane was the Shadow Stalker, she could take it to the sheriff when she escaped.

"Will you take me back to town when the weather clears?"

He didn't answer, but his dark eyes settled on her again. She tried to hold his gaze, but found she couldn't. She was too nervous and felt like he could see right through her.

"Depends," he said finally. "Who shot you?"

"I told you—"

"No, you lied to me."

Shit. He didn't believe her memory loss story. "I really don't remember. Please, I just want to go home."

Shane's eyes narrowed as he studied her. "I don't believe you."

Her heart sank. She had to think of something fast, or he was going to kill her.

"I swear, I don't remember," she said, and let her fear and exhaustion creep into her voice, making it tremble. "I was hiking in the woods, and someone shot me from behind. That's all I know."

Shane said nothing for a long moment, and she held her breath, waiting for his reaction.

Finally, he shook his head. "More lies. The exit wound is on your back. You saw who shot you."

She curled her hands into the blanket—which, she realized now, was fur. This man was a killer. Animal. Human. It didn't matter to him, and she was stupid to think he had any intention of letting her go.

"Please," she whispered. "I won't tell anyone."

He shut the grate on the wood stove, and the metal hinges screeched in protest. As he turned toward her, she could see the madness in his eyes. The fire in the stove cast his not-right face in an eerie light, making him look like a demon.

He took a step closer to her, towering over her. "You're lying. And I don't tolerate liars."

Alexis's heart pounded in her chest as Shane reached out and grabbed her chin, forcing her to meet his gaze. His touch was rough and calloused, and she could feel the heat of his breath on her face. She wanted to pull away, to scream and fight, but she knew that would only make things worse.

"I'm not lying," she said, trying to keep her voice steady. "I don't remember anything."

Shane's grip tightened, and she winced in pain. "You can save yourself a lot of suffering by telling me the truth. Who sent you here? Are they after me?"

Alexis shook her head frantically, tears streaming down her face. "No one sent me. I don't even know who you are or what you're talking about. I was just hiking. Please, I don't want any trouble."

His grip on her chin loosened slightly, and she pulled away.

"You're a terrible liar," he growled. "I can smell the fear on you. You're hiding something, and I'm going to find out what it is. And if they sent you to kill me—"

What? He wasn't making sense. She'd known the Shadow Stalker was crazy—any man who held a woman captive for weeks only to set her free so he could hunt her must be crazy. But in all the weeks he'd held her in that underground bunker, she hadn't realized he was actually clinically insane. Maybe he didn't even know what he was doing.

"No one sent me. I swear."

Shane let go of her chin and took a step back, his eyes still fixed on hers. "You're not leaving this cabin until I figure out what's really going on."

Oh, God. She closed her eyes and took a deep breath,

trying to calm herself down. She had to keep her wits about her if she was going to survive, but her mind was foggy from pain and fear. She couldn't fight him, she couldn't outrun him, and she couldn't reason with him. He was a madman, and she was at his mercy.

But...

She remembered the podcast series she did a few years ago focusing on survivors of violent crime. The one thing they all said, the one thing they all had in common, was that they made sure their captors saw them as human.

It was her only chance.

"Shane?" She made his name into a pleading question. "Can I... clean up a little? I feel disgusting."

Shane hesitated for a moment, then nodded toward the back of the cabin under the loft. "Don't try anything stupid."

Alexis nodded, relieved, and slowly rose to her feet, choking back a scream when she put weight on her injured leg. Tears tracked down her face, but she would not give him the satisfaction of hearing her whimper. She limped over to the partition and found a small bathroom with a sink, shower stall, and a composting toilet, like something you'd find in a camper. She tried the faucet. The water was freezing and little more than a trickle. There was no mirror, so she could only imagine what she must look like. She swished a handful of water around in her mouth, then splashed another handful on her face. Hot tears mixed with the ice-cold water as she tried to hold back a sob.

Shane was a monster.

She had to get out of here. But how? She had no weapons, no way call for help, and no one knew where she was.

She tore off a square of toilet paper and wiped her face. She had to stay calm, stay focused. She looked around the tiny bathroom, searching for anything that could help her. Her gaze landed on the composting toilet. It had a crank handle on the side made of metal. If she could get that off, she could use it as a weapon and—

She heard a noise outside the door, a faint click like a padlock snapping shut, and froze. Sweat broke out on her forehead as she realized what was happening.

Shane was locking the bathroom door.

chapter
seven

HE'D FRIGHTENED HER.

Shane watched her halting steps toward the bathroom with something close to shame burning up the back of his neck. He'd treated her horribly, but he didn't trust her. How could he when every word out of her mouth since she woke up had been a lie?

Alexis.

He liked the sound of it, but was it even her real name?

Ever since he arrived home and found her, the bit of hair he still had on the back of his neck had been standing at attention. Like someone was watching.

No, not just watching.

Stalking.

Hunting.

Waiting for the right moment to pounce.

If someone had sent her...

Ridiculous. He shook his head to clear his thoughts. She was obviously in no shape to hurt him.

But what if she was the bait?

He looked at the front door, then back at the bathroom.

That would explain the feeling of someone watching. And all that shit she'd said about getting shot while out on a hike.

What if she had injured herself so he'd lower his guard and—

No, he told himself firmly. No. She couldn't have shot herself in the chest, not with the angle of entry. He needed to chill out. If the paranoia took control, he'd show his vulnerabilities.

But was it paranoia or just good sense?

Fuck.

He needed to keep her contained until he had more information.

Before he could second-guess his plan, he grabbed the padlock from the front door. When he first moved to this cabin, the bathroom had been a pantry, and he'd had a lock on it to protect the food inside from bears. The hasp was still there, rusted now, but usable. He forced it over the eye and clicked the padlock closed. He couldn't take any chances. If his demons had finally come after him, he would not let them get to him through this woman.

Alexis screamed his name.

He turned away from the door and walked back to the wood stove, grabbing his rifle. The fire crackled and cast dancing shadows on the floor through the grate. It reminded him of his last mission with the SEALs, of the fire that stripped him of his face, his sanity, his life.

He had been a different man back then. A man who had believed in honor, duty, and country, and who had wholeheartedly believed he was working for the greater good. Fearless, unrelenting, deadly.

He missed that man.

He missed the fearlessness especially, the sense of invulnerability that came from a combination of youth and the extreme training he'd endured to become a SEAL.

Now he was always afraid. An unexpected sound, a surprise visitor on his mountain... hell, sometimes even his own damn shadow triggered him. He'd shot at it more than once, thinking it was someone following him.

He closed his eyes and took a deep breath, trying to push the memories away. He had to focus on the present, on the woman he had locked up in his bathroom. The woman who claimed she didn't remember anything, who begged for mercy.

He scoffed at the thought. Mercy was a luxury he couldn't afford.

When he opened his eyes, he saw his hunting knife lying on the table. He mainly used it to skin animals, but it could also be used as a weapon. He picked it up and turned it over, the blade catching in the firelight. It felt good, reassuring, to have it in his hand. He needed to be prepared for anything.

He heard Alexis crying in the bathroom, but ignored it. He wouldn't let her get to him. He couldn't let his guard down for a pretty face and crocodile tears. Not even for a second.

With his blade in one hand and his rifle in the other, he sat on the floor with his back against the wall, where he could easily see his front door, the cabin's one window, and the bathroom door.

The storm raged outside and he could only hope it was winter's last blaze of glory before spring claimed its life. The wind howled like a wild animal, and snow piled up on the window ledge, obscuring the glass. It was the perfect cover for anyone trying to sneak up on him.

He had to stay vigilant.

He had no idea how long he sat there. Long enough that the storm died and the ink of night faded to a soft morning, with snow flurries dancing in the cold air.

He heard a sound from the bathroom that didn't fit with the rest of the noises she'd been making. A hard thunk.

What if she was trying to escape?

But there wasn't a window in there and breaking through the cabin's solid walls would take more effort than she was capable of in her wounded state.

But what if she was trying to find a weapon to use against him?

He stood up and shouldered his rifle, but kept his knife handy as he walked across the room to the bathroom door. He pressed his ear against the wood, listening for any movement from inside. All he could hear was the sound of her breathing, ragged and uneven.

"Alexis." Her name came out of him in a growl.

No answer. His grip tightened on the knife as he hesitated, taking a deep breath to steady himself. Then he removed the padlock and pushed open the door.

She was curled up on the floor, unconscious but shivering wildly. Her leg had started bleeding again, and she'd tried to use the toilet paper to stanch the flow before she passed out.

Jesus. What had he done?

At that moment, he forgot about her lies. The paranoia. The fear. All he saw was a woman about to shake hands with the Grim Reaper if he didn't act now.

He moved quickly, scooping her up in his arms and carrying her back to her cot. He stripped off her wet clothes and wrapped her in a blanket, trying to warm her up.

He cursed himself for being so selfish. He should've noticed her dire condition earlier. But he'd been so focused on protecting himself that he'd forgotten about her wounds.

He sat on the edge of the cot and watched her. Her face was pale, her lips blue, her hair matted with sweat. She looked nothing like the confident woman who had confronted him earlier. She looked like a victim.

Guilt punched him in the gut. He'd hurt her, physically

and mentally. And for what? For what she might know? For what she might be hiding?

And what if she wasn't hiding anything?

Had he just killed her because he was a paranoid fucking bastard?

He shook his head and stood up, pacing back and forth as he weighed his options. She'd lost too much blood and needed a transfusion if she had any chance of surviving, but he couldn't take her to town. For one thing, she might not survive the journey. For another, if he rolled into town with a half-dead woman, the sheriff would arrest him and he'd lose what little he had left of his mind in jail.

So, he had to do the transfusion right here. He was O negative, a universal donor. He'd been a walking blood bank for his teammates.

He pulled a chair to the bedside and sat, shucking his flannel and rolling up the sleeve of his undershirt. He rifled through the first aid kit until he found a needle and tubing. He sterilized everything with the alcohol pads from the kit.

It had been a while since he had done something like this, but muscle memory kicked in as he began drawing his own blood. His skin resisted at first, and he had to press hard on the needle to get through the layers of scar tissue. It hurt like hell, but he didn't stop until he had a vein. He prepared another needle, taking extra care to make sure everything was sterile, then turned to Alexis, taking her arm in his hand and searching for a suitable vein. He found one and inserted the needle, connecting the tubing between them. The blood flow slowly, steadily, from his arm to hers.

He watched her face, waiting for any signs of improvement. But she remained pale, her breathing shallow and ragged. If he hadn't come to his senses in time, she would've died right there in his bathroom.

"Jesus. I'm so sorry. This isn't me. I'm not a monster."

She didn't respond. Not even a flicker of her eyelid.

He knew he had to stay with her, to monitor her condition, but he was so tired, so bone-weary. He needed to close his eyes. Just for a moment. But as soon as he did, his mind dove back to his last mission, the one that had left him with so many scars, both physical and emotional. He tried to push it away, but the memories consumed him like a wildfire...

Despite the chill of the desert night, sweat dripped down Shane's spine as his well-armed team of six followed a narrow, winding pathway through the rocky mountains to Ahmed Al-Mansoor's heavily guarded compound. They settled on an outcropping overlooking their target and waited, watched until they had a firm grip on the pulse of the place. Their intel had been correct— Al-Mansoor was traveling light with only two armed soldiers at the gates and another two patrolling the perimeter.

So why was Shane's stomach twisted into uneasy knots? So far, Operation Ember Storm had gone off without even the slightest hiccup.

"We a go?" his second-in-command, Echo Two, Jaxon Thorne, asked close to his ear.

He shifted to look at his best friend, his brother. They'd been in the same BUD/S class, had lived through some of the toughest training in the world, had completed an untold number of missions together and had risen from tadpoles to Master Chief and Senior Chief, respectively. He trusted the man more than anyone else on the planet.

"What's wrong?" Jax's face was a blur of dark paint in the inky night, but Shane knew the man's expressions almost as well as his own. Jax was nervous, too, and Jaxon Thorne usually had

nerves of pure titanium. It was why their teammates had nick-named him Steady. "You getting bad vibes from this?"

Shane shifted his gaze back to the compound. Everything had gone according to plan. There was no reason he should be hesitating. He was just seeing his own nerves reflected in his men, so he had to buckle down and do the job. "No. We're a go, but..." He made a split-second decision that would change all of their lives. "Change of plans. Echo Two and Echo Five will secure the perimeter."

Jax frowned. "Are you sure about that? I should go with you—"

"No, I want you on overwatch."

"Fuck," Jax said softly. "You're getting bad vibes."

Shane stared at him, willing him to shut the fuck up before doubt infected the entire team. "Secure the perimeter, then set up overwatch, Echo Two."

Still scowling, Jax nodded. "Copy that, One."

Shane looked at Ethan "Mack" Mackenzie. "Five, I want you with us to breach the compound after you and Two taking out the perimeter guards."

Mack nodded, his face grim. "Hooyah."

"Echo Four, be ready to neutralize any traps we might encounter."

Zeke "Fuse" Mitchell grinned, all white teeth against his camo-painted face. "They ain't yet dreamed up an explosive I can't defuse."

"Don't get cocky, Fuse."

The big Texan waved a hand dismissively. "This is a milk run, Chief. We'll be home in time for the Cowboys game."

Shane's gut churned, but he swallowed it down, reminding himself of the stakes. Too many people had died at Al-Mansoor's hands, and intel suggested he was planning another attack on an American airbase. More service members and innocent civilians would die soon if the bastard wasn't taken off the board.

They had to complete their mission, no matter the cost. "Three, Six, stay on me."

Alejandro Ramirez—Echo Three—and the newest member of Echo, fresh off of Green Team, Rylan Cross—Echo Six— stacked up behind him.

"Remember," Shane said, "our primary objective is to capture Al-Mansoor alive, if possible. If not possible, we're to end his reign of terror tonight, quickly and quietly, with minimal civilian casualties. We good on ROE?"

"Hooyah," Alejandro said, and everyone nodded in agreement.

"Then let's move out."

With practiced efficiency, the team split into their designated positions.

Shane silently moved toward the main building with Alejandro and Rylan on his six, his senses alert for any signs of danger. He heard the muffled pops of Jax's and Mack's guns as they took out the guards. Fuse moved out ahead of them to place a breeching explosive charge on the door...

And the world erupted into chaos.

Gunfire exploded from every direction, ripping through the quiet darkness. Tracer rounds streaked across the sky like deadly fireworks and filled the air with an acrid stench of cordite that burned Shane's nostrils.

"Hostiles incoming from the west!" Mack bellowed into their comms, his rifle responding with sharp cracks that echoed over the grounds.

"Door's charged," Fuse said.

"Blow it," Shane said.

"I've got your six covered, Echo One," Jax said through his comm. "We'll hold 'em off. Finish the mission."

Jax was a sniper, one of the best the Navy had ever seen, but no way he could hold off the swarm of enemy combatants alone.

Alejandro pulled a grenade from his vest and heaved it into the growing crowd of fighters. "Grenade out!"

But when his grenade hit the ground, more than one explosion shattered the air, illuminating the havoc with blinding flashes.

"RPG incoming!" Jax shouted a second too late.

The building rumbled from the force of the explosions, and the ground seemed to heave under their boots. Flames burst at Alejandro's feet and in the second before the fire swallowed the four of them in a maelstrom of destruction, the medic looked up at Shane with stark terror in his eyes. Then a wave of intense heat blasted Shane out of his boots, searing skin, melting his clothes to his body, his weapon to his hand.

Somewhere far away, he heard a voice shout, "One is down! I repeat, Echo One is down!"

And then more garbled shouts, like splinters in his ears.

"Echo Six is down!"

"Four is down!"

"Three is—Jesus. Alejandro is gone. Just fucking gone."

Time fractured, and Shane's senses became a jumble of sights, sounds, and pain. He saw Rylan laying next to him. The kid was barely old enough to drink legally and he—

Or, no.

It wasn't Rylan.

It was his arm.

Just his arm, still clutching his gun.

He saw Fuse, wounded but struggling to his feet, still trying to fire at the enemy with a melted weapon. A hail of bullets sliced through the air and Fuse fell, his eyes blank and his mouth, usually so quick with a big grin, now slack, blood staining his lips...

chapter
eight

SHANE CAME BACK to reality and sucked in a sharp breath, his heart racing, his hands shaking. He was lightheaded.

He wished he could go back and change things. He should've listened to his gut feeling and scratched the mission before it ever started. He'd lost so much that night. His team — no, his family. His sense of purpose.

And now, here he was, bleeding into a woman he barely knew, hoping to save her life.

He turned to look at Alexis and realized he'd given her too much blood when his vision swam. That was why he felt woozy—not the flashback. He slid the needle from his arm and pressed a cotton pad to it to stop the bleeding, then did the same for her. When he applied pressure, she stirred, groaning softly as consciousness returned to her.

He stood up, wobbling a little on his feet as he leaned over her. "Alexis?"

She shied away from his touch, her eyes wide in terror. Only then did he realize how he must look, looming over her with his face still streaked in winter camouflage paint. He stepped back, then collapsed into his seat as his knees wobbled.

Yeah, he'd let the transfusion go on too long. He needed to eat something.

Alexis watched him warily for a handful of seconds, then her gaze flicked to the tubing and bloody gauze still on the bed by her leg. Horror filled her expression, and she scrambled back until she hit the wall, her breaths coming in short, fearful gasps.

"What did you do to me, you psychopath?"

"Shh." He held up his hands in a placating gesture. The same one the sheriff always used on him, which never actually calmed him down, and in fact did the opposite by pissing him off. And now he was doing it to her. He dropped his hands. "It's okay. You shouldn't try to stand up yet. You lost a lot of blood, and I gave you some of mine. I'm a universal donor."

She stared at him for another moment, then glanced down at her arm. "What...?" Her eyes narrowed with suspicion. "Why?"

"Why?" Shane repeated. Good question. One he didn't have an answer for. He didn't even know her last name, and yet he'd given her something that was a part of him, something he couldn't ever get back. "I couldn't just let you die," he said finally. "It's not who I am. I'm not a psychopath."

"You locked me in the bathroom." She looked like she was going to say more, but then snapped her mouth closed and tears spilled from those amazing green eyes.

Shame heated the back of his neck. Despite all of his claims of wanting to help her, she had every right to be suspicious. He had treated her like shit. "I... didn't trust you. I'm sorry. Sometimes..." He trailed off.

How much should he tell her?

The truth, he decided. All of it. After the way he'd treated her, she deserved it. But he'd never explained to anyone the way his brain played tricks on him and found the words difficult to voice.

"Sometimes... even though I'm here and safe, I sometimes still think I'm deployed, and the lines between then and now blur in my head. When that happens, everyone looks like an adversary, a potential threat— even a frightened, wounded woman. I could tell you were lying to me, and my paranoia got the better of me."

Some of the tension eased out of her shoulders, but she still stayed close to the wall, keeping as much distance as possible between them. "Deployed where?"

"A lot of places I'm not at liberty to discuss."

"You were military." It wasn't a question. "Which branch?"

"Navy. Once upon a time."

"And now you live..." She eyed the small cabin. "Here?"

He sat back in his seat and exhaled a long breath. He'd decided to be honest, so he was going to give her the full, ugly, unvarnished truth. "I can't trust myself around people. I might snap and hurt them like I hurt you."

Alexis studied him for a long time, eyes narrowed as if she was trying to puzzle him out.

"You're not him, are you?" she said finally.

"Not who?"

When she didn't respond, he looked pointedly at the fresh bandage on her bare thigh. "I'm not the man who shot you, if that's what you're asking. If I'd wanted to shoot you, you'd be dead."

She nodded and ducked her head as tears spilled from her eyes. "I thought you were him. That's why I lied. I thought you were playing mind games with me."

"Who is he?"

"I don't know."

"What did he do to you?"

She shook her head, but didn't answer.

Shane realized he had a stranglehold on the arms of the

chair and forced his fingers to open. Why was the answer so important to him? And why did the idea of anyone hurting her boil his blood?

He pushed himself out of the seat and blinked against a wave of dizziness. "We should both eat. I gave you too much blood and I'm feeling it."

Alexis gripped the edge of the cot, a shiver scraping down her spine as she watched Shane rummage through the cupboards in the small kitchenette. If you could call a small locked pantry and single burner on top of the wood stove a "kitchenette."

"Please, just take me back to town." She hated the tremor in her voice. Even if he wasn't the Shadow Stalker, he still made her uneasy. He was clearly unstable and dangerous...

And yet he had saved her life.

She couldn't quite make sense of it all.

"I can't do that," he said, his back to her as he warmed some canned soup on the stove.

"Why not?"

He didn't answer. He simply dumped the soup into a bowl and brought it over to her, shoving it into her hand. "Eat."

When she hesitated, he growled low in his throat. "It's not drugged or poisoned or anything."

She slowly lifted the spoon to her lips. She didn't want to seem ungrateful, but she still didn't completely trust Shane.

Would she ever trust any man again?

The stew warmed her belly. Only then did she realize how incredibly hungry she was. She ate several more bites, and the tension eased from her shoulders as her gnawing hunger abated.

But then she realized Shane wasn't eating and fear twisted her stomach. The strew threatened a return visit. He said it wasn't drugged, but if that was true, wouldn't he be eating it, too?

She dropped the spoon into the bowl. "Why aren't you eating?"

"I only have one bowl. One spoon."

She looked down at the dented metal bowl. It was like something you'd take on a camping trip, not the kind of dish you'd use for everyday meals. She returned her gaze to him.

He still hadn't moved.

Between the layers of camouflage paint obscuring his face and her missing glasses, which she'd lost somewhere in the woods, his expression was nothing but a vaguely human-shaped blur to her. And yet she thought maybe he was embarrassed by his lack of amenities.

"What, you don't host many dinner parties?"

"I don't like visitors." If he picked up on her sarcasm, he didn't show it. He turned away and grabbed a can of fruit from the haphazard stack of canned goods on the floor by the front door. He cracked it opened and dug in with his fingers, pulling out a peach slice, not the least bit embarrassed to eat without utensils.

Okay, so maybe she was projecting, trying to assign him feelings he didn't have because he didn't quite seem human. Part of her wondered if he was a figment of her imagination. What if the Shadow Stalker had killed her, and she was lying in the forest somewhere, hallucinating vividly in her final moments?

God.

She shook off the eerie thought. She hoped if her brain

were going to hallucinate a savior, he'd at the very least be more pleasant than this guy.

She sat back on the cot, the bowl of soup still untouched in her lap. "Then take me back to town."

Shane turned to her, his eyes narrowing. "I told you I can't do that."

"Why not?"

He gestured out the window to the raging blizzard outside. "You want to travel in this? Be my guest. But I don't have a death wish, so I'm staying here until it passes."

Panic rose in her chest. She'd been abducted from her motel, imprisoned for weeks, abused in ways she couldn't even think about yet, then set free to be hunted down like an animal. She refused to be trapped anywhere a second longer.

"But I can't stay here with you," she said, trying to keep her tone reasonable even as her voice broke. "I'm sure you don't have enough supplies for the both of us."

Shane finished the can of fruit and wiped his hands on the threadbare towel hanging beside the stove. "You still don't trust me."

"I don't know you." She set the bowl of soup aside. "Why should I trust you?"

"Because you don't have a choice. We're stuck here together, whether we like it or not. You saw what's outside."

"I don't care." She rose from the cot, trying to make herself seem taller than her diminutive height, but pain zinged up her leg and she limped. "I'd rather take my chances out there than be stuck in here with a man like you."

"A man like me," he repeated with a low, dangerous edge in his voice. "What does that mean?"

"You know what it means. A man who abducts women, who hurts them, who keeps them prisoner."

Shane took a step forward. "I didn't abduct you, Alexis. Why would I? I hate having you here."

"But you're still keeping me against my will!"

"I'm keeping you for your own safety. This mountain is a nasty bitch." He crossed to the door, his heavy boots thudding on the wooden floor, and flung it open. Snowflakes swirled inside on a frigid gust of wind.

It was white out there.

Just... white.

She couldn't even see the trees beyond the cabin.

"You won't make it to the snowline, and even if by some miracle you do, you'll still freeze to death because it will only be a few degrees warmer and raining."

Alexis took a step back, fear knotting in her stomach. But she knew one thing for sure— if she couldn't see anything, then the Shadow Stalker wouldn't be able to see her either. This storm might be her one chance to escape from this fucking mountain.

"I'll take my chances."

Shane stepped aside and waved an arm at the open door. "Then go. Get the hell off my mountain."

She hesitated for a moment. It was foolish to wander out into the blizzard, wounded and half-starved, but the thought of staying trapped in the cabin with Shane was too much to bear.

"Go!"

She jolted at his sudden roar and grabbed the bloodstained jacket and snow pants the Shadow Stalker had given her. She pulled them on, then stepped outside. The cold hit her like a punch to the chest, stealing her breath, and the cabin door slammed at her back.

Oh, God. This was a mistake.

chapter
nine

ALEXIS LOOKED at the closed door. Considered pounding on it and begging Shane to let her back in. But, dammit, she refused to trade one prison for another, one captor for another. Shane might not intentionally hurt her like the Shadow Stalker had, but he obviously wasn't stable and he'd already proven he was capable of violence. She was safer on her own, so she bowed her head and trudged off the porch, into the calf-deep snow.

It couldn't be that hard to get off the mountain, right? There were all kinds of cabins and vacation rentals and camp-grounds scattered around the area. There were National and State Parks all around the mountain with patrolling rangers. All she had to do was go downhill, and she'd eventually run into someone who didn't want to hurt her.

She hoped.

She stumbled forward, eyes squinted against the blinding white, and struggled to keep her footing as the wind whipped around her, blowing snow into her face and hair. She had no idea where she was going, but anywhere was better than staying with Shane.

Her body ached with every step, her injured leg dragging

behind her, the cold seeping into her bones, numbing her fingers and toes.

This was stupid.

She never should've left the cabin.

Why had she thought this was the safer option?

Maybe she was the unstable one.

She turned to go back the way she'd come, but the wind had filled in her footsteps. She turned again. Nothing looked familiar. She couldn't even tell if she was going uphill or down.

She heard something—a faint sound, almost lost in the wind's howl. A voice.

Alexis squinted through the snow, trying to pinpoint where the sound was coming from. The voice grew louder, and she realized it was a man's voice. He was calling out, trying to find someone.

Shane?

Had he changed his mind about taking her to town?

She cupped her hands around her mouth, shouting into the wind. "Over here! I'm over here!"

The man's voice faded away and she once again heard nothing but wind as a figure loomed out of the white void. It was definitely a man, his tall frame wrapped in a thick white coat, his face obscured by a scarf and goggles.

Definitely not Shane.

And she realized she'd made another horrible mistake in thinking he wouldn't still be out in the storm, hunting her.

The Shadow Stalker.

Alexis stumbled back a step, tried to turn and run, but her injured leg gave out. She landed hard in the snow, face-first, biting her lip and jarring her wounded shoulder. She tasted blood on her tongue.

The Shadow Stalker approached with a slow, deliberate gait, his boots crunching through the snow with every step.

The metal of a blade glinted in the light, and she gasped, instinctively scrambling backward, away from the danger.

But then she saw something else. A flash of movement behind him—something big and furry.

Shane.

He threw himself at the Shadow Stalker with a feral roar. Their bodies collided as they fought fiercely, violently tumbling across the ground. The snow whipped into a frenzy around them, obscuring her vision, but she heard grunts of pain and the sickening thuds of flesh being pummeled.

Shane burst out of the tangle of limbs, his fur coat spattered with blood and rage blazing in his wild eyes. He had the Shadow Stalker's knife in one hand and grabbed her by the arm with his free hand.

"Come on!" he shouted, dragging her uphill.

A searing pain shot down her leg and she fell to her hands and knees in the snow, unable to bear any weight. She'd pushed the injury too hard for too long, and her leg had gone numb.

Shane scooped her into his arms, barely breaking pace as he charged headfirst into the storm. Blinding wind and snow whipped at them from all sides, but Shane's determination kept them pressing forward. Fear and adrenaline coursed through her veins like fire. She clung to him, his body heat radiating around her, warming her icy limbs as they ran for what seemed like an eternity. She tried to thank him for saving her life, but found that the words were stolen from her lips by the vicious wind.

Finally, they reached the cabin and Shane kicked the door shut behind them with one hard knock of his boot. He locked it, then leaned against the wood heavily, panting hard.

"Are you okay?" he asked, voice hoarse, as he set her back on her feet.

Alexis nodded, still too shaken to speak. She collapsed

onto the cot, her knees too weak to hold her. "Did you kill him?"

"I don't think so." He wiped a hand across his face, smearing the paint and blood. "But he won't try for you again anytime soon."

"But he will try again." She shuddered at the thought of the Shadow Stalker still alive out there, waiting for her to show her face again. "What are we going to do now?"

Shane grunted as he sat down heavily in a nearby chair, his eyes fixed on the door. "We wait. When the storm passes, I'll take you to town and let the sheriff deal with you. I don't need your kind of trouble in my life."

She watched him for a moment, unsure of what to say. She had thought she knew him, had thought he was just another monster like the Shadow Stalker. But now she wasn't so sure.

Yes, he was dangerous. There was no denying that, but maybe he was the kind of danger she needed right now. He had saved her life, after all, had risked his own to protect her when he had no reason to. So maybe there was more to him than she had originally thought.

"Thank you," she finally said, her voice barely above a whisper.

He grumbled. "You shouldn't have left."

"Well, you shouldn't have been an asshole!"

The grumble hardened into a growl. "I'm not the asshole in this situation."

She closed her eyes for a moment, more exhausted than she cared to admit. "Okay."

"Okay."

She heard him shift in the chair and opened her eyes to see him watching her intently. His eyes were the same color as the paint he wore, a pale blue-gray, almost like the pigment had been sucked out of them.

The intensity of his gaze made her feel exposed, vulnerable, and yet there was something in the way he looked at her that was almost... soft. It was a contradiction that she couldn't wrap her mind around.

She thought about the way he had fought for her, how he had risked his life to keep her safe. He could be terrifying and he was capable of extreme violence, but there was something else there too, something sad and maybe broken beyond repair. But he wasn't broken in the same way as the man who had taken her captive. She could see that now.

What had happened to Shane to make him the way he was?

She wanted to ask, but didn't know how, so she went with what she thought was an easier question. "Why do you wear face paint?"

"Camouflage."

She opened her mouth to make a smartass remark because, duh, of course it was for camouflage, but there were no trees dressed in winter white to hide behind indoors and he still hadn't removed the paint. In fact, she had yet to see him without his face painted or covered.

Before she could speak, Shane stood and gave her his back as shrugged off his coat. Her mouth went dry, and she pushed to her feet before she remembered the bullet hole in her thigh.

"Shane! You're bleeding." His furs were bloodstained, but she had assumed it was all from the Shadow Stalker. It never crossed her mind that he'd been hurt. He seemed so... invincible. But at least part of the blood had come from a deep gash across his shoulder blade.

He grunted in acknowledgement as he stripped off his shirt, revealing a heavily muscled torso. Alexis watched him, trying not to stare, but it was hard. He moved with a fluid grace, every movement precise and deliberate. Deep scars crisscrossed his skin in ridges and valleys. She'd seen scars like that before during an interview with a woman whose abusive boyfriend held her arm over an open flame after she tried to leave him. But that woman's scars, as horrific as they were, only covered one arm. Shane's scars extended down his entire back and disappeared under the waistband of his winter camouflage pants.

He tore a strip of cloth from his shirt and wrapped it around his shoulder, wincing as he pulled it tight. "It's not as bad as it looks."

Alexis wasn't convinced. "You need to let me clean that up and bandage it properly. It could get infected."

He eyed her over his shoulder. "I'm not the one who needs to worry about infection."

She looked away, breaking eye contact. "Right. Sorry."

Shane finished bandaging his wound and turned back to her. "Who is he?"

She sucked in a sharp breath. This was the moment—she had to decide whether or not to trust Shane. Was he an ally or an enemy? Her instincts told her he was a little of both, but also that she didn't have any other options at the moment.

"He's a man I've been investigating for a while now—"

She saw his shields go up as clearly as if he'd built a wall between them. "You're a reporter?"

"Sort of. I used to be a producer for a news station in Chicago, but I left when my true crime podcast took off. Now I do that full time."

Shane scowled. "What's a podcast?"

She blinked at him in disbelief. "Exactly *how long* have you lived up here?"

"Nine years."

Her mouth dropped open. Nine years. Nearly a decade. So much had changed in that time—more than just the rise in popularity of podcasts. Nine years ago, she'd been in college, trying to figure out what she wanted to do for a career, going out on the weekends with her friends, and just enjoying life as a young adult.

And he'd been here.

Alone.

With his demons.

When he growled softly, she realized she was staring at him and clamped her jaw shut again.

"Okay," she said after taking a second to gather her thoughts. "Well, a podcast is like a radio show, but it's on the internet. People can listen to it on their phones or computers. I talk about true crime cases—mostly cold cases—and try to uncover new information that wasn't previously known."

He made a face that said he still didn't quite understand, but didn't press the issue. "And you came all the way out here to investigate this guy? Why?"

"Because nobody else was. Everyone thinks he's a myth, like Sasquatch, and, I don't know, maybe he did start out that way. The legend has been around a long time, so unless he's immortal, it's probably not the same man who originally sparked the Shadow Stalker myth. But there's a killer using that legend to his advantage, preying on vulnerable women. I thought I could get more information if I came to his hunting grounds."

"That was a mistake."

Alexis winced at the truth in his words. "Yeah, I can see that now. But I didn't expect to draw his attention because I'm not like his usual victims. He goes for brunettes who are isolated, vulnerable—addicts, prostitutes, runaways. He chooses young women who won't be missed. I'm none of those things. I'm thirty-one—five years older than his oldest known victim—and I have a sister I'm very close to. I have a big friend group, a high-profile job. And I'm blonde. I honestly didn't think I'd be a target."

"You should have called the police."

"I did. I went to the sheriff with my research, but he was distracted by other crimes happening in town. I thought I could investigate on my own and bring him something more solid than a hunch."

"And you nearly got yourself killed," he said bluntly.

"I have two bullet holes in me. To say I'm very aware of that fact is an understatement."

Once again, her sarcasm seemed to go right over his head. "What did he do to you?"

She hesitated. She wasn't sure if she was ready to talk about everything that had happened to her, but she also knew that if she wanted Shane to help her, she had to be honest.

"He... he took me from in front of my motel. He pretended to need help." She closed her eyes against the memory, but still saw the whole scene play out again in her mind. She'd gone over that moment repeatedly while stuck in the Shadow Stalker's bunker, analyzing it, wondering what she could've done differently. But it had all happened so fast. She'd been in the middle of unlocking the door of her room, could hear her dog yipping with excitement inside. The man had approached her with a heavy limp and said something about needing directions to the nearest hospital. When she turned toward him in concern, everything went black. Next thing she remembered was his bunker and him coming in to—

She shuddered at the memory, her skin crawling with revulsion. She opened her eyes and looked at Shane.

Weirdly, his presence soothed her unraveling nerves.

She swiped at the tears leaking down her cheeks. "Crime is my job. I research the worst of the worst cases. I talk about murderers and victims all day, every day. I constantly warn my listeners about the danger, and share with them all the ways women can avoid becoming victims themselves—but when push came to shove, I fell for it, too. I fell for the oldest trick in the serial killer playbook."

Shane's face was still hidden by a layer of paint, but she sensed a shift there, a darkening. He knew she was stalling.

"What did he do to you?" he asked again.

"He kept me in a bunker for weeks and…" Nope. Still couldn't talk about it. She cleared her throat. "Then one day, he threw that at me." She nodded toward the bloodstained jacket on the floor. "And told me to run. He wanted to hunt me like an animal. I think that's how he killed the others. The jacket already had bloodstains and bullet holes in it."

Shane said nothing for several long minutes. Then, in a burst of movement that startled her, he pushed up from the stool. "Rest. You're safe here."

The weight of exhaustion settled in her bones, weighing her down. "Where will you sleep?"

He gestured to the pile of furs on the floor. "Over there."

"I don't want to kick you out of your bed."

"You're not. I usually sleep up there." He pointed to the loft. "It's warmer. When your leg stops bleeding, I'll move you up there. But I'm not planning on sleeping."

A chill danced over her skin in a blast of cold air even though the cabin was warm and the blankets were cozy. "Do you think he'll try for me again?"

"I know he will. He can't let you live. You know too much about him."

"Oh, God." She sank back onto the cot and the events of the day replayed in her mind like a movie on fast-forward. "But I've never seen his face."

"You've seen other parts." He didn't elaborate, and she was glad for it. She didn't want to think of what other body parts he meant. She didn't want to think about the birth mark. Just… didn't want to think about any of that. Not yet. Maybe not ever.

"You've seen his bunker," Shane continued. "And know approximately where it is."

"But I don't think I could find—"

He spoke over her protest: "You have a jacket with his

other victims' blood on it. My furs are covered in his blood. We have his DNA. He's not going to let either of us live through this storm. His life—his freedom—depends on it."

He was right.

Of course he was right.

She was being stupidly, dangerously optimistic about their situation. Blame it on the blood loss.

Nausea swirled in her stomach at the thought of being hunted again. But Shane was calm, collected—calculating, even.

Like he was used to being hunted.

Like he had a plan.

God, she hoped he did, because she had no idea how to survive another encounter with the Shadow Stalker. She'd barely survived the first two and doubted she'd get lucky a third time.

Shane seemed to sense her fear. He crouched down beside her, his hand hovering over her shoulder. He didn't touch her, though. "I won't let him hurt you again."

She searched his eyes and saw something in his gaze that she couldn't quite name. A mixture of determination and... something else. Something softer.

"Why are you helping me?"

He hesitated for a moment before answering. "Because you need help."

The fact that this man, who had more than his own share of demons, was willing to fight hers, brought tears to her eyes again. And with the tears came a fresh surge of terror.

"You don't have to do this," she whispered. "He's not human—he's a monster."

Shane's smile was slow and hard and a little bit grotesque. "So am I."

chapter
ten

IT TOOK A LONG TIME, but Alexis finally fell asleep.

Shane sat beside her cot and watched the slow, steady rise and fall of her chest. Her color looked better, the pallor fading from her cheeks. She was fighting—just as she had fought to survive out in the wilderness, bleeding and alone. This woman had strength and grit and wasn't going to give up.

Neither was he. Shane had failed to protect people before, had watched friends die because he wasn't fast enough or strong enough or smart enough. He wouldn't fail Alexis. No matter what it took, he was going to keep her safe.

Even if it meant going back to the life he'd left behind. The life of violence and shadows he'd walked away from after his injury. He flexed his scarred hands, remembering the way his flesh had melted and fused together. The pain had been unbearable, but the loss of his career and purpose had cut deeper.

Until now.

Looking at Alexis, he felt that old drive ignite in his chest. The need to fight, to defend, to destroy anything that threatened the innocent.

Shane stood and pulled his chair over to the window,

planting himself there. He scanned the thick forest outside. The storm had eased somewhat, but Mother Nature wasn't done yet. This was just a timeout for her to catch her breath. More snow was coming down the mountain, and if the dark clouds at the summit were any indication, it was going to be here soon.

If the killer was smart, he'd crawl back into his bunker and wait it out.

But Shane could sense him out there, waiting. Watching.

The bastard had made a huge mistake coming after Alexis while she was under his protection. Because now Shane had a reason to stop running—and start hunting. The Shadow Stalker wanted to cast darkness over his mountain? Well, he'd stepped into the shadows with the wrong fucking man this time.

Shane leaned back in his chair again, and stared out the window, clocking every snowflake, every twig snap…

But then suddenly, it wasn't snow anymore. It was sand. It was hot. So hot. Fire everywhere. Everything burning. The world, his skin, his teammates…

Then Jax was there on the ground in front of him, listless, bleeding.

Shane stooped to pick him up. Couldn't leave him behind. Then he saw an arm. Just an arm, a few feet away, with an intricate compass tattoo on the wrist. Rylan's tattoo. He picked the limb up. Couldn't leave any piece of his men behind.

This time, he'd get them out. He'd save them.

He took another step. Stumbled under the weight of his dead teammates. Collapsed to one knee—and a woman reached out, took his hand in hers. He looked up into striking green eyes. Her long blond hair cascaded over her shoulders and she wore a simple white dress that flowed around her like a cloud. She smiled at him, and for a moment, he forgot about the pain and the death that surrounded him.

"Come with me," she said, pulling him forward.

His men disappeared. The blood vanished from his hands. Everything shifted around him, the harsh desert heat fading to a misty, deep green forest.

His forest.

His mountain.

His... woman?

No. That didn't make sense. And, yet, it didn't sound wrong either.

As he followed her, a sense of peace washed over him. He couldn't remember the last time he felt peace. Certainly before the war. Before the SEALs. And he smiled as they walked through a field of wildflowers to a small cabin.

His cabin.

But not like his at all.

Instead of moss-covered logs and a sagging roof, it was all bright and clean and new. Flowers bloomed in window boxes and the porch didn't creak and groan when she led him onto it.

The interior was cozy and warm. The old cast iron wood stove was now a fancy stone fireplace with a fire crackling merrily in the hearth. The woman sat him down in a comfortable leather chair and tended to his wounds. Her touch was gentle and soothing, and he relaxed for the first time in years.

When she finished bandaging him up, she handed him an ornate gold mirror, like something out of a fairy tale. He tried to give it back. He didn't want to look. Didn't want to see what he'd become. But she turned it gently in his hand and lifted it toward his face and—

It was *his* face.

Not melted and twisted and nightmare-inducing, but the face he'd had before that night in the desert. Classically handsome with symmetrical features, a straight nose, a strong jaw, and dimpled chin. Hair that was not blond, but not brown—a mix of colors, like a lion's mane—and a little too long, but not shaggy. Blue eyes, crinkled at the corners, bright against skin that was whole and healthy with the perpetual tan he'd cultivated from spending his every free moment on the beaches of Southern California. Even the little scar above his lip from a bike accident when he was a boy was there. His dad had called it his "Elvis scar" because it pulled his lip up into a tiny permanent sneer. He lifted a hand to it in wonder. He'd always hated that imperfection, but now he was so happy to see it that tears filled his eyes.

The woman leaned in close and whispered in his ear, "You're still you. I think you've forgotten that, but inside, in your heart, you're still as beautiful as you ever were."

He looked up at her, struck by wonder. He had never met anyone quite like her before. She radiated kindness and understanding, something he had been missing for years. "Who are you?"

She smiled gently. "You know."

He leaned in closer, suddenly needing to kiss her more than he needed anything else in his life. She met him halfway, and a spark ignited in him. It was the first time he had felt anything remotely resembling passion in years.

As they broke apart, she smiled at him, her eyes filled with warmth and affection as she pulled him to his feet. "You need to go back now."

Shane woke up slowly, and for the first time in a long time, he wasn't anxious. He'd never had a dream like that before, one that soothed and calmed. Usually his dreams were all terror and blood and death and pain. But this was different. It was like a glimpse of something he had long forgotten, something he had buried deep inside himself. Or maybe something that hadn't happened yet? A look at the future. He felt a deep sense of longing, a desire to find that woman again, to stay in that cabin forever.

How weird to be homesick for something that didn't exist. That never existed. That never will exist.

He scrubbed a hand over his face, disappointed but not surprised to find all the ridges and valleys and waxy ropes of scar still there.

It was just a dream, after all.

And the woman wasn't real, either. She was a figment of his exhausted mind and—

His gaze landed on the cot. Alexis lay still and silent under the heap of blankets and, for a heartbeat, he worried that she'd started bleeding again. What if she bled out while he'd been lost in dreamworld? He got up and crossed to her bedside. Her breaths came evenly, and her pretty face was flushed, but relaxed in sleep.

Blonde hair.

Intense green eyes.

Was his dream woman Alexis?

Shane shook his head, dismissing the thought as ridiculous. Alexis was beautiful by any measure. She had friends and family and a thriving career. She had a life to get back to off the mountain. He was a scarred beast of a man with no manners, crippling paranoia, and severe social anxiety. Not to mention all the blood on his hands. He would never be worthy of someone like her, and she would never be interested in someone who looked like him. It was stupid to fantasize about such things, even in his dreams.

And yet he couldn't get the thought out of his head. He stood there, staring down at her, trying to find any resemblance between the woman in his dream and Alexis. Her hair was the same shade of blonde. And her eyes, though closed now, were the same shade of green. Her lips looked as soft as they'd felt against his in the dream. Her hands were elegant, with long fingers, and she had touched him with such tenderness as she tended to his wounds.

Okay, no denying the dream woman had been Alexis. Obviously, his mind had inserted her because she was the first person he'd had more than a few minutes of conversation with in years.

It meant nothing.

He wondered what she dreamed about. Were they like his dreams, filled with death and destruction? Or did she dream of joyful things, of love and family and all the things he would never have?

She made a small sound, like a frightened whimper, and without thinking, he reached down to smooth her hair back from her face.

Shit.

She was burning up.

Shane tore through the first aid kit. He'd seen a thermometer in there, though he'd never used it. In the rare times he'd gotten a fever, he just rode it out, and waited to see if it would finally be the thing to kill him. But he wasn't about to risk Alexis's life like that. So where was the damn thing?

His hand closed around the sterile package and he exhaled in a rush until he saw it was digital. Hopefully, it wasn't dead because he didn't have batteries on hand for it. He ripped it open and hit the power button. The screen lit up. He lifted the blanket off Alexis long enough to place the tip under her arm.

As he waited for it to take the reading, guilt twisted his stomach into uncomfortable knots. How long had she been feverish? He shouldn't have fallen asleep. He should have been paying closer attention to her.

The thermometer beeped.

One-oh-three point one.

Fuck.

He had to cool her down.

He scooped her up and flung open the door, trudging out into the snow. The icy air hit him like a thousand knives, but he couldn't go back in for his furs now. Holding Alexis tightly in his arms, he ran towards the creek that snaked through his land. It had still been flowing when he found the dog, and he hoped it hadn't frozen over it the last few days.

There was a fresh glaze of ice on top, but he easily broke through it. As snowflakes swirled around them, he waded in until the water was up to his waist, then lowered Alexis into it, being careful not to dip her head under. She gasped and shivered as the cold water hit her, but she didn't wake up. He held her there, keeping a close eye on her for any hint of stress. It was too cold—she could go into shock—but it was his only option to lower her fever until she woke up and could take some Tylenol from the first aid kit. After a few seconds, he lifted her out and carried her back to the cabin, holding her close to his chest.

The whole time he felt eyes on him.

The killer was out there, watching, waiting for another chance to strike.

Or was that his own paranoia talking?

Maybe.

Hell, probably.

He'd stabbed the asshole at least once, and the knife had gone in deep. It was highly unlikely the guy was just hanging around in a snowstorm without shelter. No, he'd retreated to lick his wounds and plan. He wasn't a threat right now.

Back inside, Shane laid her down on the cot and checked her temperature again. It was slowly coming down, but the reprieve wouldn't last unless he combatted the infection causing it. And the only way to do that was with antibiotics, which he absolutely didn't have.

He had to take her to town.

But would she survive the ride down?

She stirred and let out a soft groan.

"Alexis?" He leaned over her, his heart pounding with worry. Her eyes fluttered open, and she glanced around with confused panic. Then recognition flickered, and the panic eased as she tried to sit up.

"No, no, don't move. Let me." He gently lifted her and stuffed blankets behind her back to prop her up.

"I'm cold," she said through chattering teeth.

"You have a high fever. I had to cool you in the stream, but it will only bring your temp down temporarily. Think you can take some Tylenol?"

She nodded. He left her side long enough to grab his canteen from its hook beside the door. Gave it a shake to make sure there was still water inside, then found two of the individual dose packages of the pills in the first aid kit. Her fever was high enough to require a double dose. Kneeling beside the cot, he ripped open the packages, dumped the four pills out into his palm, and offered her one at a time. She took each pill slowly with sips from the canteen, swallowing like her throat hurt. When she finished, she lay back as if that small bit of movement had exhausted her.

Shane set the canteen aside and pressed the back of his hand to her forehead. "That will work for the short-term, but you need antibiotics."

A small smile tilted up the corners of her lips. "I don't suppose you have a pharmacy nearby?"

His scars pulled uncomfortably as he scowled. "The nearest one is in town."

She gave a weak laugh. "I know. It was a joke."

He grunted in response, stood up, and paced back and forth across the cabin as he thought through the problem. She watched his every move with those green eyes.

How could he get her to town safely? Could he bundle her

up in the cargo trailer like he had the dog? But the ride down had nearly killed the dog. For all he knew, it had killed the animal. But what other choice did he have?

Finally, he stopped and turned to her. "I have to take you to town. You need more medical attention than I can provide."

"How far away are we?"

He hesitated, unsure if he should tell her the truth. But it was her life in the balance. As much as he wanted to scoop her up and carry her down the mountain himself, she had to make this decision.

"It's a long ride. On my ATV, it's half a day's ride, and that's in good weather. I can load you into my trailer with my furs, but it will be dangerously cold. We'll be exposed to the elements for hours until we reach the snowline. If we're lucky, it won't be raining down there. If we aren't, hypothermia will be almost a given." Of course, with how high her temperature was, maybe hypothermia wouldn't be a problem for her.

"And if we stay here?" Her voice was hoarse.

"The infection could reach your blood. You'll go septic, your organs will fail, and you'll die within twelve hours."

"So either way, I'll probably die." She gave a small smile, trying to be brave, but he could see the fear in her eyes. He didn't blame her. It wasn't exactly a reassuring situation.

"I won't let that happen," he said with more confidence than he felt.

She closed her eyes and didn't speak again for a long moment. Then she looked at him, and her tears made something clench painfully in his chest.

"Take me home, Shane."

"Done." He went to the door and opened it, peering out into the blizzard. The wind had picked up, howling as it whipped snow into his face, and he squinted to see beyond the cabin. It was going to be a hell of a treacherous journey.

But they didn't have a choice.

"Is he still out there?" Alexis whispered behind him.

"I don't think so." He shut the door and tried to ignore the icy claw of paranoia scraping down his spine. "But we'll leave after dark. Minimize the chances of being seen."

Her eyes widened. "In this weather?"

"We don't have a choice."

chapter
eleven

ALEXIS DIDN'T KNOW how she'd managed to fall asleep, but she felt a hand on her shoulder and peeled her eyes open to see Shane leaning over her with concern in his pale eyes.

He exhaled softly. "There you are."

"Where did I go?"

"Your temperature spiked again and you wouldn't wake up."

She smiled faintly. "Nope, still here."

"Yeah." He took her hand and pressed his fingers to the flutter of her pulse. "You're too stubborn to die easily."

Her smile widened briefly before fading into a grimace. "Hurts like hell, though."

"I know." He checked the bandages at her chest and leg, and seem satisfied by what he saw. "It's dark. Time to go. Can you get up?"

It took more effort than she expected. Her body was stiff and ached all over. She gritted her teeth and forced herself to sit up as her muscles protested.

Oh, this was going to suck.

She took a deep breath and pushed herself to stand. A bolt

shot through her leg and she cried out, gritting her teeth, willing the pain away.

Shane steadied her with a hand on her back. "Okay?"

"Uh-huh." She shuffled a step forward, but her legs wobbled, and Shane caught her again.

"You're not going anywhere on your own just yet." He wrapped his arm around her waist, supporting her weight.

"Thank you." She leaned heavily against him. He was solid, muscular. Safe.

God, she hadn't felt safe in weeks.

He lowered her into his chair by the wood stove and picked up her blood-stained coat and snow pants. "You gotta put these back on."

She stared at the garments, bile rising in her throat. The white camo was darkened with more than just her blood, speckled with more holes than had been shot into her. How many other women had worn those? Died in those at the Shadow Stalker's hands?

"But it's evidence," she protested.

"It's all we have to keep you warm on the ride down. I'll also wrap you in my furs, but every layer counts." He didn't wait for her to agree and instead knelt in front of her, lifting her bad leg into the pant leg first. She winced, but didn't argue and lifted her butt off the seat so he could slide the snow pants the rest of the way on. As he fastened the snaps, she noticed his hands were painted like the rest of him. They were big hands, rough and capable...

And horribly scarred.

She looked up into his eyes and, for the first time, she saw past the camouflage face paint. Those scars weren't just on his hands and back. She remembered thinking his face didn't look quite right. Now she knew why she'd had that impression when they first met.

Shane's expression was unreadable as he stood up, but

Alexis saw the flicker of pain in his eyes. She opened her mouth to say something, but he turned away and shoved the jacket at her.

"I need to load the ATV. Put that on and stay here until I come back."

Without waiting for an answer, he grabbed an armful of furs from her cot and flung open the door, disappearing into the night. The blast of cold air he let in sent a shiver rattling through her, even though she felt like she was roasting slowly over a fire.

Just how high was her temperature?

Obviously high enough that a recluse like Shane thought it prudent to drive her off the mountain in the middle of the night.

Alexis struggled into her coat, wincing as she raised her arms. The pain was all-encompassing, but she refused to let it show. She was a survivor, damn it. She'd made it this far, and she wasn't going to let some bullet holes and a fever stop her now.

She glanced around the cabin, taking in the sparseness of the place. There were no photos on the walls, no decorations to speak of. Just the bare necessities of life on the mountain.

Who was Shane?

Where had he gotten all of those scars?

She was jolted out of her thoughts by the sound of his boots crunching through the snow outside. He came back in, cinching his coat tighter around him before scooping an arm around her waist and pulling her to her feet.

"More snow is coming in. We need to move now."

She limped beside him. Each step was agony, but she refused to make a peep.

Out on the porch, she stumbled to a halt. "It's dark."

"Usually is in the middle of the night."

Her hand tightened around his arm. "Not like this."

She'd never seen anything like the inky blackness surrounding the cabin. It was as if the world had disappeared and left them alone in a void of nothingness. It was the kind of darkness that whispered of danger, of the unknown waiting to pounce on them, with no stars in the sky and no moon to light their way. The wind howled, whipping snowflakes into a frenzy, and the trees creaked and groaned around them. But she couldn't even see their outlines in the darkness. It was just noise. Strange, terrifying noise.

Shane didn't seem bothered by the darkness. He just tugged her towards the ATV, which was already loaded up with supplies.

When she didn't move, he looked at her and some of the stiffness eased out of his shoulders. "Welcome to winter on my mountain."

"How can you see anything?"

"I'm used to it. I know this land." He tugged at her again, but her feet still wouldn't move forward. She didn't want to leave the soft pool of light cast by his cabin.

Then he extinguished that light and shut the door. She couldn't help the tiny squeak of alarm as the world plunged into blackness. It was disorientating.

"Shane? Where's the light?"

"No lights. We can't risk it." His arms circled her waist, and he pulled her close. "I've got you," he murmured, and scooped her up. "You need to trust me. I'll get you off this mountain."

Trust him? She didn't know him. Twelve hours ago, she'd thought he was the man who had tortured her for weeks and tried to kill her.

But what choice did she have? It was dark and snowing. She was injured and feverish. And there was a killer somewhere on this mountain waiting for another shot at her.

Maybe it was wrong, maybe her intuition was all out of whack from the fever, but he felt safe.

She curled against his chest, and felt the warmth of his breath on her temple, the roughness of his scars against her cheek as he carried her. It was an intimate embrace, one that made her heart race despite the pain ripping through her body.

He deposited her in the cargo trailer behind his ATV. It was slightly shorter than her height, but she could fit if she bent her legs. The steel mesh was icy even through the fabric of her snow pants.

"Lay down on your side and curl into a ball to preserve body heat."

She did as Shane instructed, and he tucked the furs around her, making sure she was as warm as possible before climbing onto the driver's seat.

"It's going to be bumpy. Stay under the furs as much as you can," he said over his shoulder as he pulled a balaclava down over his face.

She didn't get the chance to respond because he fired the engine and the whole rig jolted forward.

Shane drove the ATV with the ease of someone who'd done it a thousand times before, weaving his way through the trees and over the rocks. Still, she felt every bump and rut of the uneven terrain jarring her already sore body.

As they left the clearing surrounding Shane's cabin behind, she closed her eyes and focused on her breathing. She couldn't see anything anyway, and the darkness allowed her to retreat into herself, to forget the pain for a moment.

She didn't know how long they drove, but the landscape around them didn't seem to change. It was all trees and snow and darkness, all the same as far as she could tell.

Every turn they took, every bump they hit, was a reminder

of how vulnerable she was. She was at the mercy of Shane and the unforgiving terrain, and her life was in his hands.

Her mind kept drifting back to his scars. What could have caused such damage to his face and hands? Was it related to the Shadow Stalker, or was it something else entirely? She wanted to ask him, to understand the man who was risking everything to save her, but the darkness and the noise made it impossible to form the words.

So she had to think of something else. She had to think warm thoughts.

Hot chocolate. Cozy socks. Crackling fireplace.

No, that wasn't working. She had to think summer warm, not winter warm.

She tried to picture herself on a beach somewhere, the tropical sun beating down on her face, but it still didn't work. All she could feel was the biting cold seeping through the mesh of the trailer and into her bones. She felt like she was freezing from the inside out. Was that possible? Would Shane get her to town only to unwrap the furs and find a Lexi-sicle?

Just when she thought she couldn't take it anymore, they hit a large rock, and the trailer bounced so hard she thought she might be sick.

But then the ATV lurched to a stop.

The engine made a sad gurgling sound and died, plunging the forest into a startling silence.

Shane's voice was muffled through his balaclava. "Fuck."

Alexis peeked out from under the furs, but she still couldn't see more than vague tree-shaped shadows. "What's wrong?"

He hopped off and, finally, flicked on a small flashlight. She was so relieved she sat up. Even though logically she knew the beam didn't give off heat, she still wanted to hover over it with her hands outstretched.

Shane unscrewed the gas cap and shined the light inside. "Fuck," he said again and smacked the side of the vehicle.

She knew little about ATVs, but she didn't think it was supposed to sound hollow like that. "Are we out of gas?"

Shane didn't answer. He just got down on his back and shimmied under the ATV with the light. After a moment, he reappeared, his bloodstained fur coat covered in snow. He paced a few steps and she could practically see the anger shimmering off him.

"Did we run out of gas?" she asked again, panic rising.

"I filled it before we left, but the bastard must've poked a hole in the tank. Small enough that we'd lose the gas slowly, but big enough that we had no chance of making it to town."

She looked around, but somehow the landscape was even darker and more ominous in the small beam of his flashlight. "How far are we from town?"

"Too far."

"So we go back to your cabin."

"He'll be waiting."

She shivered and pulled the fur up under her chin as the wind picked up and snow blasted her in the face. "How do you know?"

"'Cause that's what I would do." He shook his head. "We can't go back. You need medical attention. We go back, and you'll die, no matter how stubborn you are."

Alexis bit her lip and looked away. She didn't want to die, but she didn't want to be stuck here with Shane either. She barely knew him, and yet he was her only hope for survival. "What do we do then?"

Shane walked over to her and crouched down. "We walk. It's the only way."

"Walk?"

"We don't have a choice. We'll have to stick to the trees, use them as cover. We can't risk being out in the open."

"How far is it?"

"About twenty miles."

"Twenty miles? In this?" She gestured at the blizzard raging around them.

Shane nodded grimly. "But it won't all be snow. Once we drop enough in elevation, it will change to rain, which will be just as dangerous. Are you up for it?"

She hesitated, looking at him, really looking at him for the first time. What was it about him that made her trust him, made her believe he would do everything in his power to keep her safe?

His eyes, she decided. Beyond the layers of camo paint, hidden behind his gruffness, he had kind eyes.

She nodded. "I'll do whatever it takes to get out of here. Lead the way."

Shane stood up and offered her his hand. "We'll have to move fast. The storm's getting worse. Can you walk?"

She pushed herself up, wincing as pain lanced through her leg. She leaned heavily on his arm. "I can walk."

He didn't call her on her lie, and they set off into the darkness, the wind howling around them and the snow stinging their faces. She stumbled a few times, but Shane kept her steady. They moved quickly, but carefully, using the trees as cover and trying to avoid making too much noise. Every sound made her jump, afraid that the Shadow Stalker was right behind them. Which was ridiculous. There was no possible way he'd followed them. Unless he wasn't human. Unless he was actually made of shadows like the legends claimed...

No. Stop.

The Shadow Stalker was human. Just a twisted, sick, pathetic human being who hid in the shadows. And she was going to make it to town and take everything she knew about the asshole to the sheriff.

She was going to bring him down.

chapter
twelve

THEY WERE STILL miles away from civilization, and the storm was not letting up. Shane could barely see five feet in front of him, and the wind was so strong it felt like it was trying to push them back up the mountain.

And Alexis was fading. Becoming quieter, slower with each passing minute.

He was losing her.

Fuck.

When she collapsed in the snow, he scooped her up and gave her a light shake. "Alexis. C'mon, stay awake."

"I'm awake." The two words slurred together. Her eyelids drooped, heavy with exhaustion, and snowflakes accumulated in her blond hair as she shivered uncontrollably.

He had to warm her up, and fast.

He opened up his furs and bundled her against his chest, trying to share his body heat with her. She relaxed slightly, nuzzling closer as he pulled the fur jacket tighter around them both. Holding her like this, so close their breath mingled in the same cloud, should feel wrong. He couldn't remember the last time he was this close to another human.

A strange sensation moved through his chest. It wasn't

just the warmth spreading from his body into hers. It was something else. Something he hadn't felt in a long time. An opening, unfurling. Maybe it was just adrenaline, or maybe it was the way she fit perfectly against him. Whatever it was, he couldn't ignore it. His arms tightened against her back, pulling her closer.

The hand she'd closed around his shirt loosened, and he shook her again. "Alexis. Talk to me." He looked up at the sky, hoping to see a break in the clouds. Nothing but darkness and more wet, heavy snow. "You said you have a sister. What's her name?"

Her eyes cracked open, and a small smile touched her chattering lips. "Ellie Mae."

"Tell me about her. What's she like?"

"She's... a lot."

"What do you mean?"

"She's energy and chaos. She's so bright, she outshines the sun. And she's just fun. She's so fun. I'm not like her. I'm a black hole that sucks the fun out of everything. I'm boring."

I don't think so, Shane thought. Boring women weren't strong and stubborn. Boring women didn't fight like hell to survive against all odds. Ask him, Alexis was the farthest thing from boring.

But he kept his mouth shut about that as he adjusted his grip on her and continued to trudge through the snow. He'd never been good at small talk, even before he'd banished himself to the mountain. But the longer she spoke, the longer she stayed awake, so he needed to keep her talking.

"What does she look like?" he asked instead.

Alexis smiled a little wider, and again he felt that thing in his chest open up, loosen. "She has curly blond hair, lighter than mine, and freckles. Lots of them." She closed her eyes again, but continued talking. "Like she has stars sprinkled across her skin. Her eyes are this bright blue.

Almost electric blue. She's beautiful, but she doesn't think so..."

When she trailed off, he prompted, "What else?"

"She loves to dance," Alexis continued, her words stronger now. "Any time there's music, she won't hesitate to grab my hand and pull me onto the dance floor. And she loves animals, too. She's like an animal magnet. She can spot a lost puppy or a stray cat from miles away."

Shane pictured the dog he'd found. Its scruffy brown fur and determined eyes. Had it survived? He wanted to think so, and how strange was that? Not that long ago, he wouldn't have cared one way or another.

For a moment, he considered telling Alexis about the dog and how he'd taken it to town, how awful his trip to the grocery store had been, how much he hated the way everyone looked at him like he wasn't human...

But that all felt too personal, like opening his veins and bleeding out all of his insecurities. And he'd already given her enough of his blood as it was. Her sister was a safer topic.

"What does Ellie Mae do for a living?" he asked.

"We work together. She's my researcher for the podcast. She loves facts, details. She can never know enough. Never play against her in trivia games. She'll win. She's relentless until she has all the answers."

"Sounds like you two have a lot in common."

"Yes, and no. She always says I'm too serious," she mumbled. "Too focused on work. Too single-minded. Driven. She can turn it on and off when she needs to, but I can't. It's just the way I am. I don't know how to be any different."

Well, hell. Didn't that hit a little too close to home? He had also been accused of being too focused on finishing the mission, no matter the cost. And then the next mission. And the next. The military had awarded that aspect of his personality, amplified it, and that had been his downfall in the end. He couldn't let go of the mission, even when it was over. Even now, all these years later. The memories and the guilt had followed him back to the real world, and he couldn't shake them off.

But here, now, he had a new mission. To keep Alexis alive. To get her to safety.

"You don't have to be any different," he said. "You're perfect just the way you are."

She looked up at him with bleary eyes, and he saw the doubt there. Doubt that he could save her. Doubt that anyone could. Yeah, well, he was going to prove her wrong.

"You don't know anything about me," she whispered. "I'm not perfect."

"I know enough. You're a fighter. You're tenacious. You're a survivor. To go through what you did, to keep fighting even now... there's nothing boring about you, Lexi."

Vulnerability flashed in her eyes. "That's what Ellie calls me."

Shit. He hadn't even realized he'd shortened her name until she pointed it out. "Sorry. I, uh, meant Alexis."

"No, I like it. I like being Lexi."

They fell into silence for several steps and, once again, he sensed her drifting away from him. "Hey, Lexi. Tell me more about your sister. Tell me more about Ellie Mae. She sounds exhausting."

She mumbled something, then lifted her head again, but winced at a blast of icy wind and tucked her face against his shoulder. "She is. Keeping her on track is like trying to harness a lightning bolt. I admire that about her, though. She has this way of making everything seem possible, like there are no limits to what we can do or achieve. I'm the voice of the podcast, but her work behind the scenes made it successful. She goes after what she wants, even when all the odds are stacked against her. She's fearless."

"Everyone's afraid of something."

"Not Ellie. She lives without fear. She's always been that way."

"What about you?"

She was quiet for a moment, and he thought she'd fallen asleep again. But then she whispered, "All I do is fear."

He knew fear. He lived with it every day. It was an old friend, and he couldn't imagine his life without it. But he doubted Alexis had been to a war zone, so why was she afraid?

He tightened his hold on her. He knew he shouldn't ask. It wasn't his business. But he still found the question rumbling out of him in a growl. "Why?"

Alexis sighed, her breath hitching in her chest. "I'm the middle child. Or I was. We had an older half-sister, Hope. She was ten years older than me, twelve older than Ellie. She disappeared when she was twenty, and nobody really looked for her because of who she was—an addict who sold herself for drugs. But she was more than that, you know? So much more. She had a huge smile and the most infectious laugh. She and Mom had issues, but she loved Ellie and me. When she was sober, she was the best big sister. Then one day she left and never came home. But I know she wasn't planning to leave. She said she'd be back in an hour. She was going to take me to the movies that afternoon. I watched her get into a car with California plates and a Mt. Humboldt sticker on the back window, and that was the last time anyone saw her. She disappeared and nobody cared. Not even our mom because, frankly, life was easier without Hope. Quieter. Less volatile. I get it now, but I was only ten at the time and I didn't understand why Mom and Dad were relieved that she'd left. It terrified me, knowing you could get into a car one day and just vanish off the face of the earth. It's why I started the podcast. I thought facing the terror in the world head-on would strip away my fear."

"Did it?"

"Yes, but then it just made me angry. So many people—so many women—don't get justice. They barely get noticed. They're just lost, forgotten."

"Like Hope?" he guessed.

She blinked hard, as if to hold back tears. "Exactly like Hope."

Shane felt an unexpected pang in the middle of his chest for Alexis and her sisters. Sympathy? Envy? Whatever it was, combined with the thing opening up in there, he didn't like it. He'd been numb for so long, and he wanted to keep it that way. Numb was easier. Numb didn't hurt.

"Do you have any siblings?" she asked after a moment of silence.

He shook his head, but kept his gaze focused on the path in front of them. "No, I'm an only child."

"Cousins?"

"No. My family was... not close."

"That must've been lonely."

It had been. Loneliness had been his constant companion throughout his childhood until he became a SEAL. Then he'd finally had a family that could be counted on, brothers he would die for.

That he should've died for.

But he didn't want to talk about it, didn't want to re-open those wounds. So he simply lifted a shoulder in an off-handed shrug. "It was what it was. I didn't know any different."

"I'm sorry."

Her apology pissed him off.

"I don't need your pity," he snapped, the words coming out sharper than he intended. "I don't need anyone to feel sorry for me."

Alexis flinched, and he cursed himself for it. She didn't deserve his wrath.

But then she lifted her head from his shoulder and looked

at him with a fierce glint in her eyes. "I'm not pitying you. I'm empathizing with you. There's a difference."

He didn't respond, the anger still simmering just beneath his skin. He didn't want her pity or empathy or whatever she wanted to label it. It was unsettling, and he didn't know what to do with it.

"I'm trying to understand you," she said finally. "We've been through a lot together, and I don't want to just leave it at that. I want to know the guy who saved my life because you're not who you seem."

A lump formed in his throat, and he swallowed it down, hard. He wasn't used to being seen, not really seen, for who he was. Most people saw the scars on his face and recoiled, or saw the Navy SEAL on his resume and put him on a pedestal. But Alexis... she saw him. The broken man beneath the scars and the snarl. The man holding himself together with nothing more than anger and stubbornness. And it scared him.

"I don't know if that's a good idea," he said quietly. "Knowing me... it's not pretty."

Alexis reached up and traced her finger along the edge of his jaw, over the mottled skin, her touch feather-light. "I don't care about pretty. I care about real."

This was a dangerous thing, letting her in like this. But he couldn't deny the tug he felt towards her, the way her softness seemed to soothe the harshness inside him.

He took a deep breath and let it out slowly. "There's not much to know," he said finally, voice rough. "I'm just... a guy who lives in the mountains and avoids people."

"Why?"

He hesitated. Did he really want to go down this road with her? No. But he was going to. "It's too much. The stares, the questions, the fear. I can't handle it. And it's safer for everyone if I stay away."

"Safer?"

He shook his head. "It doesn't matter. Let's just say I'm dangerous and I don't want to hurt anyone else. That's why I need to get you away from me."

Alexis studied him for a long moment, her green eyes searching his face. "You saved my life, Shane. That's not something a danger to others would do."

"I also locked you in the bathroom because I thought you were a threat." Again, there was that ache in the center of his chest. He hated the way he's treated her when he found her. His paranoia had almost cost her life.

She didn't argue. She couldn't. She had to know he was right. "But when you realized I wasn't a threat to you, you gave me your own blood to make sure I survived. You took care of me."

So she was putting him up on a pedestal, seeing him as some kind of hero savior.

"I did what I had to do," he grumbled. "It wasn't about being a hero or anything like that. If you had died in my cabin, they would've come for me. The sheriff. The town. I'm their bogeyman, the guy they blame for everything bad that happens around here. Saving you was just... survival. That's what I do, Alexis. I survive. Even when I shouldn't."

She nodded slowly, as if she understood. "Survival is still heroic, Shane. You did what you had to do to stay alive, and in doing so, you saved me. That's something to be proud of."

He snorted, the sound bitter. "Proud of being a scarred, paranoid hermit who can't stand the thought of being around other people? Yeah, that sounds like something to be proud of."

Alexis didn't flinch at his harsh words. Instead, she leaned closer to him, her hand still resting against his jaw. "It's not about what you look like, or even how you behave. It's about the person you are inside. And from what I've seen, Shane, that person is brave and kind and fiercely protective. And that is something to be proud of, scars and all."

Her words hit him like a punch to the gut. He didn't know how to respond to her praise, didn't know how to accept it. He'd spent so long hiding from the world, from himself, that the idea of being brave or kind felt foreign to him.

But as he looked at Alexis, with her battered body and her unbreakable spirit, he realized that she was showing him a different kind of bravery. The kind that came from facing the worst of humanity and still finding a reason to hope.

He reached up and took her hand from his face. He had little feeling left there, but still mourned the lost contact as he tucked her hand back under his furs. "You need to stay warm."

She smiled faintly. "See? You're doing it again. You can't help yourself. It's who you are." She nuzzled against him. "And I really like who you are."

She liked him?

Jesus.

Nobody liked him.

He didn't even like himself.

He realized she'd gone quiet and still in his arms again.

"Hey," he said, nudging her awake with another jostle. "Stay with me, okay? We're almost there."

She roused, but slowly. "Town?"

"Yeah," he lied as the snow shifted into a sloppy rain and the terrain became slick with ice under his boots. They'd reached the snowline, which in some ways made the rest of the trip even more dangerous. Because it was still cold, and now they'd both be wet.

Hypothermia was a real threat now.

He tucked his furs more tightly around her and picked up the pace.

chapter
thirteen

EVERY MUSCLE in Shane's body ached, and he was soaked to the bone, but he gritted his teeth and kept putting one foot in front of the other. Alexis had gone limp in his arms hours ago. Too still. He'd stopped multiple times to make sure she was still breathing.

The rain hadn't let up.

If anything, the closer they got to town, the heavier the rain fell, until it was coming down in sheets that obscured everything beyond a few feet in front of him.

Shane stumbled over an uneven patch of ground and almost fell, but caught himself before he dropped Alexis. She was still unconscious, her head lolling against his chest. He pulled her closer, trying to shelter her from the worst of the rain.

He didn't know how much longer he could keep this up. His body was screaming for rest, for warmth, for dryness. Every step was agony, but he couldn't stop. He had to get Alexis to safety.

He suddenly remembered his BUD/S instructors taunting from the shore as he and his classmates swam for hours in the cold Pacific: "How's the water, boys?"

And they would all respond between chattering teeth: "Toasty warm!"

Weirdly, it worked. The more he told himself the water was warm, the warmer it felt.

That experience had taught him that life was all a mind game. He could accomplish anything as long as he tricked his mind into believing it.

"Toasty warm," he muttered to himself now and kept putting one foot in front of the other.

The air was warm.

The rain was warm.

He wasn't cold.

He wasn't in pain.

Pain was his best friend because it told him he was still alive.

Finally, in the late afternoon, he emerged from the trees onto a paved road and he took a second to orientate himself. He was closer to town than he'd thought, could even see the yellow glow of the streetlights reflecting off the low-hanging gray clouds. The sheriff's station wasn't much farther. He adjusted his grip on Alexis and exhaled in a rush of relief when she let out a low groan.

"Hang on, Lexi. We're almost there."

He summoned up all the energy he had left, tightened her against his chest, and ran toward the lights.

As he stumbled into an intersection, a car stopped in front of him. The driver stared at him, at the soaked and shivering woman in his arms, with horror on her face. For once, he didn't care. He staggered up to the window, but as he opened his mouth to ask for help, she hit the gas. The tires squealed as they tried to gain purchase on the wet pavement. She blew through the stop sign and was gone.

Shane wiped rainwater out of his face. He's taken the balaclava off hours ago when it became soggy and uncomfortable, but maybe he should've left it on.

Then again, the woman probably wouldn't have stopped for a man with his entire face covered, either.

Okay. Back to plan A. Get to the sheriff's office.

At the next intersection, he noticed a dark green Tahoe parked at the curb in front of the Mad Dog Pub. He'd know that vehicle anywhere.

Ash.

The sheriff was there.

He detoured toward the pub, hesitating only when he realized how many cars were parked in its small lot and along the curb.

So many people.

He could still go to the sheriff's office. There would be deputies there. He didn't have to see the sheriff specifically.

But he trusted Ash. The man was the only person in the world he could say that about. Well—Ash and now Alexis.

He looked down at her. She was too pale, with hot slashes of color riding high on her cheeks. Her eyes twitched under her lids as if she was trapped in a nightmare she couldn't escape from. She needed help now, and it was steps away, right there inside the pub. So he needed to suck it up and do the mission. He was a goddamn SEAL. He'd breached buildings scarier than this pub, in situations with a much higher pucker factor than this.

He could do this.

He had to do this.

For Alexis.

He held her tighter to his chest and, heart pounding, pushed his way inside.

The pub was warm and inviting, with a fire blazing in the hearth and music playing from a jukebox that looked older than him. Most of the tables were taken, and everyone seemed to be having a good time...

Until they saw him.

Conversations tapered off. Everyone turned to stare. He ignored them all and zeroed in on Ash, sitting at the end of the bar and smiling at the black-haired bartender like she was the center of his universe.

"Holy shit," someone said.

The bartender turned toward the voice, spotted Shane, and gasped, her hand flying up to cover her mouth. She also wore a shiny ring like Ash's. She must be the sheriff's new wife.

"Oh my God," she said. "Ash, look."

The sheriff followed her stare, and his entire demeanor changed. His smile vanished as he jumped to his feet, knocking his stool over. "Shane..." He approached slowly, one hand held one hand out while his other hovered over the gun holstered at his hip. "What are you doing in here?"

Shane opened his fur coat, uncovering Alexis's pale face. "She needs help." His voice came out in a harsh rasp that he barely recognized as his own.

Ash's eyes widened in shocked recognition. "Jesus. What happened?"

"Shot. Infection." Each word felt like it was coated in spikes. He cleared his throat and tried again. "She needs a doctor."

Ash stepped forward to take her from his arms, but he couldn't let her go. Not with all these people here. Any of these men could be the man who hurt her. Hell, in a small town like this, the probability of one of these men being the Shadow Stalker was high.

He backed up, snarling as two other men tried to approach. One had a metal leg, so he definitely wasn't the Shadow Stalker, but the other guy? He was big, with close-cropped dark hair and full-sleeve tattoos. That man could be.

Or the man in the corner booth, sitting in front of a laptop, watching everything unfold with rapt attention. Why was he just sitting here in a pub by himself with a laptop? That wasn't right.

The Shadow Stalker could be any of them.

Any of them could be dangerous.

Any of them could want Alexis dead.

No.

"Get back," he growled, holding her tighter to his chest as he backed toward the door.

Ash held up a hand. "Wait, Van, Zak, don't approach him. Let me talk to him." He eased a step closer. "Shane, you need to let me take her. You want her to get help, right?"

"She's not safe here."

"Why?"

"Someone tried to kill her."

"Who?"

Shane shook his head.

"But *I'm* not going to kill her," Ash said. "You know that. You know I only want to help her, and so do my friends, Donovan"—he indicated the tattooed man—"and Zak." He motioned to the man with the missing leg.

Shane relaxed a degree as he studied Zak's metal leg. "I remember you. Ash's friend with the bad attitude and the dog."

Zak nodded. "Yeah, we met a few years ago on the mountain. It wasn't under the best of circumstances, but you found my daughters when they were missing. Bella told me you helped them, gave them food and water and shelter. I really appreciate that, man."

More tension eased out of Shane's shoulders. "I remember the girls."

"You took care of my girls," Zak said gently. "Now let us take care of your girl, okay?"

"C'mon, Sheriff," one patron muttered and shoved away from a high top table filled with empties. He had a full beard and a 49ers cap pulled down low over his forehead, shadowing his face. He pointed an accusing finger at Shane. "You know this crazy fuck did it."

"Yeah," another guy piped up. "He's been terrifying people for years."

"Just the other day, he attacked Sophie Foley at Roger's Market," an older woman added. "She told me herself."

Shane's blood boiled. He had never attacked anyone, at least, not without provocation. And he didn't hurt that girl at the market. He definitely didn't hurt Alexis. He glared at the group of people, daring them to say anything else.

But Ash stepped in, his voice firm. "That's enough, all of you." He pointed at the man in the 49ers cap. "Especially you, Jacoby. You keep this shit up, and I won't wait for Rose to throw you out. I'll do it myself. I was there at the market that night and Shane didn't attack anyone. Now," he said more gently and turned back to Shane, holding out his arms. "Let me take Alexis and get her help. That's why you came here, isn't it?"

Shane hesitated. He trusted Ash. The sheriff was one of the good guys—maybe the only one in this entire fucking town. He relaxed his grip on Alexis.

Ash carefully took her from his arms and carried her to a back room, issuing orders as he went. "Rose, we need blankets."

The bartender nodded and pushed into the room ahead of him.

"Zak, call for an ambulance."

"Already on it," Zak said and lifted his cell phone to his ear.

Shane watched them disappear, then turned to face the angry patrons. "I didn't hurt her. Someone else did."

"How do we know that?" the bearded man in the 49ers

cap—Jacoby—demanded. "You've got a history, Trevisano. You're a ticking time bomb, just waiting to go off."

"He should be arrested," someone else shouted. "Do your fucking job, Sheriff!"

Shane's hands clenched into fists. "You don't know anything about me."

"Oh, we know enough," Jacoby sneered. "Ex-Navy SEAL with a record of violence. Lives off the grid like some kind of psycho. And now you show up with this girl bleeding in your arms?"

Anger boiled in his chest, threatening to erupt in a violent outburst. But he took a deep breath, trying to calm himself down. He needed to think, to figure out what to do next.

Then he noticed the man in the corner booth, the one who had been watching everything with intense interest. He was typing something into his laptop, and as Shane watched, he hit enter.

Suddenly, a high-pitched beeping sound filled the room, and the man's face twisted into a grin.

"Bomb!" Shane launched at the man, his fist colliding with his jaw.

The bar erupted in chaos. People shouted, scrambling to get out, but Shane's entire focus zeroed in on the threat.

Eliminate the threat.

The man crashed backwards, his laptop clattering to the floor, but Shane didn't stop. He tackled him to the ground, his hands wrapping around his throat. The man's grin had disappeared, replaced by a look of terror. Shane squeezed harder, feeling the man's windpipe collapse under his fingers. He didn't care. This was the man who tried to kill Alexis. He had to be. Why else would he plant a bomb in the pub?

He deserved to die.

Strong arms banded around Shane's waist and arms,

pulling him up and away from the gasping man. It was Ash and Zak, their faces filled with shock and anger.

"What the fuck?" Ash demanded. "What the hell's wrong with you?"

Shane struggled against their hold, still wanting to kill the man on the ground as Donovan helped him to his feet.

"You okay, Connelly?" Donovan asked.

The man touched his neck and tried to clear his throat. When he couldn't speak, he simply nodded and bent to pick up his cracked laptop. He cleared his throat again and winced. "Fuck, I hope that chapter saved."

It wasn't until Ash and Zak wrestled Shane to the ground and Ash snapped a pair of handcuffs on his wrists that reality seeped through his rage and terror.

There was no bomb.

There was no threat.

He had snapped, attacked an innocent man in the crowded bar, and now he was going to jail.

He had become the monster they all thought he was.

ELLIE SAT in the local cafe, her coffee steaming as she scowled out the window at the slushy rain splattering Main Street.

The weather was not cooperating.

For the third day in a row.

Just like the last three days, she'd woken up early, ready to march up that damn mountain and find Alexis. And just like the last three days, the sheriff had called her and told her the search was off. The conditions on the mountain were too dangerous. With a blizzard raging above the snowline, there was no way they were getting anywhere near Shane Trevisano's cabin until the weather broke.

But she couldn't just sit around doing nothing until then.

Frustrated, Ellie had grabbed her laptop and walked to the cafe. They had better coffee and more reliable Wi-Fi than the motel.

She was a researcher.

It was time to do some research.

She took a sip of her coffee—shit, too hot!—and winced as she opened her laptop. She needed answers, and the sheriff was reluctant to give her any, so she'd find them herself.

She typed "Shane Trevisano" into the search engine.

The first thing to pop up was a picture. He was a serious man in Navy dress whites, with pale blue eyes, dark hair, a straight blade of a nose, and a small scar that pulled his lip up into a weirdly appealing sneer. Like Elvis. It gave him a dangerous, sexy vibe.

Okay. Not what she'd expected, given the sheriff and Cal's conversation about the man. Alexis so would've gone for this guy if she'd met him in a bar. He was exactly her type.

What if they were all wrong about the abduction and she'd gone with him willingly?

But that didn't make sense. She wouldn't have left without, at the very least, leaving a note for Ellie, explaining where she was going. She wouldn't have left her dog behind to starve. Or all of her clothes.

No. If Shane had her, it was against her will.

Ellie scrolled down to the first article and sucked in a sharp breath of surprise.

"Unwavering Valor and Resilience: Navy Commends Wounded Veteran's Heroic Service."

She clicked the link. The top image of the article was a generic stock photo of a mean-looking military helicopter with a soldier dangling from it on a rope. She scrolled past it and several ads, skimming until she found the meat of the article.

"In the face of unimaginable adversity, Master Chief Petty Officer Shane Trevisano exemplified unwavering courage, unbreakable determination, and unmatched devotion to duty. His indomitable spirit and unyielding commitment to the team served as an inspiration to all who had the privilege of serving alongside him. Master Chief Trevisano not only faced the crucible of combat with valor, but also displayed remarkable resilience in the aftermath of injury. His unselfish sacrifices and relentless pursuit of excellence embody the finest traditions of the Navy SEALs. We commend Master Chief

Trevisano for his extraordinary service and salute his enduring legacy as a warrior, teammate, and hero."

What? He'd been a SEAL?

Ellie blinked and sat back, staring in stunned horror at the next image in the article. It wasn't a stock photo this time. It showed a heavily scarred man looking miserable in a wheelchair while the Navy presented him with some kind of metal. That couldn't possibly be the same man, could it? She pulled up the first picture of Shane Trevisano on a split screen and compared the two.

His little scar on his lip. It was still there, nestled in among all the new scar tissue. It was him.

She pressed a hand to her mouth. "Holy shit. What happened to him?"

She didn't realize she'd spoken out loud until the two women at the table next to hers scowled in her direction.

Ellie flushed and looked back at her laptop, scrolling through the article to find more information about Shane. She found a section about an IED explosion during a mission in Afghanistan, but there was precious little other information available. Which, she supposed, was to be expected if he'd been a SEAL. Weren't all of their missions classified?

The article detailed his injuries—severe burns, shrapnel wounds, and limited mobility. It also mentioned that he had been awarded the Purple Heart for his injuries and the Navy Cross for his bravery in trying to save one of his teammates.

Ellie's heart ached with sympathy for the man. She couldn't imagine the pain and trauma he must have gone through. And now she understood why the sheriff was reluctant to blame him for Alexis's disappearance.

How could a hero like this turn into the kind of monster who abducted women?

Of course, she also knew from her research work on the podcast that all kinds of men became monsters. Any many of them had much less reason for it than Shane. Maybe it had always been in him, and he'd just been able to hide his violence behind a shield of patriotism and duty until he was injured.

Maybe the explosion had just given his true ugly self a face to match.

Oh, God.

The sip of coffee gurgled uncomfortably in her stomach. She pushed her laptop aside, took off her glasses, and rubbed her temples. She needed a break from all of this. Just for a few minutes. Maybe a quick walk around town to clear her head. As she stood up from her seat, her cell phone rang. She fumbled in her purse for it and started to tremble when she saw the sheriff's name on the screen.

She stabbed the answer button. "Ash?" In her panic, she forgot to call him by his title, but he didn't correct her. "What's wrong?"

"We found her."

For a moment, she couldn't breathe. She had prepared herself for the worst, but now that she was hearing the news she had been hoping for, she didn't know how to react. She sank back into her seat.

"Alive?" she finally managed in little more than a squeak of sound. "Is she okay?"

"She's alive," Ash confirmed, his voice as gentle as she'd ever heard it. "But she's in bad shape. She's on her way to the hospital now. You should come down here as soon as you can."

"I'm on my way." She snatched up her computer and purse and rushed out of the cafe, leaving the cup of coffee behind. Dread curdled the little bit she'd drank as she broke all the speed limits on the way to the hospital.

Had Shane done this to her sister?

How serious were the injuries?

Sheriff Rawlings was waiting for her at the emergency

room entrance, his face grim. He caught her before she could shove by him. "Ellie, wait. She's in surgery. She's been shot multiple times and has an infection. One bullet is still in her. They're getting it out now."

"I need to see her." Ellie's knees gave out beneath her, and someone caught her before she hit the ground.

"As soon as the doctors give the okay, you'll be the first one in there."

She glanced up at the familiar voice, ashamed of what it did to her belly even under these circumstances. Cal Holden. She was strangely grateful to see him. His presence felt like a life raft, and she'd been drowning since Ash called her with the news. "Thank you."

The sheriff scowled faintly at Cal. "You can't promise her that, Holden."

Cal ignored him and wound a supportive arm around her. "Okay now? Not going to faint on me, are you?"

She gulped in a breath and shook her head. "Thank you for catching me."

"Anytime." He gave a quick flash of a smile, then faced off with Ash. "She needs to see her sister. C'mon, I know you would've busted down the surgery suite's door by now if that was Anna in there."

Ash's scowl darkened. He obviously didn't like that thought. "I'll talk to the nurses and make sure she's added the approved guest list."

Ellie blinked at him in shock. "What do you mean, approved list?"

"Your sister is part of an ongoing investigation. Someone held her captive for weeks and then tried to kill her. For her safety, we need to make sure that only authorized individuals are allowed to see her."

"Do you think whoever did this will try again?"

"It's only a precautionary measure."

Which meant, yes. He absolutely thought the killer would try again when he realized Alexis was still alive.

Ellie may be a chaotic mess on her best days, but that didn't mean she was stupid. She could read the subtext. "You know who did this."

"We're following up on some leads, and that's all I'm willing to say at this time. When I have something more concrete, you'll know. Until then..." He waved a hand at the two men standing behind him. One was the big tattooed guy she'd seen with the border collie in the agility yard at the rescue the day they found Clue. The other man had only one leg. Though she'd never met him in person, she knew he was Zak Hendricks—the sheriff's brother-in-law and the head of Redwood Coast Rescue's tactical K9 team.

"Zak, Donovan, and I will take turns watching over her," Ash said. "I trust these men implicitly. Nothing will happen to her on our watch."

The tattooed man, Donovan, nodded. "Nothing will get by us."

He was Donovan Scott, she realized suddenly. The man Lexi had accused of murder last fall on the podcast. The man whose life they had nearly ruined.

And he was willing to protect Lexi now?

Ellie's eyes filled with tears. "Thank you."

"Why don't you go wait in the family room where it's more comfortable?" Zak said. "We'll stand here and let you know the moment she's out of surgery."

She looked at Cal, silently pleading with him to come with her. He nodded and squeezed her shoulder. "I'll walk with you."

As they made their way down the hall, their footsteps echoed in the empty corridor and Ellie couldn't shake the feeling of dread that had settled in her stomach back at the coffee shop. Her sister had been through hell, and now they were being told to wait and hope for the best.

Cal opened the door to the family room and motioned for her to go in. "I'll grab us some coffee," he said.

Ellie nodded even though the last thing she wanted was more coffee, then stepped into the room. It was small and cramped, with beige walls and a few uncomfortable chairs. She sank into one of them and tried to take some deep breaths. She needed to calm down. She needed to be strong for Lexi.

But all she could think about was the last time she had seen her sister. They had been arguing over Lexi returning here, to this corner of the world where their older sister had disappeared twenty years ago.

The last time Lexi had come here to investigate a case, things hadn't gone well. They'd really thought Donovan was guilty. Well, Ellie had. Alexis had been less convinced, felt the investigation had too many holes. In hindsight, it had. And the actual killers almost slipped through the holes unnoticed, leaving Donovan to take the heat for them.

After that mess was resolved, Alexis had been determined to come back to Steam Valley and redeem herself and the podcast. She'd become obsessed with the legend of the Shadow Stalker, and more convinced with each missing person case she studied that their sister Hope had been one of the killer's first victims.

And then she'd almost become a victim herself.

Ellie leaned her head back against the chair's cushions, suddenly bone-deep exhausted.

Cal returned a few minutes later with two cups of coffee and sat down next to her. "You doing okay?"

Ellie shook her head. She took the coffee he offered and wrapped her hands around the paper cup, grateful for the heat. She was freezing. "I don't know."

"You're allowed to not be okay," Cal said. "This is a lot."

"We never should've come back here. This place is cursed."

Cal gave a small, teasing smile. "That's the rumor. "

"I'm serious. The last time we were here, it was a disaster. We almost ruined an innocent man's life. And now Lexi's been shot and—was it Shane? Did Shane Trevisano do this to her?"

Cal said nothing for a long moment, then set his coffee down and turned to face her. He took her coffee from her and also set it aside, then pressed her icy hands between his. "He showed up at the Mad Dog with Alexis in his arms and blood all over his coat. Ash arrested him. He's sitting in a jail cell at the sheriff's office as we speak."

That wasn't a comfort. "What if we're mistaken? What if he's innocent like Donovan was? What if he was just trying to help her?"

"Why don't we wait until Alexis wakes up, see what she can tell us?"

"Okay, but I don't think Shane—" She broke off and shook her head again because she couldn't find the right words to go with the unease swirling through her. "I was reading about him before Ash called and he was a hero. Something's just not right about all this."

Cal squeezed her hands. "Hey, I'm a lawyer, remember? I made sure Donovan stayed out of jail, and if Shane is also innocent, I'll do the same for him." His dimples made a flash appearance. "Defense is kinda my thing."

Right. She'd forgotten that about him. "I thought you did, like, corporate law for the rescue?"

"Nah. I handle the lawyer shit for RWCR because..." He trailed off, released her hands, and shrugged as he reached for his coffee. "Well, don't tell Zak, but I like him. And Ash. And Donovan. I like all of them. I believe in what they're doing. And defending criminals, as much as it needs to be done, can be soul-sucking sometimes. Working for the rescue gives me a little piece of my soul back."

Ellie smiled despite herself. Cal always had a way of making her smile, even in the worst of times. "I'm glad you found something you believe in."

He flashed her another dimpled grin. "Yeah, me too. But enough about me. How are you really holding up?"

She sighed and leaned back in her chair. "I feel like I should be doing something, but I don't know what."

"You're doing the best thing you can right now," Cal said. "You're waiting for your sister to wake up. And then we'll go from there."

"Will you wait with me?"

He laced his fingers through hers. "There's nowhere else I rather be."

chapter
fifteen

A SMUG DEPUTY led Shane to a holding cell at the sheriff's department and shoved him inside. He swore the door slamming shut with a resounding clang sounded like the chop of the guillotine's ax.

This was it. They were going to lock him up, either in prison or a mental institution, and throw away the key. He'd never see his cabin again. Never breathe the crisp mountain air.

Fuck.

He sat down on the cold, hard bench, his head in his hands. He called himself every name he could think of for losing control like everyone said he would. He probably should be locked up. He was a danger to himself and to others.

And to Alexis.

It was only a matter of time until he snapped and hurt her again, too. And next time, he might not come to his senses in time to save her.

He heard footsteps approaching and looked up to see Ash standing outside the cell. The sheriff's expression was grim as he unlocked the door and stepped inside.

"Shane." Ash sat on the bench beside him and exhaled hard, rubbing a hand over his beard. "We need to talk."

Shane nodded, not trusting himself to speak. He knew what was coming. Ash was going to tell him he was under arrest for assault or, worse, attempted murder. He deserved it.

"She's going to be okay," Ash said, surprising him. "The doctors say she's lucky to be alive, but she's stable now and they're optimistic about her prognosis."

Shane breathed a sigh of relief, a weight lifting off his shoulders. Alexis was going to be okay.

"Thank you," he muttered.

"But that doesn't change what you did. You attacked a man."

"Is he okay?"

Ash sighed heavily. "Connelly's fine. He'll have a sore throat for a few days, but he's agreed not to press charges. I told him what you've been through, and he was sympathetic. He was Pararescue in the Air Force, so he knows how this PTSD can fuck with you. You got lucky there, but I can't just let this go. I know you didn't hurt Sophie Foley at the market, but you scared her. And everyone else there."

"Didn't mean to."

"I know. You're not a bad guy, Shane. You just need help. Professional help. And I'm going to make sure you get it." He got up and left the cell.

A moment later, he returned. An older woman with neat wire-frame glasses and graying brown hair followed him.

Ash motioned to her. "This is Dr. Firestone. She's here to talk to you about what happened."

"Hi, Shane." Dr. Firestone spoke softly, her voice soothing. "I'm a psychologist, and I specialize in treating patients with PTSD. I want to start by saying that I respect your service to our country and the sacrifices you've made, and I'm so sorry we've failed you since you came home. I hope to change that, if you'll let me."

Shane eyed the woman warily, not sure what to make of her. Eight years ago, he had managed to avoid the VA therapists by telling them everything they wanted to hear until he was discharged from the hospital. Now, he wasn't interested in having this woman poke around inside the dark recesses of his brain. All kinds of ugliness could come spilling out.

But Ash was right. He needed help. He couldn't keep going on like this, living in fear of what he might do next.

The doctor nodded to Ash, and he let her into the cell. She lowered herself to the bench beside Shane. "Sheriff Rawlings has told me a little bit about what happened at the pub, but I'd like to hear it from you. Can you tell me what led up to the altercation?"

Shane remained silent, staring at his hands. He couldn't talk about it. He didn't want to relive it. He just wanted them both to leave so he could be alone again. Alone was more comfortable.

After a long moment, Dr. Firestone nodded. "It's okay. You don't have to talk now. I know tonight has been a lot, but please know you did a very good thing by bringing Alexis to us. She would have died without your help."

He squeezed his eyes shut. He couldn't look at the doctor's kind face. Her compassion was a lifeline he wasn't sure he deserved.

"Why don't you try to rest?" she suggested and stood. "I'll talk to the sheriff about moving you to more comfortable accommodations and we can try again tomorrow?"

She left the cell and as Ash pulled the door shut behind her, Shane heard the two of them murmuring to each other. Ash said something about a "psych hold" and panic sizzled down his spine.

"No!" He jumped to his feet and rushed the bars, hitting

them harder than he'd intended. The doctor gasped and took a startled step back. Ash just stared at him with a mix of concern and resignation.

"Please, Ash." He tried to gentle his voice, but it came out all growly and shaky. "I can't be locked up like that. Just let me go home and I'll stay away from town. I won't come back. Please don't do this to me."

Ash sighed heavily and scrubbed a hand over his beard again. "I don't want to, but you attacked a man tonight. You could have killed him. I can't just let you walk out of here like nothing happened, but we're not going to lock you up forever. It's just a hold for observation."

"Your safety and well-being are our top priority," the doctor added. "We want to make sure you're getting the care you need."

"I don't need that kind of care," Shane protested, and the walls closed in around him. Suddenly, he couldn't draw a full breath. "I just need to be left alone."

"I'm sorry, but we can't do that. You're a danger to yourself and others. You attacked a man."

"I didn't mean— I-I thought he was—"

The doctor didn't seem to hear him. "And you've been living off the grid for years with no support or help. Sheriff Rawlings said you practically starved to death this winter rather than come to town for supplies. You need psychological help, or it's not going to end well for you."

The idea of being locked up in a psych ward was unbearable. The only thing he had left in life was his freedom, and now even that was being taken away from him.

"Please, let me go home and I'll come back for therapy, I swear." And now he'd resorted to pleading. Bitterness coated his tongue, but he saw no other options. "Please, just don't do this to me, Ash."

Ash looked at him for a long moment. Shane saw the

conflict in the sheriff's eyes, but in the end, he knew what the decision was going to be.

"I'm sorry, Shane. I really am, but this is out of my hands now."

He watched as the sheriff and the psychologist left. The door closed with a finality that made his stomach clench. He was trapped in this cell with nothing to do but wait.

Wait for the inevitable breakdown...

For the panic attack...

For the nightmares that would surely come...

chapter
sixteen

THE WORLD SWAM into focus as Alexis slowly regained consciousness, head throbbing and body aching. The sterile scent of disinfectant filled her nose as the harsh fluorescent hospital lights seared her retinas, coaxing a groan out of her parched throat. She tried to sit up, but every movement sent waves of pain radiating through her.

"Hey, take it easy."

At the familiar voice, she relaxed back into the bed and closed her eyes.

Ellie.

Her sister was here.

She blinked back a rush of tears.

Ellie's pale blond curls shimmered in a wild halo around her head and her red-framed glasses were slightly askew. Out of habit, Alexis reached out and straightened them, making Ellie smile her bright, sunshiny smile.

"Hi, sis. I'm so happy you're back." Ellie sat on the bed and her blue eyes filled with relief as she folded her hands around Alexis's. Her fingers were warm and comforting. A lifeline to cling to as she tried to piece together blurry memories.

Pain.

Fear.

Suspicion.

Uncertainty.

Hope.

Trust.

Safe.

She shook her head slightly. She couldn't make sense of the jumble of feelings and flashbulb images. "Where am I?" Her throat was so raw, those three words made her cough.

Ellie squeezed her hand. "You're safe now. You're in the hospital. They got you here just in time."

"Who...?" She blinked, trying to bring a blurry face from her memories into focus. It felt very important that she remember, but all she could see was camouflage paint. "Who brought me here?"

"The sheriff and his friends, Zak and Donovan."

But that didn't make sense. She didn't know why, but she knew it didn't. "How did they find me?"

Ellie's expression changed, closed down despite her trying to keep a placid smile firmly in place. She'd never had much of a poker face. "You've been through a lot, Lexi. Just try to rest and we'll worry about everything else later—"

And the face she'd been trying to remember snapped into focus.

"Shane!" She struggled to sit up, and this time, Ellie didn't stop her. "Where is he?"

"Um." Ellie looked toward the door. "He's here, too."

"*Here?*"

Ellie leaned forward and brushed a lock of her limp, dirty hair back from her forehead. "Lexi, rest. Please."

"Why is he here? He shouldn't be here. He doesn't belong here."

Ellie exhaled a long, slow breath. She was stalling. "He's...

being held against his will on the psychiatric floor. They say he's unstable. All that time alone in the mountains has damaged him."

With each word, a growing sense of urgency clawed at her insides, threatening to consume her entirely. Shane—the man who had saved her from the clutches of the Shadow Stalker, who had shown her that there was still hope amidst the darkness—was now locked away, suffering and alone. She couldn't bear the thought of him trapped with only his demons for company.

"I have to see him."

"Not a good idea."

"Why not?"

A crease formed between Ellie's brows. "They said he's dangerous."

"No. No way. I know him." She swung her legs over the side of the bed, ignoring the protest from her aching muscles. She had a fresh bandage over the bullet wound on her thigh and she pulled at the tape, wondering how many stitches she'd needed to close up the hole.

Ellie stilled her hand. "Leave it alone. They had a hell of a time trying to stop your bleeding."

"Okay, Mom." She rolled her eyes, but gave up on the bandage and pushed to her feet, limping only slightly when her weight settled on her wounded leg. "Shane's not dangerous."

"He attacked a man," Ellie said dubiously. "Completely unprovoked, or so I've been told."

Dammit.

But, also, she wasn't surprised. Shane was made for the wilderness, not for civilization.

"Okay, yes, he's damaged. And probably scared, but he's only here because he was trying to get me to a doctor. He doesn't deserve to be treated like a feral animal. He just... needs someone to help him."

Ellie searched her face for a moment, then sighed softly. "Someone like you?"

"He saved me, Elle. I would be dead and buried under a pile of snow on the mountain if it weren't for him. How could I not return the favor? I need to see him."

Ellie sighed again and pushed up her slipping glasses. "I suppose I owe him a favor, too, for bringing you back to me. All right," she agreed after a beat and popped to her feet. "I'll help you see Shane, but you need to sit down before you fall down. Oh!" She went to her oversized purse sitting on the windowsill and dug through it until she found what she was looking for. She handed Alexis a black glasses case. "I thought you'd need these. It's your old prescription, but it's better than nothing."

Alexis opened the case and found an old pair of her glasses. They were a trendy cat eye in electric blue that Ellie had convinced her to buy from a discount online retailer—"Your glasses are so boring! You always go for black or brown or navy. Try something fun!" She'd wore them a grand total of two times before going back to her comfort zone with the black-framed pair she'd lost on the mountain. She'd honestly forgotten about this pair until now. She slid them on. Everything was still a little blurry, but at least she could see again.

"How do I look?"

Ellie made a face. "You were right when we bought them. They're not your style. I'll go find a wheelchair."

"Thank you." She dutifully sank back to the bed and stared at the hospital's parking lot beyond the window. The sky was gray and a damp mist hung low, but the foliage was a deep, verdant green. On the mountain, she'd almost forgotten there was any other color than white.

In Chicago, it was either winter or spring. Or sometimes it

was winter in the morning and spring in the afternoon. But the two seasons never existed in the same place simultaneously, like they did here. Outside the hospital, it was spring, but she knew winter still ruled with an icy fist a few miles away on the mountain.

She shivered at the thought.

Ellie returned with a wheelchair and a nurse who was none too happy with either sister. She cautioned Alexis against pushing herself too hard, walking too soon, moving too fast... basically, she wanted her to climb back into bed and not move a muscle. Which so wasn't happening.

"I got it from here, thanks," Ellie said, all sweetness, and took the IV pole from the nurse's hand. "I'll have her back in bed in no time."

Unsurprisingly, the nurse gave in and left them alone. Everyone always gave in to Ellie. Alexis had to badger or annoy to get her way, but all Ellie had to do was aim that stunning smile.

"How do you *do* that?"

Ellie grinned and wiggled her fingers in the air. "Magic." She hooked the IV pole to the back of the wheelchair, then took hold of the handles and pushed Alexis out into the hall.

It was cooler in the corridor than in her room, and the sterile walls seemed to close in on them as they moved deeper into the hospital. Alexis's heart pounded in her chest as Ellie's footsteps echoed through the cold, clinical hallways. The antiseptic smell assaulted her nostrils, while the harsh fluorescent lights cast shadows that danced along the linoleum floors.

It reminded her of the bunker.

Jesus.

The bunker.

The memories came back in a rush that left goosebumps on her skin, and now she wished she was still blissfully amnesic. The things he'd done to her...

She felt cold and hollow and dirty. And so ashamed she suddenly wanted to melt into the floor.

No.

She sucked in a deep breath and sat up straighter in the wheelchair. She had nothing to be ashamed of. She'd done nothing wrong. And if she had any dirt on her, she'd gotten it from the bastard who hurt her.

If the Shadow Stalker thought she was just going to curl up into a terrified ball like she had in the bunker, he was dead wrong. Yes, she was his victim. There was no denying that. But she refused to be *a* victim. She could fight him now, and she was going to use every weapon at her disposal to expose him for the coward he was.

"Are you sure about this?" Ellie asked, her voice betraying a hint of uncertainty as she glanced down.

"More than anything." She couldn't explain it to her sister, but imagining Shane confined within these walls made her sick to her stomach. Every fiber of her being demanded that she find him and make sure he was all right.

Because she had a feeling he wasn't.

As they turned the corner, they came face to face with Ash Rawlings. His gaze zeroed in on them and his lips compressed into a thin line. He excused himself from the conversation he was having with a small middle-aged woman and walked over, blocking their path.

"Alexis, Ellie, you shouldn't be here."

"Please, Ash." She'd always called him Sheriff Rawlings in their past interactions, but it felt like they were well beyond those social niceties now. "I need to see him."

Ash hesitated, his eyes flickering between them and the woman he'd been speaking with. "You don't understand. Shane's mental state is... unstable. At best. Dangerous at worst. I can't let you in there. He could hurt you."

"He won't."

"You don't know that. He might not mean to, but he—"

"He won't," she said again, leaving no room for doubt in her tone. "If he wanted to hurt me, he had plenty of opportunities to do so, but instead he went out of his way to help me. He gave me his own blood when I was on the verge of bleeding out."

Behind her, Ellie made a soft sound of distress.

"Are those the actions of a dangerous man?" Tears she couldn't control welled in her eyes, and she impatiently swiped at them. "I have to be there for him, Ash. I can't let him face this alone."

As silence settled around them, Ash's gaze softened. He cursed under his breath and dragged a hand over his head. His hair was a deep, dark auburn, but currently looked more brown than red from either the rain outside or a recent shower. It was longer than the last time she'd seen him and rumpled adorably under his hand. He looked tired, and she had the inexplicable urge to throw her arms around him and hug him even though Ash Rawlings was about as huggable as a porcupine.

"All right," he relented and turned back to the woman who had been watching their conversation with a clinical interest. "What do you think, Doctor?"

She stepped forward and held out a hand to Alexis. "I'm Dr. Firestone. Sheriff Rawlings called me in to evaluate Shane." She wasn't a big woman, but she had an air of calm command around her, and kind eyes behind the lens of wire-frame glasses that were so vintage they were cool again.

"I'm Alexis." She accepted the handshake. "And this is my sister Ellie. Is Shane okay?"

"Why don't you come with us and see for yourself?"

chapter
seventeen

"HE HAS one of the worst cases of PTSD I've ever seen," Dr. Firestone said as she led them into a small room. She motioned to the window that stretched across one entire wall.

On the other side was a hospital room much like the one Alexis had just left, except everything was bolted down. Shane paced the small space like a caged beast, desperate for freedom. Out in the hallway, a dietary aide pushed a cart full of empty lunch trays. Such an innocuous sound, just the ebb and flow of the hospital, but Shane flinched away like the noise had been a physical blow.

"And I've seen a lot of it over the years," the doctor continued. "In his condition, the VA never should've released him from the hospital eight years ago."

His eyes were too wide, showing too much white. His ratty clothes had been taken, and he wore only a hospital gown tied around his neck. Hair hung in limp, tangled strands over his shoulders and his face was still streaked with faded remnants of his camouflage make-up. But for the first time, Alexis could see the full extent of his scars. The thick ridges wound around his neck and shoulders and extended down his back, butt, and legs. His hands and most of his right arm were likewise covered with scar tissue, save for a small patch of skin on his bicep that still had a partial tattoo. It might have been a skull at one time, but his burns had blurred and warped the black ink.

God.

Tears blurred her vision. She had known Shane was scarred, but seeing all of it up close was something else entirely, like looking at a topographic map of pain. It was a miracle he'd survived.

"Will he be okay?"

The doctor sighed. "His physical wounds have healed— though probably not as well as they would have had he not gone off the grid. But it's the mental scars I'm worried about. They run deep. He's been avoiding any kind of therapy or treatment for years, and he shuts down every time I attempt to talk to him."

"Is he beyond help?" Ash asked and Alexis glowered at him.

"What kind of question is that? Of course not. Nobody is beyond help."

Ash crossed his arms over his chest. "I'm surprised you think so, given your career choice. And given what you've been through. You've seen the worst of humanity."

"Exactly." She motioned to Shane's room. "And I know for a fact he is not it. He's wounded and scared and, yes, that makes him unpredictable, but he's not evil." She faced the doctor again. "How can we help him?"

"Well, I don't recommend he stay here, locked up in a hospital," Dr. Firestone said. "I don't think it's beneficial for him in any way and, in fact, might even be detrimental. I've seen a marked decline in his responsiveness since he came here. He's shutting down, withdrawing deeper into himself."

"So what do you recommend?" Ash asked. "We can't just let him go back to the mountain."

Dr. Firestone shook her head. "Certainly not. He needs support. We need to find him a place where he can rebuild his connections with society. He needs to learn how to function among people again, and he can't do that if he disappears into the woods. If we let him return to the mountain, we will never see him again."

The thought of never seeing Shane again made Alexis's heart clench. She turned away from the observation window. "I'll help him."

Ash's hard expression softened. "You've been through enough. Shane is my problem now."

She scowled at the sheriff. She knew he was well-meaning, but she still kind of wanted to punch him. "He's not a *problem.*"

Ash winced slightly. "I didn't mean it like that."

"Yes, you did, but Shane is not a problem to be solved. He's a hero. He saved me when he didn't have to get involved. And all that was after he already lived through absolute hell overseas, protecting our country. He is not a problem."

The doctor nodded. "She's right. Shane needs someone who understands his pain, not just someone who sees him as a problem to solve. His condition is delicate, and he's not exactly the most cooperative patient, but I think he might respond well to Alexis's presence."

"Absolutely not," Ash said at the same time she said, "Let me talk to him."

Ash scowled. "Alexis."

She glared right back. "Sheriff Rawlings."

"This is not a good idea."

"You should know by now that I don't always do what's good for me."

His gaze dropped to her sling. "And look what happened."

She flinched. "Low blow."

He cursed under his breath. "You're right. I'm sorry." He dragged a hand over his head and, for the first time, she noticed the silver band on his finger.

She smiled to soften the sudden tension between them. "That's new since I last saw you, Sheriff. I'm surprised. I thought you were married to the job."

He looked at his ring, and a rare smile tipped up the corners of his hard mouth. "Surprised me, too, but Rose makes it hard to say no."

Her eyebrows climbed up in surprise. "You married Rose, the bartender from the Mad Dog Pub?"

"She's the owner. And, yeah."

She never in a million years would've paired the by-the-book sheriff with the free-spirited Rose, but now that she thought about it, it made a strange sort of sense. Ash needed someone fun in his life to balance his workaholic tendencies and Rose, who laughed loud and loved hard and didn't take anyone's shit, was just the right person for the job.

"I'm happy for you. I really am." She touched his arm and waited until he met her gaze.

His smile faded, and he cursed softly. "You're not digging through his trauma for a story. Shane doesn't deserve that."

"No, he doesn't," she agreed, although it pissed her off that after everything, Ash still saw her as a podcaster before anything else. Which, all right, maybe was fair. She had almost ruined his friend's life with her podcast, after all. "I have no interest in Shane's story."

Ellie, who had been making herself unobtrusive until that moment, gave her a look that clearly said, *Liar.*

She bugged her eyes at her sister in a non-verbal *shut-up.* Okay, yes, she wanted to know everything about him, but not for the podcast. Her curiosity was entirely for personal reasons, but telling Ash that wouldn't help her case, so she went with another version of the truth.

"He saved me. Let me return the favor. Please."

Ash hesitated, his eyes flickering over to the observation window. Shane was standing in the middle of his room now, staring out into space. He looked resigned. No, more than that. Defeated.

"All right," Ash said finally. "But I'm going with you."

She shook her head. "He won't talk to me if you're there. Let me try alone first."

"I'm trying to protect you, Alexis. I'm not about to let you get hurt again on my watch."

The flash of guilt and regret in his eyes caught her off guard. He was always so equanimous that it hadn't even crossed her mind he would blame himself for her disappearance. But in that instant, she saw it. He'd been tearing himself apart with guilt over the last month as his department searched for her.

"And I appreciate that so much," she told him and gave his big hand a squeeze. "I really do, but Shane is the last person I need protection from."

After a stubborn moment, Ash exhaled a long breath and pinched the bridge of his nose. "You just love giving me headaches, don't you?"

She grinned at him, knowing she'd won. Despite all of his grumpy growliness, Sheriff Ash Rawlings was a good man at heart. She liked him.

He shook his head, then indicated the door to Shane's room with the jerk of his chin. "Go ahead. Fifteen minutes, and Dr. Firestone and I will be right out here if you need us."

"Me, too," Ellie said and passed her the IV pole.

"Thank you." She leaned on the pole as she entered the hospital room, limping with each step. It didn't hurt as much as she expected it would, but that was probably due to whatever was dripping into her arm from the IV.

Shane went still, suddenly looking less like prey and more like a predator. He was standing by the window, his back to her, but she felt the tension radiating off his body. She took a deep breath and stepped closer to him.

"Hi," she said softly.

He didn't turn around, but she saw his reflection in the glass. His face was blank, unreadable. She took another step closer until she was standing beside him. For a long moment, they both looked out the window in silence.

"I'm so sorry," she said finally. "I didn't mean to cause all this trouble for you."

He still didn't say anything, but the muscles in his cheek tightened like he was clenching his jaw.

"The doctors said I survived because of you. If you had given up when the ATV ran out of gas, or after I collapsed, if you had taken me back to your cabin, I wouldn't have lasted another day. So, thank you."

He finally looked at her. "SEALs don't give up."

Those four words told her so much more about him than anything else he'd said over the last few days. She'd known he was military, and had figured he was special ops, but to have it confirmed explained so much.

She reached for his hand. He didn't pull away like she half-expected him to, and instead let her lead him over to the bed. She sat beside him.

Shane's gaze flickered to her sling, then up to the IV pole. "How are your shoulder and leg?"

"Healing," she said. "Thanks to you."

His fingers twitched in hers, and a jolt of electricity raced through her body. It was a strange sensation, but not an unwelcome one. He was nothing like the men she usually found attractive, and not just because of his scars. He was danger personified. He was anger and pain and fear. He was so damaged, and she wanted more than anything to fix him. The need to make him whole nagged at her, surpassing everything else.

No doubt Dr. Firestone would have something shrink-like to say about that, like she was deflecting her own trauma by focusing on Shane's.

But whatever.

She owed it to him.

For a moment, they sat in silence, Alexis not sure what to say next. She sensed his gaze on her, but she didn't turn to look at him. Instead, she focused on the hand she was holding, tracing the rough lines and scars on his skin.

"Does it hurt?" she asked softly.

He didn't answer for a long moment, and she was afraid she'd overstepped, but then he spoke. "Every day."

She got up and crossed to the small bathroom, where she found a wash basin and filled it with warm, soapy water. She returned to his side with some towels and placed the basin on the tray table beside his bed.

She touched his face, her fingers lightly brushing his cheek. "May I?"

His hard swallow was a dry click in the room's silence. Finally, he gave one sharp nod.

He watched with weary eyes as she dipped the edge of one towel in the water, but he didn't stop her as she lifted it to his cheek and started washing away his remaining camouflage.

As the last of the paint came off, Shane braced himself for her inevitable reaction. He had seen it hundreds of times before, the disgust and fear that people showed when they saw his scars. He had accepted it as his punishment for the things he had done, the violence he had inflicted during his time in the war. But it still hurt, deep in his bones, to be judged so harshly by strangers who didn't know him or what he had been through.

But once again, Alexis surprised him. She didn't recoil in horror or pity. Instead, she continued to look at him with the same steady gaze, her fingers tracing the jagged lines across his cheek and over his lips.

He flinched away from her touch.

"It's okay," she murmured. "It's just skin. It doesn't change who you are."

A lump rose in his throat at her words. He couldn't remember the last time he had been touched with such tenderness. He had been alone for so long, isolated from the world, that he had forgotten what it was like to have loving human contact.

Loving?

No. Where had that thought come from? She didn't love him. She was only being nice because she was grateful.

He drew away from her touch. "I shouldn't have let you do that."

"Why not?" she asked, her voice gentle. "I only washed your face."

"You don't have to pretend around me. I know what I look like."

"I'm not pretending." She lifted her gaze to his. "I don't care what you look like. You saved my life, Shane. I owe you everything."

Her words only confirmed his fears. She felt like she owed him. He should disabuse her of that notion and let her go back to her life, but no one had ever seen him like this before, scars and all, and accepted him so openly. He should push her away, tell her to leave him alone, but he couldn't bring himself to do it. He wanted her to stay, to keep looking at him like he was a hero, not a monster.

Without thinking, he reached out and took her hand in his, the roughness of his scars contrasting sharply with the softness of her skin. They were like sandpaper and silk. If he kept touching her like this, he'd tear her to shreds.

Just another reason he should tell her to go.

She didn't pull away, but instead squeezed his hand gently. Something stirred low in his stomach. Something that he hadn't felt in a long time. Something he thought he had lost forever, buried under the trauma of war and the pain of his scars.

Desire.

A beautiful woman like Alexis would never be interested in a man like him. Her only interest in him stemmed from her insistence that he'd saved her life. But he could hold on to that spark of desire, pull it out and warm himself with it on lonely, cold nights. He'd never had that before, and even if she'd never feel the same for him, he was grateful to her for giving him a little piece of his humanity back.

"Thank you," he said, his voice barely above a whisper.

"For what?" she asked, looking up at him with those piercing green eyes.

He couldn't tell her the truth. Didn't dare.

"For not being scared of me." His throat was so tight with emotion, he barely got the words out. "For treating me like a person."

"You are a person. A damn good one, from what I've seen. You just need help."

All of that warmth inside him vanished as if doused with a bucket of water. He should've known she had ulterior motives. The doctors weren't just going to let her come in here with the crazy man for a friendly visit.

He stood and put as much distance between them as possible in the small room.

"Shane, wait."

He glared at her, then at the window to the hall. He couldn't see anything on the other side, but he knew the sheriff and the doctor watched his every move like he was a zoo animal.

"I don't need their kind of help."

Alexis tossed the dirty towel into the basin of water, which was now murky with the paint she'd cleaned off him. "Except you do."

He shook his head, panic clawing at his throat. "I can't stay here. I can't. I'll go crazy. Crazier."

Alexis stood up and walked towards him, her hand outstretched. He flinched at the movement, but she didn't stop. Instead, she took his hand in hers and looked up at him with those piercing green eyes again.

"Listen to me, Shane. You don't have to stay here if you don't want to. We can find a more comfortable place for you, but you can't just run away back to the mountain. You need help, and there's nothing wrong with that. I need help, too. We both went through hell. Different kinds of hell, but still hell. So I'll be here for you every step of the way if you want."

He took a deep breath, trying to calm the storm of emotions inside him. He wanted to believe her, to believe that he could be helped, but he'd lived with the fear and paranoia for so long, he no longer knew who he was without it.

Would he even like who he was without it?

Probably not.

But he also hated who he was now.

It couldn't be worse.

"What if I try it their way and it doesn't work?" It was his biggest fear and giving voice to it made his chest tighten until drawing breath hurt. He'd long suspected he was beyond help.

It was why the forest was easier. Nothing in the forest cared that he was broken.

"Then we try something else and we keep trying until you feel whole again."

"Not possible."

She smiled, but it was sad. "Maybe not, but don't you think it's still worth a shot? What do you have to lose at this point?"

part two
man

"Love isn't a state of perfect caring. It is an active noun like struggle. To love someone is to strive to accept that person exactly the way he or she is, right here and now."

- Mr. Fred Rogers

chapter
eighteen

"DADDY?"

Zak Hendricks bolted awake from a sound sleep and looked around the dark room. For a minute, he was back *there*. Deep in the mountains of Afghanistan, at the mercy of men who delighted in torturing him.

But then the room snapped into focus. *His* room. With his wife in bed beside him, snuggled deep into her nest of blankets, sleeping off the two orgasms he'd given her before bed. His dogs were in their beds by the window, awake but unworried. And his daughter was a small silhouette in the open doorway, her blond hair lit like a halo from the nightlight in the hall.

"Daddy?" she said again, a tremble in her voice.

His heart rate slowed back to a normal level, and he smiled. He hoped he never got used to her calling him "daddy" because every time she did it, he felt like the biggest, bravest man on the planet instead of a soldier with a missing leg and a head full of demons.

"Hey, Popstar," he whispered and lifted the blankets, beckoning her over. "Did you have a nightmare?"

"There's a shadow man outside." Poppy raced across the

room and jumped into bed next to him. He lifted her to the middle of the bed and tucked her in.

"A shadow man?"

Anna rolled over and brushed the girl's blond hair back from her face. "Oh, honey. It's okay. It was just a bad dream. Ghosts aren't real."

She shook her head emphatically. "No, he's real. And he's not a ghost. He's from the woods."

And Zak's heart rate spiked again. "Where did you see the shadow man?"

"On the edge of the yard. He likes the woods. He disappears there and nobody ever sees him."

Anna lifted her gaze to his, her eyes wide. She wrapped her arms around Poppy and pulled her close.

Zak swore under his breath. He swung his foot off the edge of the bed and grabbed his prosthetic leg, fitting it into place over his stump. Then he crossed the closet, pulled on a sweatshirt, and retrieved his gun from the safe. "Stay here. I'll send Bella in, and when she gets here, lock the bedroom door."

"Should I call Ash?" Anna asked.

He leaned over the bed to press a kiss to his wife's head, and then to Poppy's. "Not yet, but keep the phone close. If you hear anything weird, don't waste time calling Ash. Call 911. He'll hear the call over his radio." He looked down at the dogs, who were both watching him with wary eyes. "Winston, stay and protect our girls. Ranger, come."

Ranger instantly jumped to his feet and fell into step behind Zak. Winston left his bed and climbed up onto the bed with Anna and Poppy. He was a goofy Golden Retriever most of the time, but when it came to his family, he could be downright vicious. Ranger, on the other hand, was always the intense, serious working dog. The Dutch Shepherd lived for a job, and if that job included biting bad guys, all the better.

Zak left the bedroom and made a beeline for his older

daughter's room, but he didn't need to wake her. Bella was already in the hallway, her pink braids peeking out from under her silk bonnet. Her eyes were impossibly wide, showing too much white against her brown skin.

"Dad, there's someone—"

"I know." He wrapped an arm around her shoulders and gave her a quick, reassuring squeeze. "Go in with Mom and Poppy and lock the door. Ranger and I will check it out."

He waited until Bella disappeared into the bedroom and he heard the click of the lock, then headed for the stairs with Ranger right on his heels.

By the time he reached the front porch, he was a black ops soldier again, focused solely on the mission of keeping his family safe. But as he circled the house and spotted the man at the edge of the woods, that tunnel vision fell away.

"Shane?"

Shane flinched at the sound of his name. He'd known Zak was there, had been aware of the other man the moment he stepped out of the house, and still the break in the silence startled him.

Zak lowered his weapon and signaled for his dog to stand down. "What are you doing out here?"

He stared into the dark woods. If he squinted, he could almost see the path that would lead him back to his cabin. Back to the silence.

"Ash gave me a room here."

"Yeah, I told him to," Zak said. "But what are you doing outside? You scared my daughters."

"Didn't mean to."

Zak was silent for a moment, then sighed. "Okay. Let me tell them it's safe, then we'll talk."

Out of the corner of his eye, Shane saw him reach into his pocket. He tensed, but Zak only withdrew a phone.

"It's okay," Zak told whoever answered. "Tell the girls everything is okay and they can go back to bed. It was just Shane."

A woman spoke on the other end of the line, her voice too muffled to make out.

"Yeah," Zak answered and studied Shane. "I think he's okay. I'm gonna stay out here with him for a bit. Yeah. Uh-huh. Okay, love you, too." He hung up and slid the phone back into his pocket. "So were you planning an escape? Because it looked like you were calculating the easiest exfil route."

Shane shook his head slightly. "I can't stay here."

"Yeah, well, that's a pisser because you can't leave, either. You heard Ash. If you leave, he'll track you down and you'll be committed to the hospital again."

"It's too loud down here."

Zak sighed and tilted his head back, looking up at the low-hanging clouds overhead. He was either praying for patience or cursing the twist of fate that brought Shane to his home.

Finally, he dropped his gaze back to earth and nodded toward the Redwood Coast Rescue facility. "Take a walk with me, Trevisano." He didn't wait for an answer, but headed back toward the cluster of buildings.

Shane hesitated and looked back into the woods. He could just go. Disappear into the life he knew. The life he was comfortable with. Despite Ash's warnings, the sheriff wouldn't be able to find him if he didn't want anyone to.

But then he would never see Alexis again.

But wasn't that for the better? He knew she was going to be okay. If he left now, it would be a clean break, the kind that heals without major deformity. If he stayed, it wouldn't be clean. Not for him. It would be messy and painful and he'd had more than enough of those kinds of wounds in his life.

Except...

Except.

She was getting out of the hospital soon, and he promised her he'd be here when she did. She'd be so disappointed in him if he broke that promise.

He turned and found Zak waiting silently by the fence enclosing the Rescue. He looked back at the forest. He could be free again. All he had to do was take a few more steps and let the forest swallow him. If he followed Zak, he'd never know that kind of freedom again. These fences were meant to keep the dogs safe, but all he saw was a prison.

Freedom or captivity.

Isolation or Alexis.

When he looked at it like that, it wasn't much of a choice, was it?

He turned and walked toward the Rescue. Zak nodded once and opened a gate in the fence, allowing his dog to run in the field beyond. He didn't move until Shane stepped through, too.

"I was like you once," he said as he turned to latch the gate. "Every little unexpected sound had my skeleton trying to jump out of my skin. I didn't sleep very much, and when I did, I had nightmares. Everything around me seemed too bright, and yet also somehow muted at the same time. I drank to dull the colors and sounds, then did coke when the world started to look too monotone. It was a vicious cycle I couldn't break out of. That, truthfully, I had no interest in breaking out of."

"We're not alike," Shane said. "I've never touched drugs." Even at his worst, when the pain was so bad he wanted to die, he never took more than what he was prescribed. And as soon as the prescription ran out, he never got it refilled.

Zak gave a tight smile and led him across the field. "You didn't need to. The mountain is your drug."

He stopped walking like he'd slammed into an invisible wall. "That's not..." He trailed off as Zak arched a brow at him.

"C'mon, man. You can't tell me you weren't just standing there jonesing for a hit."

Fuck. That was exactly what he'd been doing, standing on the line between civilization and wilderness, trying to decide which side he most wanted to be on.

He crossed his arms over his chest. He felt too exposed in this field, and in this conversation. "How did you... break the cycle?"

"Anna. My wife. She pulled me back from the brink when I'd've rather just jumped over. Hell, I tried to jump over. Multiple times. She kept me here, even when I didn't know I wanted to be here. She held me until I realized I wanted to live." Zak sent him a sly sideways look. "What made you step back from the woods just now and follow me?"

Alexis, he thought, but didn't respond. He couldn't because it sounded ridiculous even in his own fucked-up head.

"My guess?" Zak said after several seconds ticked by without an answer. "A certain nosy podcaster."

Shane scowled.

"Uh-huh. That's what I thought." He changed directions and headed for one of the buildings. "Let me show you something."

Shane recognized the building from his first time here, when he brought the dog off the mountain. It was the back side of the vet clinic.

Zak used a set of keys from his pocket to open the door, and a square of pale yellow light spilled out. It looked cozy and welcoming, but felt dangerous, and Shane hesitated just outside the light's reach.

Zak noticed and turned back to him. "You don't have to

come in if you don't want to. But I have a feeling you want to see this."

Shane took a deep breath and stepped into the light. The room was warm and smelled of antiseptic, but underneath that, there was a hint of something else. Something familiar, earthy and comforting.

Wet fur.

Animal.

Zak led him into a room lined with kennels and he sucked in a surprised breath when the dog inside the first one stood. Tan fur, pointed black ears, fluffy tail. It was the dog he'd found on the mountain, but stronger, healthier.

Alive.

She pushed her nose between the bars of her cage and he crouched down to get a better look at her. She was still too skinny, but already her ribs were less visible than they had been. Her tail whipped the air as he rubbed her nose and he found his lip twitching into something that might have been a smile. "She survived."

"She did."

"I didn't think she would."

"Well, she's a tough girl. Just like her owner."

Shane looked up in time to see Zak's quick flash of a grin. "Her owner?"

"Alexis."

He exhaled in a rush. "What?"

Zak leaned against the wall and crossed his good leg over his metal one. "I'm not usually one to believe in divine intervention or fate or whatever, but even I gotta wonder about the coincidence of this. Makes a guy think maybe you and Alexis were meant to find each other."

He stared at the dog again, and something unfurled in his chest. It was soft and sweet, and he didn't think he'd ever felt anything like it before. He certainly didn't have a name for it. "How?"

Zak shrugged. "We'll never know for sure, but Ash thinks the dog followed Alexis up the mountain when she was captured, but lost her scent when the Shadow Stalker took her underground. Then Clue couldn't find her way back into town and got lost."

"Clue?"

"Named for the board game."

That sounded exactly like something Alexis would name her dog.

Clue pushed her head under his fingers, seeking an ear scratch, and he obliged. "I believe that. She's stubborn, just like her owner. She wouldn't have known when to give up, even when she was putting herself in danger."

"Yeah, that too. I haven't had the pleasure of meeting Alexis in person yet, but I've heard the stories of her legendary stubbornness." Zak smiled down at the dog and there was real affection in his eyes. "Anna and I both think Clue has what it takes to be a SAR dog. When she's stronger, and if Alexis agrees, we're going to test her."

"For search and rescue?"

Zak nodded. "If you're interested, we'd love to have you stick around and help out. We could use someone with your knowledge of the wilderness on the team."

Team.

His heart clenched with something like... homesickness. He hadn't been part of a team in years. And, in his quietest moments, when all he could hear was his own breathing, his own heartbeat, he could admit to himself he missed it.

"Hey," Zak said, breaking into his thoughts. "You okay?"

Shane blinked and shoved to his feet. "Why bring me in here?"

"I thought you'd want to see Clue again."

"You're just trying to keep me from leaving."

Zak shrugged, completely unapologetic for the manipulation. "Maybe. But I also think you needed to see that she's healthy—all because you brought her to us. She's alive because of you, and so is Alexis. So maybe there's something here worth staying for."

Shane opened his mouth to argue, but the words died on his lips as he looked down at Clue. She was still nuzzling his hand, her tail wagging. It was... nice. Peaceful, even. He couldn't remember the last time he felt that way.

"So?" Zak asked, breaking the silence. "Wanna stick around and be part of the team?"

Shane didn't know what to say. He wasn't used to people wanting him around. He'd spent years pushing everyone away, but Zak's easy acceptance made the idea of being part of a team again tempting.

He turned back to the kennel and met Clue's amber eyes. The dog's tail thumped against the cage, as if agreeing with Zak's proposition. Maybe it was foolish, but a spark of hope flickered to life inside him.

"I'll think about it," he said, surprising himself with the words.

"Fair enough," Zak said and turned away. He went back to the door and whistled. "Ranger, come."

A moment later, his dog came barreling through with a big grin on his face. Zak gave his radar dish ear a scratch, then shut and relocked the door. He pulled out his phone and tapped out a text before turning back. "We'll give it a trial run. And since we're both up and probably not going back to sleep, how about some coffee? I'll show you around, introduce you to some of the dogs. Pierce is coming in at eight for a training session with his dog, Raszta. They're our urban SAR team, not wilderness, but you can still watch how they work. Let's just see if you're interested, huh?"

chapter
nineteen

SHANE *WAS* INTERESTED, much to his surprise. He'd hadn't been interested in anything but survival for years, but as he watched Pierce and Raszta work through the rubble pile out behind the Rescue, his curiosity was piqued. He'd worked with dogs before, even had one on his SEAL team for a short time during one of his deployments. He knew what they were capable of, but he'd never watched a training session before.

Pierce and Raszta weren't what he expected when he thought of a K9 team. He pictured Ash and that big black German Shepherd of his, or even Zak and Ranger with his brindle coat, radar dish ears, and intense yellow eyes. But Zak had explained that Ranger's specialities were cadaver detection and apprehension, and Ash's dog, Dante, was a police K9. Neither of them did much search and rescue. Not like Pierce and Raszta.

Pierce was a serious man with dark blond hair and hard hazel eyes. He nodded at Shane when they were introduced, and there was no flicker of disgust or revulsion in his eyes. Maybe because he had his own share of scars. His neck looked like something had tried to take a bite out of him, and the sight of it made Shane weirdly uncomfortable.

Was this how people felt around him? Like they were looking at something they shouldn't be? Like they were voyeurs to another person's private pain?

No wonder people ran in the opposite direction when they saw him.

While Pierce still looked every bit the soldier he used to be, Raszta looked more like the love child between a mop and a bear than a SAR dog. He was a medium-sized dog, thirty pounds at most. Dreadlocks covered his sturdy body and spouted from a ponytail on top of his head. They bounced with every jaunty step the little animal took.

"Gotta watch out for that one," Zak said, a smile pulling at his mouth as he watched the pair. "He's manipulative."

"Pierce or Raszta?"

Zak let out a burst of a laugh. It was deep and genuine and Shane wondered when the last time he'd laughed like that was. It hadn't been in a very, very long time.

"Both," Zak said. "But in this case, I was referring to Razzy. That little dog is probably the smartest animal I've ever met." He reached down and rubbed Ranger's radar dish ear. "And Ranger's no dummy, but he's like class valedictorian next to Raszta's Einstein. Razzy is twenty-nine pounds, and I swear most of that is his brain."

Shane watched Pierce run Raszta through some simple find exercises to warm up. The dog was smart. And fast. He ran literal circles around his handler, but Pierce didn't seem to mind. He grinned at the dog and made a huffing sound that might have been a laugh.

"What happened to—" Shane broke off, surprised at himself for speaking his thoughts out loud.

"To Pierce?" Zak finished.

He hesitated. He didn't know the protocol here. Did these guys talk about their injuries openly or did they all brush them aside and pretend everything was A-okay? He wasn't sure which he preferred. If he was going to be living here with these men, he didn't want to piss them off or make things awkward.

If Zak noticed his hesitation, he gave no indication. "Shrapnel damn near decapitated the guy in Iraq."

"Jesus," Shane muttered and rubbed his own scarred neck. "Fuck."

Zak nodded. "It's not only amazing he survived, but to walk away and only lose his voice? Dude's about as close to a miracle as I've ever seen." The way he slid a look in Shane's direction when he said those words put a knot in his stomach.

All of his doctors had called him a miracle for surviving second and third-degree burns over seventy percent of his body. But he wasn't a miracle. Surviving hell didn't make him special or worthy of admiration. It just made him lucky. And it certainly didn't feel like a miracle. It felt like a curse. A curse that followed him everywhere he went, reminding him of all the things he'd lost.

Shane turned his attention back to Pierce and Raszta, trying to shake off the feeling of discomfort that had settled in his gut. Their movements were fluid and synchronized as they worked through the piles of concrete and rebar, looking for the small canister containing human scent that Zak had hidden earlier. They moved together flawlessly, like a well-rehearsed dance, communicating only with whistles and hand signals.

The dog was impressive, but so was his handler. Pierce radiated a sense of calm confidence and the way he talked to Raszta, even though he couldn't speak, was almost like a conversation between equals.

It was fascinating.

And the way Raszta looked up at Pierce with complete trust and adoration made Shane's chest ache with a strange longing.

It wasn't until the end of the training session, after they

successfully located the "victim" and Pierce called Raszta to him with a sharp whistle and the dog bounded over with his prize—a stuffed elephant toy—in his mouth, that Shane realized what that strange feeling was.

He wanted that kind of trust.

He wanted that kind of connection.

He wanted someone to look at him with that kind of unconditional love.

And he knew, deep down, that he would never have that. Not with the way he looked now. Not with the nightmares that plagued him every night. Not with the way he was broken inside.

But... maybe he didn't have to stay broken?

Zak and Pierce had both faced the demons of war. They'd both been broken and had put themselves back together. Was it foolish to hope he could do it, too?

The next few days passed in a blur, but life at Redwood Coast Rescue wasn't as awful as he feared it would be. He liked helping with the dogs, and if ever the social interaction got to be too much, he could retreat to the woods behind the Rescue for some solitude. By his third day there, he started taking Clue on his walks with him. By his fourth day, he was even feeling like he had a handle on things.

That was when Alexis showed up.

Nobody told him she'd been released from the hospital. Of course, he hadn't asked. He'd assumed it wasn't his place to ask.

But now here she was, standing in the doorway of the main building, talking to Zak, looking like a completely different person than the woman he'd seen in the woods just days before. Her hair was brushed, her makeup was done, and she was wearing a pair of sunglasses that hid her eyes. But when she took them off and looked at him, his heart stuttered in his chest.

"Shane," she said, and he heard relief in her voice. She took a limping step toward him, but stopped short of touching him. "Oh my God. You're okay."

I wasn't the one shot twice, he wanted to say, but the words caught in his throat.

"Yeah," he said finally, his voice rough. "I'm okay."

"He's been helping out with the dogs," Zak added. "They like him."

Alexis nodded, her gaze flickering back to Shane. "That's good," she said softly. "I was worried about you. I'm glad you're finding some peace here."

Except he wasn't finding peace. He was still just trying to survive one day at a time. But he couldn't bring himself to tell her that when she looked so hopeful. Instead, he just nodded again and stared down at Clue, who was sitting obediently at his side, all but vibrating with excitement.

She followed his gaze to Clue and then did a double take and gasped. "You found her?" She slowly lowered to her knees and held out her hand for Clue to sniff. "Hi, my baby. Do you remember me?"

Clue gazed up at him in question. He nodded, releasing her from her sit, and she bounded into Alexis's arms, frantically licking her face. Alexis's laugh settled all the nerves fluttering around in his chest.

She looked happy, genuinely happy, and it was a sharp contrast to the haunted look he had seen in her eyes before.

"I can't believe you found her," Alexis said to Zak, tears brimming in her eyes.

"I can't take the credit." Zak held up his hands and took a step back. "That was all Shane."

Her gaze tracked over to Shane. "*You* found her?"

"Right before I found you." He didn't know why the admission made him feel so self-conscious, but it did.

Tears shimmered in her eyes. "You saved both of us?"

"I'll give you guys a minute," Zak said and pulled open the door, disappearing inside.

"I didn't know she survived until I got here. She's a good dog."

"Yes, she is." Alexis wrapped her arms around Clue's neck and buried her face in that fluffy tan fur. "Thank you. Again. I'm starting to feel like you're my guardian angel."

That strange longing pulled at his gut again. But this time, it wasn't just for the kind of trust and connection he saw between Pierce and Raszta. It was for Alexis herself.

He couldn't explain it, but she was the first person he'd met in a long time who didn't seem to see him as a monster. Who didn't flinch when she saw his scars or avoid looking at him altogether.

He shouldn't let himself get attached. He had nothing to offer her. But as he watched her hug her dog, he let himself wonder what it would be like to have someone like her in his life. Someone who looked at him with kindness and understanding. Someone who might be able to help him put himself back together.

He shook his head. "I was just in the right place at the right time."

"Or the wrong time," Alexis said and gave Clue a kiss on the head before straightening. She limped slightly, and he had to stop himself from scooping her up into his arms. He hated to see her in any kind of pain.

"I really am sorry I pulled you into this, but..." She hesitated. "Can I ask a favor?"

Anything, he thought. *It's yours.* He said, "You can ask."

She drew in a breath, held it for a second, then exhaled slowly. "So I have to go in to the sheriff's office tomorrow and — and relive it all. Tell them what I know. What little I remember. And I was hoping... would you come with me? I know I have no right to ask when you're dealing with your own problems, but... I feel safe with you. I don't know if I can do it without you."

He knew all too well what it was like to drown in your own trauma, and the only thing keeping you afloat was the presence of someone you trusted. Except in his case, the only person he'd ever trusted was himself.

Until her.

For reasons he couldn't begin to comprehend, he trusted her.

"Of course I'll go with you," he said, his voice thick with emotion. "You didn't even have to ask. I'm here for you, Alexis." The words sounded hollow, even to his own ears, just like the nice, meaningless platitudes all of his friends and fellow SEALs uttered after he was shipped home looking like a charred marshmallow. She'd never know just how much he meant it, that he was literally here in this place for her. If it weren't for her, he'd have disappeared back to his cabin the moment the sheriff released him from custody.

She smiled through her tears and he felt something shift inside him, like a door he'd kept locked for years was cracking open, letting in a sliver of light.

"Thank you," she whispered. "Thank you so much."

He nodded, but before he could say anything else, Zak appeared in the doorway again. "Hey, guys, sorry to interrupt, but Dr. Firestone is here."

Shane swore under his breath. He'd been dreading this all day, and stared longingly at the woods. Should've stayed out there. The shrink couldn't dig around in his mind if she couldn't find him.

But Alexis's hand on his arm stopped him from fleeing. "It's okay," she said softly. "I'm here for you, too. I'll be here when you get back."

He nodded, then, not trusting himself to speak, turned and followed Zak into another building. He was learning the facility's layout and knew this one served as a community center. The Rescue rented it out to various groups throughout the week and had plans to use it for future fundraising events. They passed a comfortable lounge area with a pool table and a larger empty room with folding tables and chairs stacked along one wall.

At the end of a short hall, Zak stopped at a door and gave it a soft tap. "Doc? Shane's here for his session."

"Come in," Dr. Firestone said.

Zak cracked open the door, but paused before stepping aside. "It's going to suck." When he met Shane's gaze, his dark eyes were serious. "I'm not gonna lie to you and tell you therapy will be easy. It's fucking awful, but it works. You got this, man."

With that, he walked away, leaving Shane to stare at the half-opened door.

If Zak had meant that as a pep talk, it hadn't worked. He wanted to run now more than ever, but avoiding it wasn't working for him anymore. If he was honest with himself, it hadn't been working for years. His anxiety, paranoia, and the overriding sense of fear had only gotten worse. If he didn't take this step, if he didn't get help, he would lose that last shred of sanity he still had.

He took a breath and stepped through the door.

chapter
twenty

THE ROOM WAS small and cozy, filled with the usual shrink's office decor: a couch, two chairs, a desk, and a bookshelf stuffed with volumes on PTSD and psychological disorders. Dr. Firestone sat behind the desk, her graying brown hair pulled back in a ponytail, her expression blandly pleasant.

"Good afternoon, Shane," she said, glancing up at him over her glasses. "You're looking better. How are you feeling since you left the hospital?"

He took the seat opposite her, nerves jangling like he was walking into a trap. "Fine."

"Fine?" She raised an eyebrow. "People only say 'fine' when they're actually not."

He wanted to tell her to fuck off. He didn't owe her anything, but he knew he had to play the game if he wanted to stay out of the psych ward. "I'm... adjusting."

"To life at the Rescue?"

"To... everything."

"Good." She wrote something down on a notepad. "Have you had any nightmares?"

The question made him clench his fists in his lap, and his scars tightened along his knuckles. He'd been having nightmares every night since he'd come here, but he didn't want to tell her that. He didn't want Dr. Firestone unraveling the threads of his trauma and laying them bare for her inspection. If he let her, he was afraid he wouldn't be able to sew himself back together when she was done.

When he didn't respond, Dr. Firestone wrote something else in her notebook and continued as if she hadn't asked the question. "I understand you've been helping out with the dogs. Animals can be very therapeutic. That's why I have Alfie here to help with these sessions."

"Alfie?"

For the first time, he noticed the dog bed under her desk. At the sound of his name, the petite brown and white dog poked its head up from the bed. He wore a green plaid bowtie and had big, fluffy ears that stuck out on either side of his head like wings. Alfie curled from the bed and trotted over to sit at Shane's feet. When Shane didn't move, he gave a small, questioning *arf*.

"What does he want?"

"For you to pick him up."

"No, thanks." But even as he said the words, Alfie launched into his lap in a jump that seemed to defy physics. Maybe those really were wings instead of ears.

The dog was soft, and the warm weight of him settled the unease swirling inside Shane's chest. Tension eased out of his muscles and his fists unclenched. He stroked a hand over Alfie's back.

"I don't want to be here," he told Dr. Firestone bluntly.

"Nobody ever does." She waited a beat, then took off her glasses and folded them on her desk. "Tell me, Shane. What made life on the mountain easier for you?"

He tensed at the mention of his mountain. It seemed like it was worlds away now, impossible to reach.

"It was quiet," he said finally. "I liked the quiet."

"You mention noise often. What kind of noise?"

"Just..." He trailed off, unable to find the right words to explain it. "People."

"You prefer being alone?"

"I prefer not having to deal with anyone's bullshit."

She leaned forward, her expression kind. "And now you're dealing with a lot of bullshit?"

He snorted. "You could say that."

"Tell me about it."

He shook his head.

"Do you consider what Alexis is going through more bullshit that you have to deal with?"

"No. Yes." Heat seethed just beneath his ruined skin. "I don't like that question."

"So you don't want to help her?"

"I don't want to talk about her."

"Okay," she said easily. "We'll talk about something else. Do you have any hobbies?"

"Hobbies?" Startled by the sudden shift, he looked down at Alfie, who had fallen asleep in his lap. He hadn't thought about hobbies in years. "No."

"Everyone has hobbies." She nodded toward Alfie. "You like spending time with the dogs here. That could be a hobby."

"That's survival, so I don't go crazy while stuck here." He paused, then amended, "Crazier."

"Okay, so what did you do on the mountain when you had all of your survival needs met? When you had plenty of food and firewood and could just relax for a few hours. What did you do then?"

Those moments had been so few and far between that he genuinely had to think about it. "I guess... fishing."

"That's a very peaceful activity. How did it make you feel when you were fishing for fun instead of survival?"

Shane's mind went back to the mountain, the memory of casting a line and feeling the tug of a fish on the other end, reeling it in and admiring its rainbow scales before setting it free. He'd liked those rare times he could set them free, when he didn't need to take them back to his cabin and cook them. It had been a small joy, one of the few he allowed himself. He remembered the way the sun felt on his face, the sound of the water rushing by. It had been a moment of peace in an otherwise chaotic life.

"It made me feel... calm. Like everything else didn't matter," he said, surprised at the admission. "There's always that noise in my head. It gets better on the mountain, but it's still there. But when I'm fishing, it's gone. It's quiet."

Dr. Firestone gave him a small smile. "That's a good sign, Shane. It means you're still capable of finding peace. We'll work on finding more activities that bring you that same feeling."

He didn't respond, still lost in memories of the mountain. Alfie shifted in his sleep, and he stroked a hand over the dog's soft fur absentmindedly.

"Can I ask you something?" Dr. Firestone said, breaking the silence.

Shane looked at her, his guard up once again. "Depends on what it is."

"I've been talking to Alexis, too, visiting her while she was in the hospital. Why didn't you go back and visit her?"

He lifted a shoulder. "She has her friends, her sister. She doesn't need me."

"I don't believe that's true," Dr. Firestone said. "And I don't think you believe it either. I know for a fact she just asked you to go with her to give her statement to the sheriff tomorrow. Why do you suppose she asked you?"

"She said she feels safe with me."

"So why would you say she doesn't need you?"

"Because I—" *I need to fix myself first. I need to be worthy of her trust.* He snapped his mouth shut before finishing the thought out loud. It was a stupid, impossible thing to want, and he wasn't about to arm the doctor with that knowledge.

Dr. Firestone nodded, her expression thoughtful. "You've both been through exceedingly traumatic experiences."

"Exactly. She has enough to deal with without having me dump my insanity on her."

"Do you think you're insane?"

"What else would you call it?"

"Injured," Dr. Firestone said instantly. "PTSD is an injury, no different from breaking a bone. Nobody is ever ashamed of seeking medical help for a broken bone. Therapy should be viewed the same."

He grunted. "But it's not."

"No, it's not." Once again, the doctor changed tactics. "Alexis seems to have formed an attachment to you. Do you feel the same way about her?"

Shane's heart stuttered in his chest. He'd been trying to ignore the growing feelings he had for Alexis, knowing that he was too damaged for anyone to love. But the thought of her being in danger again, of her being hurt, made his blood run cold.

"I don't know," he said finally. "I... worry about her and I haven't worried about anyone but myself since I left the Teams."

Dr. Firestone studied him for a moment before nodding. "That's okay, Shane. You don't have to have everything figured out right now. Just know that if you do start to feel something more, it's okay to explore that bond. It would be good for you. For both of you, I would think."

He was good for *Alexis*?

For a split-second, the thought gave him hope. But it was bullshit. He wasn't good for anyone. Not even himself. He ruthlessly crushed that fragile flame of hope and let rage seep into its place, cold and familiar.

This doctor was toying with him, playing with his feelings like a child with wooden blocks, seeing what she could build just so she could tear it down again.

No.

He exploded up out of the chair, startling Alfie. The dog yelped and ran back to the safety of his bed.

Dr. Firestone gasped and pushed back from her desk as he leaned over it. "I don't need someone with more degrees than sense telling me how to feel or what to do. I don't need someone prying into my life and trying to fix me when I know damn well that isn't going to happen. That I'm broken beyond repair. How fucking dare you presume to know anything about me? About what I want or need?"

Dr. Firestone stood, her hands held up in a gesture of peace. "Shane, I don't presume anything. I'm only here to listen, judgement free, and offer advice. I'm here to help."

"I don't need or want your fucking help." He was shaking with rage and fear and frustration, all battling for supremacy, a boiling cauldron of emotion that threatened to erupt any second now. His fists clenched and unclenched as he tried to gain control over himself. But it wasn't enough.

The buzzing in his head was too loud.

The room too small, too hot.

And the doctor was getting too fucking close to truths he didn't want to examine.

"Shane—"

The rage won out and exploded from him in a guttural roar. "Stop!"

He grabbed his chair and threw it into the bookshelf. Several books crashed to the floor, but it wasn't enough. He wanted to destroy all of those texts that thought they knew what he was going through and how to fix him.

He couldn't be fixed, dammit. If he could, the doctors at the VA would have done it all those years ago.

He stalked over and swept his arm across the shelf until all the books were at his feet. And it still wasn't enough. He wanted to pulp them. To demolish the entire bland office.

But then he caught sight of Dr. Firestone's wide, terrified eyes. She was standing against the wall behind her desk, Alfie clenched protectively to her chest. She was trying to hold it together, but tears glassed her eyes and her lower lip trembled.

Fuck.

He had to get out of here.

He stalked to the door, leaving a heavy silence in his wake.

chapter
twenty-one

ALEXIS SAT on a couch in the community room, tossing a ball for Clue while she waited for Shane to finish his therapy session. For the millionth time, she glanced toward the hall he'd disappeared down. She couldn't hear anything, but that wasn't really a surprise. Zak had given her a quick tour of the facility before leaving her here to wait, and he'd said they had invested in military-grade sound-proofing when they built the place because, as he put it, "Dogs are cute but so fucking loud."

God, she hoped the session was going well.

Shane needed it.

The front door opened a crack, only far enough for a woman to slip inside. She was thin and pale, her dark hair pulled back into a messy knot on top of her head. She all but vanished inside her oversized green sweatshirt.

When she spotted Alexis and Clue, she froze like a deer in the headlights. It wasn't the normal kind of surprised you saw in people when they met someone unexpected. It was terror. The woman's reaction was so extreme that Alexis's own heart rate spiked, and she looked behind her, half-expecting the Shadow Stalker to be standing there.

But, of course, the room was empty.

Alexis stood up slowly, trying not to startle the woman any further. She spoke in a low, calm voice, "Hi, I'm Alexis. This is my dog, Clue. We're just waiting for a friend."

The woman didn't respond, but she didn't bolt either. She just stood there, staring at Alexis and Clue with wide, frightened eyes.

Alexis took a step closer. "Are you okay? Do you need help with anything?"

The woman shook her head frantically, then seemed to realize what she was doing and forced herself to stop. She swallowed hard. "I'm sorry. I didn't mean to intrude. I just..."

She trailed off, biting her lip so hard that Alexis could see the faintest hint of blood. The woman's hands shook, and she stuffed them into the front kangaroo pocket of her sweatshirt, balling it up around them. Her breaths came in sharp inhales and choppy exhales, like she couldn't get enough oxygen. It was clear that the woman was in the middle of a panic attack.

"Hey, it's okay," Alexis said softly, trying to diffuse the situation. "I won't hurt you."

The woman hesitated for a moment before slowly closing the door behind her and taking a few cautious steps closer.

Clue, sensing that something was wrong, trotted over to the woman and nuzzled her hand. It was a small gesture, but it seemed to help. The woman relaxed a little, and she even managed a small smile as she petted Clue.

"Sorry, I wasn't expecting anyone else to be here," she said in a whisper. "I'm looking for Dr. Firestone."

Alexis smiled warmly, hoping to put her at ease. "No problem at all. My friend is with the doctor right now. Do you have a session scheduled, too?"

"No, I'm just..." The woman shook her head, her gaze flicking down to the floor. "I hoped she could make the time."

"I'm sure she will." Alexis paused, waiting for the

woman to say more, but she didn't. The room fell silent except for the sound of Clue's tail thumping against the floor.

"Are you okay?" she asked after a moment.

The woman's eyes widened slightly, as if the question surprised her. She nodded, but her body language said otherwise.

"Are you... have you been through something?"

The woman hesitated for a moment before nodding again, a single tear slipping down her cheek. Alexis felt her own heart break. This woman was hurting, and she didn't know how to help.

"I'm so sorry," Alexis said softly. "No one deserves to feel scared or alone."

The woman looked up at her, her dark eyes red and puffy. "I just want it to stop. I want to be... normal. To feel like myself again."

God, could she relate to that. She hadn't felt like herself since before the Shadow Stalker took her. "What's your name?"

The woman hesitated for another moment before quietly saying, "Veronica."

"Hi. I'm Alexis," she said again because she didn't think Veronica had heard her the first time she introduced herself.

"I know," Veronica murmured. "I listen to your podcast. You have a very soothing voice, and I like the way you tell the victims' stories."

"Thank you. That means a lot." Flattered, she scooted over on the couch to make room. "Do you want to sit down and wait with us? It might help to have some company."

Veronica took a tiny step toward the couch when a door slammed open somewhere deeper in the building and she flinched like she'd been shot. Without a word, she turned and ran out the door.

God, Alexis thought as she watched the woman flee. Veronica was so broken.

And that could be her, too. Haunted by her own past and trapped in a never-ending cycle of despair. She could so easily see herself falling into that same abyss, unable to escape the memories and nightmares.

Clue came over and laid her head on Alexis's knee, looking up with sad brown eyes. She rubbed a finger along the dog's long nose. "That's not going to be me. I won't let fear consume me. That bastard wins if I do."

And she'd do everything in her power to make sure he didn't win. She had to keep moving forward, keep fighting for justice for the victims of monsters like the Shadow Stalker.

Shane burst from the hallway, strode across the room, and shoved out the side door, never even sparing her a glance.

Clue watched him go, then looked back at Alexis with a question in her brown eyes like, *What's wrong with him?*

"I don't know," Alexis answered and stood. "Let's go see."

The outside air had cooled considerably as the sun sank toward the ocean. It smelled crisp and clean, but had a bite that became downright vicious as Alexis followed Shane under the thick canopy of the forest. She hugged herself and squinted into the damp gloom, trying to spot him.

There.

He sat on the thick log of a downed tree, his chest heaving with every breath he took.

Alexis approached slowly, not wanting to startle him. His scars stood out starkly against his pale skin as his breathing grew more labored with each passing second.

"Shane," she said softly, kneeling down in front of him. "What's wrong? Are you okay?"

He didn't answer at first, just continued to gasp for air as if he'd been running for miles. She reached out to touch his arm, but withdrew when he flinched away, his eyes wild and panicked.

"Shane, please. Talk to me."

He shook his head, his breaths turning into whimpers as he hunched over, his hands clutching at his hair. His eyes flooded and she could see pain etched into every line of his face, and her heart ached for him.

"Come on." She kept her voice low and soothing. "Let me help."

"Why does everyone want to help?" he burst out.

She touched his arm again, but this time he didn't flinch away. "Because we care about you."

He stabbed a finger back toward the rescue. "They don't know me."

"But I do. And I care about you."

"You shouldn't."

"Why not?" Alexis asked softly. "Why do you think you don't deserve to have someone care about you?"

Shane's shoulders slumped, and he finally looked at her, his eyes glassy. "Because I'm broken, Alexis. I'm not the man I used to be. He was funny and had friends and could make small talk even though he hated it... but now I'm just so fucking broken, and everyone keeps saying they can help, but what if they're wrong? What if I can't be fixed?"

"No one expects you to return to the man you used to be," she said, her voice firm and unwavering. "It's impossible. But I like the man you are now. That man might not be able to engage in small talk, but he saved my life. That man is grumpy, but also kind and brave and strong."

He shook his head, tears streaming down his face. "I'm not

strong. I'm weak." He stared over her head at the Rescue. "I just scared the shit out of that doctor. Trashed her office all because I couldn't take the questions."

"Oh. I see." She straightened and moved to sit beside him on the log. "So the session didn't go well?"

"No, it didn't fucking go well," he snapped.

"You're not weak," she said, scooting closer to him. She took his hand in hers, lacing their fingers together. "You're the strongest person I know. You've been through so much and you're still here, still fighting."

"I don't want to fight anymore." He sounded exhausted.

"I know." She thought of Veronica, and a chill raced down her spine. "But what's the alternative?"

Shane's hand tightened around hers, his scars standing out starkly against her smooth skin. "Give up. Ring out."

Her heart clenched. "Is that really what you want? To give up?"

For a long moment, he just looked at her, his gaze flickering over her face as if he was trying to read her thoughts.

"No," he admitted. "I'm not a quitter. But I don't know how to keep going. Everything is just... too much."

Alexis leaned closer to him, her hand still clasped in his. "How did you survive SEAL training?"

He released a burst of bitter laughter at the change of subject. "Sheer stubbornness."

"Come on. There had to be more to it than just that."

He rubbed a hand over his face, swiping away the tears. "I guess... I just kept telling myself it was only one more step, one more stroke, one more run, one more push-up. Just one more. One more. One more. Until, finally, there wasn't another 'one more' and I was done."

"See? You don't have to know how to keep going. You just have to take it one step at a time, like you did in training. And I'll be here with you every step of the way."

Shane looked at her, his eyes softening. "You don't have to do that, Lexi. You have your own demons to deal with."

"I know," she said and offered a smile. "But you're going with me tomorrow to help me slay them, and I want to do the same for you. You saved my life, Shane. It's the least I can do."

They sat together in silence for a long time as evening faded, the only sound the rustle of leaves in the chilly March wind and the forest nightlife waking up. Then Clue nudged her snout under their combined hands, seeking attention.

Alexis chuckled and scratched Clue behind her ears. "She likes you."

Shane released her hand to stroke the dog's back. "Yeah, she has from the moment she saw me. Don't know why."

"Because dogs have a sense for good people."

"That sounds like bullshit."

Alexis laughed and bumped her shoulder against his. "It's true. And you're a good person, Shane. Don't forget that."

He leaned into her, his cheek resting on the top of her head as he sighed. "Thank you."

"Anytime," she said and wrapped an arm around his waist. "We'll get through this together, okay?"

He nodded against her shoulder, and she hugged him closer, feeling his scars under her fingertips. She didn't care about the scars, though. She didn't care what he looked like, or how broken he claimed he was.

To her, Shane was a hero.

And she was honored to call him her friend.

THE AIR from the vents overhead felt too cold and seemed to wrap around Alexis like a shroud. Or maybe that was her nerves chilling her to the bone. Probably that was her nerves, because she doubted the sheriff's office kept their A/C on full blast in March.

The sheriff's secretary, a kind woman named Janine, led her and Shane to a room that wasn't at all what she'd expected. It wasn't the stark, austere box she'd seen on cop shows, with harsh lighting, a beat-up table, and two chairs. Instead, there were two small couches, a round table with four chairs, and a small fridge stuffed with water, soda, and juice boxes. A bookcase held board games, coloring books, and novels for readers of all ages. Landscape paintings hung on the walls, all featuring different points of interest around the county, and the little plaques underneath each said the local artist's name.

Okay, this wasn't so bad.

She could handle this.

Logically, she knew that interrogation box probably existed somewhere in the building, and she appreciated Ash's consideration in doing the interview here instead. This cheery room somehow made the idea of revisiting her captivity less daunting. Her jangling nerves calmed and her breathing slowed.

Shane paced between the door and window, looping around the table. He looked a little panicked and a lot wild, just as he had in his hospital room. The man really wasn't built for enclosed places and she suddenly regretted asking him to come. It was too much for him. She should've asked her sister, but the thought of Ellie hearing all the awful details made her sick to her stomach. Ellie didn't need to know. Shane didn't need to know, either. She should've been strong enough to do this on her own.

"You don't have to stay," she said after watching him make his fourth lap around the room.

He froze, and his gaze slid to the window and the mountain that was just a faint outline in the gray sky beyond. He was debating it. Every sense he had was probably screaming at him to leave, but he took a deep breath and turned to face her. His eyes were dark and intense, and she could see the raw emotions he was struggling to keep under control.

"I'm okay," he said, his voice tight. "I promised you I'd stay for this, so I'll stay."

It was too much to ask of him. She knew it, but she couldn't help the rush of relief. She really didn't want to face this alone. "Thank you."

The door opened, and Ash stepped inside carrying two paper cups of coffee from the cafe in town. He paused when he spotted Shane. But the hesitation only lasted a second. He closed the door behind him and placed one coffee on the table in front of her.

"The coffee here sucks, so I brought you one from Hot Shots. Ellie told me you like vanilla lattes?"

"Yes, thank you." She wrapped her hands around the cup, grateful for the warmth.

Ash held out the other cup to Shane. "I didn't know you'd

be here, or I'd have brought you something, too. You can have mine if you want. It's as black as motor oil."

Shane shook his head, which was probably the right call. He was twitchy enough without adding the jitter of a caffeine high.

Ash shrugged and took a drink from his cup before setting it down and pulling out a chair from the table. He dragged it over, placing it on the other side of the coffee table from her seat on the couch. As he sat, he removed a digital recorder from his pocket and placed it next to his drink.

"How are you?" he asked.

"I'm okay." She sucked in a breath and released it in a rush. "If it's all the same, Sheriff, I'd like to cut the small talk and just get to the questions. I don't know if my nerves can handle more than that."

He nodded, and his gaze was full of sympathy. He was such a hard, gruff man most of the time that his compassion now somehow made her more nervous.

"I know this will be difficult," he said gently. "But I need you to tell me everything you can from the moment you were abducted. I have to record everything for the investigation. Is that okay?"

Her tongue suddenly felt like sandpaper, her throat a dry pipe that clicked when she swallowed. She nodded.

Ash reached forward and started the recorder. "This is Sheriff Ash Rawlings in interview with Alexis Summers. It's ten-thirty a.m., March twenty-ninth, twenty-twenty-four. Also present is a friend of Ms. Summers, Mr. Shane Trevisano." He looked across the coffee table at her. "Okay, whenever you're ready, start at the beginning. What do you remember from the day you were abducted?"

She gave herself a moment to just breathe, then clasped her hands tightly in her lap. "I had just met with Cal Holden. You told me to get in touch with him about Peter Galasso's wrongful conviction case, and so I set up a meeting with him at Hot Shots in town. We talked for a while and I took some notes on my laptop. It really was an excellent case for the podcast."

"While you were sitting there, did you notice anyone paying undue attention to you? Anyone acting suspicious? Set off your internal alarm bells?"

She shook her head. "No, not really. Just the usual people coming and going from the coffee shop. I didn't think anything of it."

"Did you see anyone there you recognized?"

"Uh..." She closed her eyes and tried to bring that day into focus. "I saw your friend... Pierce, I think his name is? He stopped, but he was only there for a few minutes. He just ordered, waited for his drink, and left. I don't think he even noticed Cal and me in the corner. He had headphones in. Then one of your deputies came in and ordered a bunch of coffees to go. And that author guy was there on his laptop. Connelly?"

She sensed Shane tense up, even though he was still over by the window. She glanced his way. His shoulders were tight and his eyes guarded as he stared at Ash, as if trying to gage the sheriff's reaction. Right. Connelly was the man he'd attacked the night he brought her into town. Made sense he'd get anxious at the mention of him.

She returned her attention to Ash. "He wasn't paying any attention to me, either. He was lost in his own world."

Ash nodded and pulled out a leather notebook. He flipped open the battered green cover to a fresh page and made a note. "Anyone else?"

She mentally scanned the tables again. It had been a busy afternoon at the cafe and she hadn't known most of the people there. "There were a couple of teachers from the school. They still had their badges on. Some kids came in at one point and gathered around a table in the opposite corner from me. Three girls. They were being kind of loud and obnoxious—not maliciously, but, you know, in that squealing way of teenage girls. Oh! The doctor was there, too. Dr. Firestone. She was with an older man with gray-streaked hair. Maybe her husband? They looked like they were having lunch and he was getting a bit annoyed at the kids, so they left." She shook her head again. "But nobody was paying attention to me. Nobody cared I was there, and I didn't know most of those people at the time. Like Dr. Firestone. I didn't know her until a few days ago."

"Okay. Let's fast forward a bit. Who left first, you or Cal?"

"Cal. He had a deposition to get to."

"When did you leave?"

"I don't know for sure. Maybe a half hour after him? I stayed for a bit, gathering my thoughts on the case. I had another coffee, then emailed all of my notes to Ellie so she could start researching. It looked like it was going to rain, so I packed everything up and went back to my motel to walk Clue before it did."

"What happened then?"

A chill scraped down her spine. "It's all fuzzy. I got out of my car, walked to my door. I think I swiped the card to unlock it. I'm pretty sure I did. I had the door partly opened and could see Clue's nose through the crack. And then... someone asked me for directions to the hospital. I didn't see him. Not really. Just got a sense from the corner of my eye that he was hurt. Limping. I turned toward him to answer, and... I think someone grabbed me from behind. I'm not sure. I don't know if that's a memory or just... a feeling. I remember being terrified, but that's it until I woke up in that bunker."

"What was the first thing you noticed when you woke up?"

"The smell. It was like mold and dirt and... something

else." She could almost smell it again and exhaled to clear her senses. "Something rotten. It reminded me of roadkill."

Ash made a note on his pad. "And then what?"

"I was tied up, my hands behind my back and my ankles together. I couldn't move. I was in this little room, with a dirt floor and walls made of cinder blocks. There weren't any windows. I was alone for a long time, just lying there in the dark. I tried to scream, but my throat hurt too much. Eventually, he came in. The man who took me."

"Can you describe him?"

She paused and took a deep breath. "He was wearing a mask. I never saw his face."

"What did he say to you?" Ash asked.

"He didn't say anything the whole time he had me. Not a word until the day he released me. He threw the bloodstained coat at me and told me to run." Her brow wrinkled. "Where is the coat?"

"It's in evidence, along with Shane's furs. We're testing the bloodstains." Ash looked up from his notebook. "This next part is going to be difficult, and if you need to stop, just say the word. What did he do to you while he had you?"

Tears flooded her eyes and spilled out. She shook her head. She couldn't say it.

Ash closed his notebook and met her gaze. "The doctors did tests when you were brought in. They found indications of repeated rape and sexual trauma."

Alexis shuddered at the memory, her chest tightening as she fought back the tears. "It wasn't sex for him. It wasn't any kind of love or connection or even obsession. It was... just about control. He was... he was so cold. So detached. But he seemed to get pleasure out of making me suffer. He hurt me so much, Ash. I didn't think I was going to make it out of there alive."

"But you did," Ash said. "You made it out. You're a survivor, Alexis."

A survivor. The word washed over her like a curse, and she had to fight the urge to curl up in a ball and hide from the world, the way she had once hidden from the dark corners of her room when she was a little girl. The way she had hidden when she'd been taken by the monster who'd stolen her will and her life and left her nothing but a shell of her former self.

Shane was suddenly by her side, his hand on her shoulder. She jumped at the contact, but then relaxed slightly at his touch as he wrapped an arm around her and drew her into his side. He was so warm, and she wanted to snuggle into him and forget it all.

But she couldn't forget. She couldn't forget the pain, the fear, the helplessness. She couldn't forget the way the man had stripped away her dignity, her autonomy, her humanity. She couldn't forget the way he had made her feel like nothing more than a piece of meat to be used and discarded.

Her body trembled as she tried to steady her breathing. Shane's arms tightened around her. She let herself lean into his embrace for a moment, but then pulled away, needing to be strong and face the reality of what had happened to her.

"I'm sorry." She wiped away her tears with her sleeve.

Ash shook his head. "You have nothing to be sorry for." He took a deep breath. "I hate that I have to ask you these questions, but I need you to tell me everything he did to you. It will help the investigation. Do you remember anything else about the man who took you? His voice, his height, his weight? Any identifying remarks?"

"I think he had light colored hair. At least his body hair was light. He was average height. Average weight. Not in bad shape—he was strong—but I don't think he was like a gym rat or anything. His stomach was soft." She tried to picture more of him.

The birth mark…

But bile rose in her throat. She clamped a hand over her mouth until she was sure she wouldn't throw up.

"No more." Shane stood up. He squared his shoulders, his face hard and his eyes flashing with anger. "She's done."

She set a hand on his arm. His muscles felt like steel under his rough skin. "It's okay. I want to do this. I need to do this."

Shane's expression softened slightly, and he nodded, but he didn't sit back down. He hovered nearby, his eyes never leaving her face.

Ash cleared his throat and flipped open his notebook again. "Can you describe the room where he kept you?"

God, why was it so cold in here? She wrapped her arms around herself. "It was small. Maybe only six feet wide and eight feet long? The walls were cinder blocks, like I said, and there was a dirt floor. The only light came from a small bulb hanging from the ceiling, but he mostly kept that off. There was a mattress on the floor with some blankets. There was a bucket in the corner for a toilet."

Ash made a note. "And he never talked to you?"

"No. He'd come in to give me food and water and… to do what he did. But he never said anything, except at the end when he told me to run. I didn't understand at first, but he had a gun and then I remembered the line from that spooky nursery rhyme about the Shadow Stalker: 'In woods so still, his hunt begins, Fear his presence, where moonlight thins.' I realized there must have been some truth to the legend, so I ran."

"What did he do?"

"He chased me. Hunted me like an animal."

A low growl pumped from Shane's throat. And, she noticed, Ash was quietly furious, too. His knuckles had gone white at how hard he was gripping his pen. But she couldn't stop now. They were almost through it. She just had to get this last part out, and it was over.

"He shot me twice, and then I found Shane's cabin and... I don't remember anything else until I woke up and saw Shane. I thought he was the Shadow Stalker at first." She gazed up at him. "I'm sorry I didn't trust you."

Shane's grip tightened on her shoulder. "It's okay. You had every reason not to trust me." If she wasn't mistaken, that was a smile pulling up the corner of his misshapen mouth. "Half the time, I don't even trust me."

"Alexis." Ash leaned forward. "Do you think you could find the bunker again?"

"I... don't know. I wasn't paying attention to my surroundings, but maybe."

"Would you be willing to try? You'll be perfectly safe," Ash added when Shane opened his mouth to protest. "I'll be there, and my deputies. And I'd like to bring RWCR in, see if the dogs pick up any scents. If you're right and there are other victims, there will be more bodies up on that mountain."

The idea of returning to the mountain made her go numb. But she had to try because she had no doubt the Shadow Stalker was already looking for his next victim. "I'm willing."

"I'm going, too," Shane said.

Ash's lips tightened, but after a moment, he nodded. "You know the area better than any of us. All right. The weather shows a few clear days up there later this week. Do you think you're strong enough to make the trip?"

No. She didn't know if she'd ever be mentally strong enough. But physically? "Yes, I can do it."

Ash closed his notebook and stood. "I'll set it up. If you remember anything else, reach out to me."

"Thank you." As he turned toward the door, something twinged at the back of her mind. "Wait. I just remembered.

Back at the coffee shop, as I was leaving, there was someone right by the door. I remember he gave me the creeps."

Ash swung back. "Did you see his face?"

"No." She closed her eyes and struggled to bring the man into focus. "I think he was wearing a hat. But... it wasn't so much how he looked that pinged on my radar. He just felt... off. Almost... angry, maybe? And he left right after I did."

Ash nodded. "That's good. I'll get the security feed from the shop and see if you can pinpoint him." He went to the door again, but paused. His eyes were full of regret when he glanced back. "You were right, Alexis. I have a serial killer in my county. He might not be the Shadow Stalker of legend, but—"

"He's using the legend to hide. If everyone thinks he's a myth, nobody will look for him."

"And I didn't." Ash's jaw tightened until a muscle ticked under his beard. "I should've listened to you sooner. I'm sorry it took this to make me pay attention, but I promise you, finding the bastard is my sole focus now. We'll get him."

chapter
twenty-three

AS ASH LEFT THE ROOM, she leaned back against the couch, exhaustion sinking in, weighing her down. Shane didn't say anything, just stood there, watching her with a look of concern etched on his face.

"Are you okay?" Shane asked, his voice low and husky.

She nodded, not trusting herself to speak. She could feel his eyes scanning her, taking in every small detail, every nuance of her expression. She wanted to reassure him, tell him she was okay, but the words caught in her throat. She didn't know if she would ever be okay again.

"Can I..." She hesitated. "Can I just be close to you for a minute?"

He sat beside her and extended an arm. "Come here," he said gruffly.

She leaned into him, her body trembling. "I don't know if I can do this. Go back there."

"You're the strongest person I know, Lexi. You can and you will and, because of it, no other women will die. And I'll be there every step of the way to keep you safe." His hand moved to cup her cheek, and he tilted her head until her gaze met his. "He's never touching you again. I'll kill him first."

A shiver ran down her spine at the intensity in his eyes, but it wasn't entirely unpleasant. She knew he meant every word. She leaned in, pressing her lips against his in a fierce kiss. His arms wrap around her, pulling her closer as he deepened the kiss. The taste of him, the feel of his body against hers, was overwhelming. She felt like she was drowning, but Shane was the anchor that kept her from being swept away.

And then, as quick as it started, it was over and he was gone. Out of her arms, out the door. She blinked in shock, then gathered her purse and chased him out of the building. She caught him at the edge of the parking lot, staring up at the mountain. She reached for him, but stopped short. He was muttering something under his breath, his fists clenched at his sides. Anxiety radiated off of him in waves.

He needed space.

She took a step back. "Shane?"

He turned to her, his eyes wild. "Why the fuck would you kiss me?"

She stared at him, uncomprehending. "Because... I like you."

"Why? Look at me." He motioned to himself. "I'm fucking hideous."

She went to him then. She couldn't stay away. She cupped his rough jaw in her hands and caressed his cheeks with her thumb. "No. You're not."

Shane squeezed his eyes shut and tried to pull out of her grasp, but she wouldn't let go. Instead, she wrapped her arms around his waist and nuzzled in against his chest. "I wish you could see yourself the way I see you."

"I know what I look like." His hands hung loosely at his sides. He wanted to wrap his arms around her and tug her in close. He wanted to bury his face in her hair and breathe in the faint berry scent of her shampoo. He wanted... all kinds of things he had no business wanting from her. Not after what she'd been through. Not with how broken he was.

"I don't care how you look, but I know it bothers you." She finally leaned back enough to meet his gaze. "There are options for treatment."

"I've seen doctors before. They couldn't do much."

"Times have changed, though. There have been incredible advancements in burn scar treatment, things that weren't available back then. Like laser therapy to resurface the skin and reduce scars. It's less painful and more effective than it used to be."

He scowled. "Laser therapy, huh?"

"Yes, and there are also silicone-based products—gels and sheets that you can wear to soften and flatten scars over time. And there are new pressure garments that are more comfortable and efficient."

"You've done your homework."

"Research is kinda my thing." Alexis flashed that gorgeous, cloud-clearing smile of hers. "And if the idea of lasers freaks you out, there are so many more options. Like microneedling, which stimulates collagen production to improve scar texture. New skin grafting techniques. Dermal fillers."

Shane said nothing for a long time, then exhaled softly. "It's not just about the scars. They don't help, especially when everyone looks at me like I'm some kind of grotesque creature they should be afraid of. But it's more..." He tapped his temple. "It's up here. That's where I'm most fucked up. I attacked Connelly because I thought he was a terrorist who planted a bomb in the pub just because he had a laptop. He's a fucking writer. Of course he had a fucking laptop. And I nearly attacked Dr. Firestone just for doing her job. She got too close to a truth I didn't want to examine, and I exploded. I can't control it. I'm dangerous."

"But there have been advancements in therapy techniques for PTSD, too. Specialized support groups, like the one here in town. And there's been new research in regenerative medicine that could help. It's not just about the physical scars. It's about your well-being as a whole."

It all sounded exhausting. Terrifying.

"It's time to rejoin society, Shane."

He stared at her, transfixed by the genuine concern in her voice. She was right. It was time to take a chance and try to move forward. He had been holed up on his mountain for far too long, wallowing in self-pity and drowning in his own despair.

"I don't know if I'm ready," he finally whispered. "It's been so long since I've been around people. I don't know if I can handle it."

"That's okay," Alexis said, her voice gentle and soothing. "We'll take it one step at a time. Maybe we can start by attending one of the support group meetings together. Zak suggested it to help me deal with..." She trailed off, took a breath, and started again. "With what happened to me. You could come with me."

When he opened his mouth to tell her he couldn't do that, she rushed on, speaking over his protest.

"I'd really like you there, Shane. You make me feel safe. And you don't have to talk if you don't want to. I'm told just being around others who understand what you've been through can be helpful."

He shook his head, then made a sound that was nearly a laugh. "That's manipulative."

Her brows slammed together, forming that adorable crease between them. "It's not manipulative. It's the truth. I need you there with me. And you need to be there for you. You don't really want to die alone on the mountain, do you?"

Shane's heart stuttered at her words, and he looked away, unable to meet her gaze. He didn't want to die alone, but he didn't know how to live among people either. What if they always saw him as the monster he felt like? What if they could never accept him?

But he also knew she was right. He couldn't keep living like this, hiding away from the world. He had to move forward, to take a chance on life again.

"Okay," he said finally, his voice barely audible. "I'll go with you to the support group meeting."

That bright smile lit up Alexis's face again, and she reached out to take his hand. "Thank you. I promise you won't regret it. We'll take it one day at a time, one moment at a time. And if it gets too much, we'll take a break. But we won't stop trying. We've already been through so much together. We can get through this, too."

As they stood there, holding hands, something stirred inside him. It was a feeling he had long forgotten— hope. Maybe, just maybe, there was a chance for him to start a new life, to leave his past behind and embrace a brighter future.

He had never met anyone like Alexis. He wondered how such a beautiful and intelligent woman could ever be interested in someone like him.

"I don't deserve you," he blurted.

Her eyes softened, and she squeezed his hand gently. "Don't say that. You deserve love and happiness, just like anyone else."

A lump formed in his throat, and he blinked back tears. He had forgotten what it felt like to have someone believe in him.

"And, if anything," she added with a self-deprecating laugh. "I don't deserve you."

"That's ridiculous."

"Is it? You're a hero. You lost everything fighting for our country. I'm just a podcaster. Even as much as I want it to be a search for justice and truth, it really just boils down to telling people disturbing stories for their entertainment. Stories like what the Shadow Stalker did to me. I'm a horrible person for exploiting trauma for clicks and likes."

Shane shook his head, his gaze locked on hers. "No. You're using your platform to raise awareness and help others. You're not exploiting anything. As for me being a hero, I'm just the guy who survived. That's all."

Alexis smiled, but it didn't quite reach her eyes. "It feels like exploitation."

"It's not." He'd listened to many episodes of Cold Truth over the last week, and he could say it with absolute certainty. She wasn't exploiting trauma for money. She truly believed in the importance of telling the stories of forgotten victims. Her conviction rang loud and clear in every word she spoke on the show. "What you do is important."

"I used to think so. I don't know anymore."

A gust of wind ruffled her hair, and he wanted to dive his fingers into the golden strands. "You said you wished I could see myself the way you do. Well, I wish you would see yourself through my eyes. I see a beautiful, intelligent, and compassionate woman. A woman I'm very lucky to know."

"And I see a man who went through hell and still came out the other side. A man who is kind, brave, and has a heart of gold. A man who deserves the world." She leaned closer, her eyes shining with emotion. "And I want to be there for you, Shane. I want to help you heal and find happiness. Will you let me do that?"

Once again, he felt that strange unfurling in his chest as he stared into her eyes. It had been so long since he'd experienced a connection with anyone, let alone romantic feelings, but he couldn't deny the way his heart seemed to soften and grow whenever she smiled at him, or the way he responded to her touch when his body hadn't responded to anything since before his final mission.

Was it possible for him to have a future, to find love and happiness despite his scars and trauma?

His heart pounded wildly, and he leaned down until their faces were mere inches apart. Electricity crackled between them. Alexis's lips parted slightly, invitingly, and even though it felt like his whole world was spiraling out of control around him, Shane knew he had to kiss her. He had to feel her soft lips on his, to know that he was still capable of love and desire.

Their lips connected and lightning jolted through his veins. A fire ignited deep within him, consuming every inch of his ruined body with desire and passion—and it was unlike anything he had ever known before. He wrapped his arms around her and drew her close, somehow both desperate and yet also terrified for more. For the first time in years, he felt alive, as if the kiss had breathed new life into him. He never wanted it to end.

Eventually, they had to break apart, both of them gasping, but they stayed locked together, their breath mingling. The air hummed with possibilities, and his chest tightened with a mixture of fear and hope. He had been alone for so long and he didn't know if he was ready for love...

But Alexis made him want to try.

chapter
twenty-four

THEY SET up base camp at Shane's cabin.

Even though he was thrilled to be home, back in his comfort zone, he hated stepping out onto his porch and seeing the tents, hearing the chatter of other people instead of wildlife. Even if he liked those other people, it still felt like an intrusion in his sacred space.

For Alexis, he reminded himself. He was playing host to keep her safe. The sooner they found the bunker, the sooner Ash could throw the bastard who hurt her into a cage.

He drew a fortifying breath through his nose and stepped off the porch. Someone had lit a fire, and the woodsy scent of it mingled with the crisp mountain air. The search team was huddled around it, their faces lit by the flickering flames. He hated feeling like an outsider on his own land, looming on the edges of the group. He wasn't a cop, and he wasn't part of the tight-knit Redwood Coast Rescue team, despite Zak's offer to join them.

As he approached, the group fell silent, turning to look at him. He could feel their eyes on his scars, the burns that twisted his face and neck. They didn't trust him any more than he trusted them.

He pulled his hood up.

He should turn around and go back inside, but Alexis was out here and he didn't dare let her out of his sight.

Pierce scooted over on the log they were using as a bench and waved a hand in invitation at the empty space between him and Alexis.

"Hey," Zak said and lifted a battered steel mug in greeting. Whatever he was drinking steamed against the cold air. He nodded toward the equally battered carafe on the grate over the fire. "There's hot water for tea or coffee. Tea bags are in my backpack, coffee's instant, but scratches the itch if you need it. And I think Van's hoarding hot cocoa over there. And stuff for s'mores."

"Jesus," Ash muttered. "We're not on a camping trip, Van."

Donovan Scott scowled at them both. "I'm not hoarding it," he said to Zak and then reached into his backpack for a bag of marshmallows. He tossed it at Ash. "Just trying to make the best of a shitty situation, Sheriff. It's not like we can do much until daylight and it's fucking cold up here. I thought s'mores would help lighten the mood."

"I'll find some sticks," Zak said and levered himself up off the log.

"We could always use your leg, Uno," Donovan called after him and got the finger in return.

Shane nodded his thanks to Pierce, then moved to sit beside Alexis. She was staring into the fire, her face a mask of exhaustion and pain.

"Are you okay?" he murmured.

She turned to look at him, and the firelight danced across her face, casting shadows in the hollows of her cheeks and the lines around her eyes. "I'm alive," she said, and it was a statement of fact, not a reassurance.

He didn't know what he had expected her to say, but not that. "It was a rough ride up."

She gave him a wan smile. "Not as bad as our ride down." She leaned into his side and rested her head on his shoulder. "I'm okay. Just tired."

"Say the word and I'll take you in to bed."

Now her smile brightened. "Oh, really?"

Damn. If it wasn't for his scars, he knew he'd be turning bright red. "I-I didn't mean it... I'd never... with what you've been through. I-I just meant, the bed's more comfortable and warmer than a tent on the ground and—" He made himself stop talking and rubbed a hand over his face. "Sorry."

"Relax. I was teasing." She bumped her shoulder into his, then stared into the fire again, but this time, she looked less frightened. "And I fully intended to sleep in the cabin with you, but I'm not ready to go in yet. This is kind of nice."

A burst of laughter sounded from the men and Shane glanced over to see Zak holding up a stick with a flaming marshmallow on the end, waving it around like a torch. He couldn't help but smile at the sight, easing the tension coiling inside him.

He turned back to Alexis. "I used to do this all the time when I was a kid. Campfires, s'mores, the whole deal. My dad was big on roughing it in the wilderness. I guess that's why I ended up joining the Navy."

"Is that what you wanted to do? Be a SEAL?"

He shook his head. "I knew I wanted a challenge. Something to distract me from the rest of my life."

"Why?"

"My dad was great, but he was gone a lot, traveling for work. My mom was... not so great. I counted the days until I turned eighteen and could leave, then never looked back."

"Did you grow up around here?"

"Drive until you nearly hit the Nevada border." He lifted his chin toward the east, where the darkness of night twinkled as the sun sank closer to the horizon at their backs. "Then turn north at the last minute before crossing over. Small desert town—smaller than Steam Valley, even. My graduating class had eight people in it, and that was big for my school. Miserable place."

"I think all high schools are miserable, no matter their size. It's like a rite of passage, or something."

"I was talking about the town. It should've died years ago. My classmates weren't so bad. They all just wanted to get out of there."

"Did you keep in touch with any of them?"

"Not really. When you join The Teams, it becomes your life. You become very tunnel vision. There's nothing before, and you think there's nothing after."

She found his hand and laced her gloved fingers through his. "But there is an after, Shane. You just have to open your heart to it."

He snorted. "Nobody wants my heart, so why bother opening it?"

"That's not true."

He stared at her. He couldn't think of how to respond, and was saved from having to formulate one by overhearing one guy say his name.

He looked at the group. "What?"

Donovan nodded toward the wildfire scar stretching down the mountain just a few miles to the east of his cabin. "We were just saying you're lucky you didn't get caught in it."

"Not lucky. I paid attention to where it was and where it was going. I've already had my skin burned off once and have zero desire to experience it a second time."

Donovan winced.

The chatter died.

"Well, fuck," someone muttered.

Alexis cleared her throat. "It's getting late. I'm tired," she said, breaking the awkward silence. She stood and stretched, then gave his hand a squeeze. "I think we'll turn in for the night. Goodnight, everyone."

She pulled him to his feet, her eyes soft with understanding.

The knots of tension faded away as he followed her into the cabin, leaving the others to stare after them in bemusement. As soon as the door shut behind them, she slid her arms around him and he was enveloped in warmth and a feeling of safety he hadn't known since his childhood days spent around campfires with his dad.

He returned the embrace, his fingers tangling in her hair as he buried his nose in the crook of her neck. Her scent was a mixture of the woods and the faint trace of her shampoo, and it was intoxicating. He took a deep breath and let out a sigh, reveling in the sense of peace and security that came from being in her arms.

In that moment, he knew he was exactly where he wanted to be. He wrapped his arms around her and pulled her closer, savoring the feel of her body against his. He could happily stay like this forever.

But then Alexis pulled back and looked up at him, her eyes dark and intense. "Shane." She took off her gloves, then cupped his cheeks in her hands, her thumb tracing over his Elvis scar. "I want you."

twenty-five

SHANE'S HEART stuttered in his chest as he stared down at her in shock. "Why me? You could have any man out there."

"I don't want any man. I don't feel safe with them."

A vicious and fiercely protective beast rose in his chest and roared. He scowled at the door. "Did one of them say something to you? Hurt you?"

"Whoa, pump the brakes there, Captain America." She laughed and pulled him back to her when he would've ripped the door off its hinges and plowed through the men around the campfire until he found the one who had made her uncomfortable.

"Come here." She tugged him toward the cot and sat down, patting the space next to her.

After one last narrow-eyed scowl at the door, he followed. The cot dipped when he sat, and she slid toward him. He automatically wrapped an arm around her and pulled her in tight to his side.

"I trust them," she corrected after a moment. "I trust them for everything except this. What happened to me... was awful." A burst of laughter escaped on her next breath, but it was bitter and full of rage. "To put it politely. To put it bluntly,

I've always enjoyed sex and that twisted fucker stole that from me. He took something I loved and warped it into something vile. I want it back and I know the longer I wait, the harder it will be, until I end up like Veronica, afraid to leave the house, terrified of even breathing the same air as a man." She lifted her gaze to his, her expression somehow vulnerable and fierce at the same time. "You make me feel safe and whole and... alive. I know I can trust you to take care of me and not hurt me."

Shane's heart ached for her. He knew what it was like to have something taken from him, to have his life irrevocably changed by someone else's actions. He understood the fear and the anger and the desperation that came with it. And he knew, with a certainty that made his blood race, that he would do anything to help her reclaim what had been stolen from her.

"I want to help you," he said, his voice low and rough. "I want to give you back what he took, but I haven't since... uh, I don't know if everything still works."

"Are you...?" Her cheeks flushed. "I mean, is everything...?"

"Intact?"

The flush deepened and she hurried to add, "It's okay if not. There are other ways to be intimate and enjoy each other."

"I'm intact. The explosion happened behind me. I started to turn toward it because I heard it—or, no. More like felt it through my boots—and I didn't realize what it was until the flames rolled over me. I dropped to the ground and curled up to protect my middle, so my back, arms, upper chest, and face took the brunt of the damage. My stomach, pelvis, and thighs sustained some burns, but they mostly healed with minimal scarring." He gave in to impulse and threaded his fingers into her hair, mesmerized by the way the honey gold strand slid through his roughened fingers like silk. He'd wanted to do this since he first saw her. "I just don't know if I can still get aroused. I don't have a lot of sensation left… well, anywhere. And I haven't been with anyone since before." He winced. "Long before."

Alexis leaned into his touch, her eyes closed in pleasure. "Do you want to try?"

Shane hesitated for a moment, his mind racing with all the reasons he wanted to, and all the reasons they shouldn't. "Even if I can… I, uh, don't have any condoms."

Her smile was full of wicked amusement. "You gave me your blood, Shane. I'm not worried about catching anything from you. And, if you're worried about me—"

"Of course not."

"The hospital tested me for everything to be safe," she continued over his protest. "I'm clean, too."

His mouth went dry as anticipation hummed through his blood. "But what about—"

"I have a birth control implant. We're safe from pregnancy."

Her eyes were so full of trust and need, and he knew he couldn't deny her this. He had to at least try. He wanted to feel alive again, to feel the heat of passion and desire coursing through his veins. And he wanted to give Alexis the same gift, to help her reclaim what had been taken from her and show her that intimacy could be beautiful and fulfilling.

He leaned in and pressed his lips to hers, his hand still tangled in her hair. The kiss was soft at first, hesitant, but it quickly deepened as their tongues met and tangled in a dance of desire he thought he'd long forgotten. Arousal ignited deep in his stomach, a slow, pleasant burn that spread through his limbs.

He broke the kiss and looked down at her. "Are you sure about this?"

She nodded, her lips parted and swollen. "I'm sure."

He leaned in to kiss her again, his hands roaming over her body, memorizing the curves and dips, the places that made her shiver and sigh. Alexis moaned against his lips, her hands fumbling with his shirt buttons, eager to feel his skin under her fingertips. He groaned as she tugged his shirt off, her hands roaming over his chest, tracing the scars and burns with a gentle touch that made him ache with longing. He wished he could feel the caress.

He pulled back to look at her, desire and uncertainty making for a messy mix in his chest. "I don't want to hurt you. I don't know if I'm... gentle enough."

Alexis smiled as her fingers played over the remains of his tattoo. "I trust you. You won't hurt me."

"You need to stop at any time, say the word."

"You, too."

No, he wasn't going to stop. He'd been living for so long with a resigned numbness, but now dead nerve endings buzzed to life under her touch. He hadn't known he could still feel like this. He was dizzy with it as he leaned in to kiss her again, his hand sliding down her back to rest on her hip. He deepened the kiss, his tongue sweeping over hers as his other hand slid up to cup her breast through her shirt. She moaned into his mouth, arching into him as he squeezed gently.

He pulled back, panting, and whispered, "Can I touch you?"

Alexis nodded, her own breath coming in gasps. "Yes, please."

Shane's hands shook as he struggled to undo the buttons of her shirt, his clumsy fingers fumbling with the tiny fastenings. Finally, he got them open, and he pushed the fabric aside, revealing the soft swell of her breasts in a plain gray sports bra. She let go of him long enough to reach behind her and unfasten the clasp. The bra fell away, revealing a perfect pair of breasts, the pale pink nipples tight with need.

She was beautiful.

Shane's throat went dry, his mouth suddenly filled with cotton. He couldn't think of anything he wanted more than to be allowed to taste those sweet buds, to swirl his tongue around them and feel her shudder with pleasure under his touch.

He dragged his fingers up the curve of her breasts, marveling at how soft she was, how smooth. Next to her, his skin looked like desert sand that had baked too long in the sun, dark and craggy, but she moaned and leaned into his touch, her head falling back. He flicked his thumbs over the peaks of her nipples, enjoying how they tightened and jutted under his touch. He watched her face, his heart threatening to pound right out of his chest as he took in the expression of pure need and arousal. He'd thought that part of him was dead, but seeing the way she looked at him, knowing that she wanted him, made that dead part of him burn with life.

He lowered his head, his lips sweeping over the skin of her breast, his tongue flicking out to tease the sensitive peak. She moaned again, and her hands dug into his shoulders as he sucked on the tight nipple. He closed his eyes and focused on the taste and feel of her, on the way her soft skin fit perfectly under his hands. This was what it was supposed to feel like— getting lost in the sensations of another person's touch. This was what he'd been missing, and now that he had it back, he wouldn't let it go.

She arched into him, gasping for breath as he licked and sucked, his tongue swirling. He moved to the other breast, giving it the same attention, and then, unable to resist any longer, he pulled back and looked down at her. Her face was flushed, her lips swollen from his kisses, her eyes glazed with pleasure. He wanted to make her glow like this over and over again until she outshone the sun.

Alexis beckoned him back to her, pulling him down on

top of her as she lay back on the cot. Her hips rolled against his as they kissed, and he groaned as his cock rubbed against her pelvis through the layers they still wore.

He was hard.

He hadn't thought it was possible. Couldn't remember the last time he'd had an erection. But now he throbbed for her, the ache heavy between his legs.

For a second, he flashed back to the last time he'd had sex, his last night with a woman before his life fell apart. He'd been in a hurry that night. Impatient. Annoyed by needing sex so much that he'd stooped to picking up a frog hog at a Coronado bar. She'd just wanted to add another SEAL to the notches on her bedpost. He'd just needed to scratch that itch before he left on his next deployment.

He didn't want to be in a hurry with Alexis. He wanted to savor every moment, every sensation, to repay her trust and her willingness to explore this with him.

He broke the kiss and cupped her face in his hands. "Are you sure?" he asked again, searching her eyes for reassurance.

She nodded, her gaze locked on his as she reached between them and stroked her delicate fingers over the bulge at the front of his pants. "I want you, Shane."

His breath caught in his throat. He could lose himself in those gorgeous green eyes.

She grinned and gave his erection a light squeeze. "Everything seems to work okay, but maybe I should take a closer look. Just to make sure."

She made quick work of his jeans, unzipping them and pushing them down his legs. She sat back on her heels, her eyes wide and hungry as she took in his arousal, thick and hard with need. As she wrapped her hand around his shaft, she kissed him again and pumped in time with her tongue, sending bolts of pleasure through him.

"Mm," she said against his mouth. "Yep, working just fine."

"Yeah," he said with an exhaled groan, his hips surging against her hand. "Definitely working."

She leaned in to kiss his neck, her breath warm against his skin. "I want to feel you inside me."

Shane sucked in a breath, his cock twitching in her hand. He wanted that, too, wanted to feel her around him as he buried himself in her warmth and made her cry out in pleasure. But he could also see the uncertainty, the flash of fear in her eyes when she said those words.

He didn't want her afraid when they came together. Didn't want her thinking of what that bastard had done to her. Didn't want her reliving the trauma. He would make her feel good, give her as much pleasure as she could take before he found his own.

He extracted himself from her grip and climbed off the cot to kneel between her legs. He reached for the button on her hiking pants, his gnarled fingers fat and clumsy on the button. She helped, and then he was sliding the nylon fabric down her long, lean legs. She wore a pair of plain, unadorned underwear that matched her bra. Serviceable. Practical for a long hike in the mountains. And yet somehow sexier than any lingerie he'd ever seen.

Her thigh was still bandaged, and he took care not to bump it as he leaned in to kiss his way up her leg to the apex where her panties were already slick with desire.

She tensed up, but she didn't tell him to stop, so he nuzzled her through the gusset of her panties and breathed in the scent of her arousal. It buzzed through him like the strongest hit of caffeine in the world, sparking all the nerve endings he had left to painful life. He drew her underwear down and tossed them aside, then leaned in to drop a kiss to the soft hair on her mons. She gasped and her fingers curled around the edge of the canvas cot.

He looked up at her as his hand slid slowly up her inner thigh. "Okay?"

She nodded, her eyes wide and glazed as she stared down at him. "I like it. Keep going."

She didn't have to tell him twice. He wanted to taste and touch and feel everything she would allow him to, to make her feel cherished and desired and never, ever have to worry about being touched without her permission.

He'd seen plenty of naked women in his life, but he'd never taken the time to really look at them, to appreciate them as a man should.

This time was different. This time, he was going to savor every moment of being with Alexis. He was going to worship her body as she deserved.

He scooped her legs over his shoulders and leaned in again, this time licking her in a long line from the base of her pussy to the swollen nub of her clit. She cried out and arched her back, her hands tangling deep in his overgrown hair, holding him tight to her. He didn't care. He'd happily drown in her. He sucked the swollen nub into his mouth, flicking it with his tongue as her hips rolled against his mouth.

She tasted like hot summer nights, like the breeze off the ocean, like pleasure. She whispered his name as she dug her heels into the mattress, rocking against his tongue. He couldn't resist the urge to reach up and pinch her nipples again, loving the noises she made as he rolled the tight buds between his fingers.

And then she was shaking, moaning loudly and lasciviously as she flew apart under his mouth. He drew back to watch the orgasm overtake her. Her face flushed, her eyes squeezed shut, her lips parted. He'd never seen anything so beautiful in his life. No sunrise over the mountains or sunset over the ocean compared, and if he saw that look on her face a thousand times, it still wouldn't be enough.

She came down slowly, her breathing ragged. He slid up the cot to kiss her again, wanting her to taste herself on his lips, wanting her to remember this night for the rest of her life, to demolish all the bad memories. She kissed him back, her tongue hot as it tangled with his. Her hands slid up to cup his face.

"Now," she said with a shaky laugh. "I really want you inside me."

She spread her thighs wide, her eyes locked on his face as he positioned himself over her. He all but whimpered as the head of his cock pressed against her entrance. She was going to feel so good clamped around him...

But something changed.

She'd gone still under him and fear flashed in her eyes.

"Lexi, look at me." He cupped her cheeks in his hands and waited until she met his gaze. "Do you still want this?"

She nodded, her eyes wide and locked on his. "I want you."

He pressed a kiss to her forehead, then shifted positions, gently lifting her until she straddled his hips. He hated lying on his back. His skin there was tight and overly sensitive in the spots it wasn't completely deadened, but he'd do anything to keep that fear from her eyes, and she needed this. She needed to be in complete control of this first time.

"Use me," he said, his voice more gravelly than he'd intended. "Take your pleasure, Lexi. Don't let him steal it. He's not worth your fear. He's not worth your time or your thoughts. Use me to banish him."

She hesitated, her gaze locked on his. He didn't know what she was seeing there, but she seemed to find whatever she was looking for, to find the reassurance she needed.

She shifted her hips experimentally, rubbing the slick head of his cock against the swollen lips of her pussy.

"Oh." She breathed the word, then slowly lowered herself, her eyes huge as she took him inside her. Inch by inch, he slipped in, until finally, he was as far as he could go. She let out a long breath, her eyes fluttering closed as she rocked her hips against him.

She took him by surprise by rolling her weight forward, shifting her hips until his pelvis brushed her clit. She smiled as she repeated the motion again and again, slowly grinding against him.

He gritted his teeth and fought the urge to thrust up into her. "God, you're so beautiful. I could watch you ride me all night."

She raised herself up and sighed as she sank back down on him again. "Good, because I'm going to be here for a while."

She kept the pace slow, taking him in small movements as she leaned forward to lick at his jaw and flick her tongue against his earlobe.

"You feel good," he said, his voice tight as he fought the urge to move and end this sweet torture. "You feel so fucking good."

"So do you," she said, then groaned. She moved faster, sliding up and down his shaft, chasing a release.

He was so close to the edge, but he wanted her there with him. He wanted to watch her come, to see her expression as she fell apart again.

He sat up to suck one nipple into his mouth, his tongue rolling against the tight bud, the rasp in stark contrast to the slick glide of her pussy on his cock. She moaned while he teased her nipples, her head falling back as she fucked him harder.

Her skin was damp with sweat, and her eyes were completely glazed as she looked down at him. Her lips parted, her breaths coming in short, shallow pants. She just needed a little push, something to take her over the edge.

He pulled his mouth away from her breast and rolled her onto her back. He moved fast, flipping her onto her stomach, not giving her time to think, to freeze up, to let the fear take over. He positioned her on her knees, then slid back inside her, her slick heat enveloping him again. She bucked against him, her head dropping back, her beautiful hair brushing his chest, and he suddenly wished he'd taken off all of his clothes. He wished they were skin-to-skin, so that he could feel those silken strands tickling him with whatever nerve endings he had left.

She cried out his name as her orgasm overtook her, and her body clenched tight around his cock. He reached between her legs to stroke her clit, to keep her riding on the edge of her climax. He wanted her trembling and needy and completely out of her mind with pleasure before he found his own release.

She was shaking with the force of her orgasm, her pussy spasming around him like a silk vise. He quickened his pace, thrusting hard and deep, teeth gritted as he fought the urge to come. He wanted to watch her again, wanted to see the bliss on her face, wanted to witness the pleasure he was giving her. He wanted to be the one person she thought of when she came, the only man imprinted on her memory.

She moaned, her head dropping back as she moved her hips in counterpoint to his. "God, I love your cock. I love how it feels inside me."

He bit back a growl as his balls drew tight against his body. Her words were such a sweet, unexpected pleasure.

She wanted this.

She wanted him.

She found pleasure in his ruined body.

"I want you to come again. I want to feel you come

around my cock again. Come for me, Lexi. Show me how much you want this."

She cried out as her body obeyed his command, climaxing hard, clamping around him in a tight vise as she trembled through it. And then he couldn't hold back, couldn't hold out. His eyes rolled back in his head as she milked him, her pussy drawing every drop from him as he came. His body wasn't his own anymore. It was Lexi's. Hers to love. Hers to command. She could bring him to his knees if she wanted to, and he'd go happily.

She collapsed onto the mattress, her body limp and satisfied. He rolled off of her and lay on his side, stroking her hair from her face.

"That was..." she trailed off with a soft sigh.

Amazing.

Earth-shattering.

Mind-bending.

Life-altering.

No. None of those descriptions worked. There weren't words to explain everything he was feeling, so he simple tucked her into his arms.

"Yeah," he said and kissed her forehead. "That was."

chapter
twenty-six

GOD, she was still shaking.

Sex with Shane was... she didn't have words. Somehow it was exactly as she had expected—dangerous and a little feral—and also not at all what she'd expected. She hadn't expected his care, his kindness, his nearly obsessive focus on her needs. By the third "Are you okay?" she'd wanted to scream at him to just fuck her already because she was deliriously desperate to feel him inside her.

Alexis smiled against his shoulder. He was still and quiet under her, but he wasn't asleep. His fingers had been tracing little designs along her back for the last twenty minutes as they lay listening to the fire crackle in the wood stove. She loved the caress, the way he couldn't seem to stop touching her, exploring her. She wanted to do the same. She wanted to know all of him, but while she was completely naked, he still wore his long-sleeve shirt and jeans.

"You're so soft," he whispered, his voice filled with wonder.

She squirmed as his fingers trailed over the dip of her waist. "That tickles."

"Sorry," he muttered. "I forgot what being ticklish is like."

She lifted her head and looked at him. "Were you ticklish before you were burned?"

He nodded. "Very."

She traced a finger down his chest, annoyed at the cotton between them. "Will you let me see you?"

He closed his eyes. "I'd rather not."

She sat up on her knees and glowered down at him. "I'm naked."

His hand slid from her waist to her hip and then over her butt. "I noticed."

"I want you naked, too."

The small smile playing over his lips vanished. "My face is bad enough. You don't need to see the rest."

"Do you think I'll like you any less?"

He opened his mouth, but closed it again without making a sound and shrugged.

"Because nothing will do that. I like you a lot, Shane. A lot more than I should because, logically, we shouldn't work. We don't make sense together. And yet I want you. I'm attracted to you." She leaned over and pressed her lips to his. "Let me see you. Please."

He froze, his hand on her hip going tight. His breath whooshed out, and a shudder rolled through him. Alexis knew he was about to say no. She wasn't even sure why she was pushing the issue, except that it felt right. He'd helped her, gave her something precious to remember instead of the trauma of her captivity. She wanted to do the same for him and he needed to take this step in accepting his body as it was now.

"You'll run screaming back down the mountain in horror," he said finally.

"I'm not so easily scared."

"No," he said on a harsh exhale. "You're not."

He didn't move for a long time, then shoved up off the cot

and stripped. He was efficient about it—boots, pants, shirt—until he stood before her wearing nothing but a scowl.

Alexis knew what to expect—she had seen most of his scars in the hospital—but she was again struck at how much of his body was covered in scar tissue. She could see the remnants of grafts and surgeries that had tried to repair the damage, but his skin was still mottled and discolored. She wanted to reach out and touch him, trace each scar, but she didn't want to make him uncomfortable. Instead, she looked up at his face. His eyes were downcast, his jaw clenched. He was waiting for her to react, waiting for her to reject him.

But she couldn't. He was beautiful to her in this moment, scars and all. She stood up and stepped closer to him, reaching out to touch his chest. His muscles tensed under her fingers, but he didn't move away.

"You're so strong," she whispered, tracing a line down his abdomen with her index finger. "You've been through so much."

His eyes flicked up to meet hers, and she saw the pain in them. "Sometimes, I wonder if surviving was a blessing or a curse."

"It's both. But look at us, a couple of survivors. We're still here—alive and breathing..." She slid her hand down to his and entwined their fingers. "And loving. They couldn't break us."

He stared down at their joined hands and gave a little shake of his head. "They broke me."

"Maybe for a little while, but you're putting yourself back together now. They didn't win." She kissed him then, slow and sweet. He let her, and she could feel his resistance slipping away.

He kissed her back, his fingers tangling in her hair, his tongue sweeping into her mouth to tease hers. Alexis lost herself in the sensation of it, in the feel of his lips and the press of his body against hers, skin to skin. She wanted to feel him inside her and arched her back, her nipples brushing across his scars.

She tore her mouth away from his and gasped as the sensation shot straight to her core. She looked up at him and saw the desire in his eyes, the fierce need. He wanted to be inside her as much as she wanted him there. His erection grew against her belly.

"I want to make love to you."

"I don't think..." His breath caught on a groan as she wrapped her fingers around his shaft. He captured her wrist to stop her from stroking him. "This isn't love, Alexis. It can't be. We—"

"Don't make sense. I know. And I don't care."

He closed his eyes and let out a harsh breath. "Fuck. I care. About you. About us. This thing between us. I care more than I should have any right to."

She curled her fingers around his and forced his hand to her breast. "Then make love to me. And let me love you."

She was offering herself to him, body and soul. She wanted him to take her. She wanted to belong to him.

He stared down at her for a long moment, his eyes dark and his breathing unsteady. She didn't move, didn't say a word. She just waited.

Finally, he lifted his hands and cupped her face, his thumbs tracing the soft lines of her cheekbones. He brushed his lips over hers.

Still, she waited, wanting him to show her he was giving this to her freely. He kissed her again, his lips soft on hers, and his tongue flicked out to tease her lips. She opened for him, letting him in, letting him taste her. He groaned into her mouth, his hands sliding down her neck to her shoulders, then down her arms to her waist.

One hand continued down, dipping between them to

stroke her inner thigh. He teased the seam of her sex, and she groaned as he found the sensitive bundle of nerves there. She arched into him, wanting more, needing him to fill her. He found her entrance, then thrust a finger inside her. She gasped, her head falling back. He pressed his lips to the hollow of her throat and added another finger, driving them in and out of her, mimicking the act of making love.

"Do you like that?" he whispered in her ear. "I want to know everything you like."

"Yes." She rocked against his hand, her only thought to feel him inside her, to be one with him. She dragged her hands down to the juncture of his thighs and stroked him. He groaned and pushed her back until her shoulders hit the wall and held her there as he kissed her. After the horror she'd survived, she thought she'd never want to be caged by a man again, but she loved the feel of Shane's body trapping hers. She loved the feel of his arms around her, loved knowing that she had brought him this far back into the land of the living.

He thrust his fingers into her again and again, and she was so close, so close to orgasm.

"Please," she begged.

He slid his thumb over her clit, then pressed and rubbed until she shattered. Her orgasm stole her breath and made her eyes roll back in her head.

When she floated back to earth, her head rested on his shoulder and her body had gone boneless.

"Jesus," he said between clenched teeth. "You're gorgeous when you do that."

She smiled and kissed his shoulder. His erection pressed against her belly, and she reached between their bodies to stroke him. "Your turn now."

In one sudden move, he lifted her off her feet, and she automatically wrapped her legs around his waist. Her breath caught in her throat as he positioned his cock at her entrance and drove into her with a low growl. She cried out at the sudden fullness, her body straining for more, but he held her still, his hands on her hips, as he stared into her eyes.

She could see the question forming on his lips and kissed him, soft and slow, stroking her tongue across his. "I'm okay, Shane."

He moved then, guiding her up and down on his shaft, and she let him take control, trusting him to take care of her. The simple act of their bodies moving together was enough to send ripples of pleasure through her. She closed her eyes as he sent her higher and higher.

"Alexis," he said on a groan.

"Yes. Oh, yes." She crushed her mouth against his, needing him closer, needing to feel penetrated and surrounded and claimed. She'd never felt anything like this, had never known that this type of connection could exist between two people.

He moved faster, the friction of their bodies making soft sounds as their skin slid together. She was so close, but she didn't want this to end. She opened her eyes and found his gaze on her, his blue eyes dark with desire and his jaw slack. She let him see all of her, what she felt for him and what he did to her. He thrust into her again and again, his movements jerky and frantic. She could feel his control slipping away, and squeezed her inner muscles around him. He groaned into her mouth and thrust even harder.

"I love you," she whispered.

She didn't question why she'd said it, didn't debate her decision to let herself fall in love with him. Not now when she was still immersed in his touch, in his kiss.

He thrust deep one final time and his groan rumbled against her neck and as he pulsed inside her. Her own orgasm caught her off guard and she cried out as she broke apart.

Shane kept his arms tight around her, hips still rocking against her, until the final shudders of their orgasms faded away. His body was hard, his skin hot, but he held her gently, as if she were the most fragile thing in the world, and they breathed together, their hearts thudding in unison.

She was still shaking when he sank to the floor and cradled her against his chest. She didn't want to move, didn't want to break the moment. He was still inside her, still partially hard, and she didn't want to lose that intimacy.

He brushed a kiss across her temple. "Still okay?"

"Yes." She touched his cheek to make sure he was real. Part of her worried maybe he wasn't. Maybe she was still in the bunker and he was a vivid hallucination. Maybe she'd dreamed up this damaged, troubled, semi-feral man to protect her and soothe away her fear. But he felt real enough, his scars alternately rough and waxy smooth under her fingertips. "I'm better than okay. For the first time since I was taken, I feel like me again."

He kissed her forehead. "I'm glad."

He didn't say anything about her confession and she didn't bring it up. She tucked her head under his chin and listened to the beat of his heart. She was so relaxed she could barely think straight, and she didn't want to think about tomorrow or the next day. Didn't want to think about the Shadow Stalker and the victims that had come before her, or the victims that would come after if she couldn't find his bunker. Didn't want to think about anything but this quiet moment with Shane. She let him hold her, let him soothe her, and she allowed herself to pretend that this was real.

That it wasn't completely crazy to be in love with him.

That he was able to love her back.

That there was a chance for them to be together, out there in the real world, away from this mountain.

And she kept pretending, even as she drifted asleep with his arms around her.

chapter
twenty-seven

SHANE WOKE up slowly from a sated and relaxed sleep, the first dreamless night he'd had in years. He stared up at the ceiling and smiled to himself as the memory of making love to Alexis played through his mind—

I love you.

His smile faded. He wasn't dumb enough to think she'd meant it. It was just something she'd said in the moment, a result of all the endorphins and hormones that amazing sex flooded the brain with. She probably didn't even remember saying it.

But fuck it. He would cherish the words, anyway. Nobody had said that to him since before his dad died, and he'd never heard it from a woman. His mom had certainly never said it to him, and he'd never let his past lovers get close enough to think they were falling in love.

So, yeah, even if Alexis hadn't meant it, he would hold the words close.

He stretched and looked around. Alexis wasn't in bed with him, and he heard her voice outside, talking with one of the men of Redwood Coast Rescue.

Time to get to work.

Shane threw on his clothes and grabbed his gear, making his way outside. The sun was just beginning to rise over the mountain, casting a golden glow over the snow-shrouded trees. The sky was clear and calm, promising a good day for their search. As he approached the group, he spotted Alexis talking to the sheriff, her face a mask of determination. Shane couldn't help but be impressed by her. She had been through so much, yet she still had the strength to keep going and face her fears. He admired her for that.

"Morning," Shane said, nodding to the group. "What's the plan for today?"

"We're going to start where you found Alexis's dog," Ash said.

Shane pointed to a spot on the map they had laid out on the seat of the ATV in front of them. "Here, by the creek."

"We'll have the teams grid search from there," Zak said, checking the straps on Ranger's SAR vest. He straightened. "Can you think of any place around there that could hide a bunker?"

Shane shrugged. "It's a mountain full of caves. It could be anywhere."

"All right," Ash said and turned to Alexis. "If you see anything that looks even vaguely familiar, even if you're not one hundred percent sure, tell us."

She nodded. The sparkle from last night had gone out of her. She was scared again, but also determined. She was not going to let the killer get away with what he had done to her.

As they set out on the trail, he stayed close to her, scanning the trees and underbrush for any sign of danger. She tensed up every time a branch snapped, or a bird took flight. He reached out, his hand brushing against hers. He didn't say anything, but the touch was enough to settle her. She gave him a small smile, and he swore he felt his heart swell in his chest.

Jesus, he was so fucking in love with this woman.

The next time his fingers brushed hers, he took her hand, wrapping it up in his. Just for a few moments, he told himself. Just to comfort her until the terrain became too rough to handle without the free use of all four limbs.

They walked for hours, the only sounds the crunch of snow under their boots and the occasional rustle of a small animal in the underbrush.

Shane had done a lot of "nature walks" while a SEAL. It was what his team had called long treks through rugged terrain —a nature walk. Nothing more than an easy stroll.

"It's a neighborly day in this beauty wood," Jax would always sing in his best Mr. Rogers voice.

"That's not how the song goes," Mack would complain. "You're butchering it."

"Nope, that's exactly how it goes. Believe me, I watched it enough times with my little brother."

And now Mack was dead. Alejandro and Fuse were dead. Rylan was living in the VA hospital, missing an arm and his mind. And Jax was... who knew where? He'd survived the mission with the least damage of all of them, but the last Shane had heard, he'd developed an opioid addiction and then fell off the grid, too. They were all dead, or if they weren't, they probably wanted to be.

Shane shook his head, trying to clear his thoughts. He couldn't let his mind drift like this. It would only lead him down a path of darkness and despair. He had to focus on the present, on finding the killer's bunker and making sure Alexis was safe.

He glanced over at her. She scanned the surrounding trees with a fierce intensity. She was unlike any woman he'd ever met. Strong, brave, and just as determined any SEAL.

Suddenly, she stopped in her tracks and let out a small gasp.

"What is it?" Ash asked, his hand hovering over the gun at his hip.

"I don't know." She pointed to a group of trees just ahead of them. "It just looks familiar. I think... I think I sat there, under those trees, after he shot me."

"How far from the bunker were you when you were shot?"

Shane's chest constricted at the question. He hated the mental image it put into his head—Alexis, bleeding and afraid, in the hands of a sadistic killer. He stepped closer to her, his hand tightening around hers.

"I don't know," Alexis said, her voice barely above a whisper. "It's all fuzzy, but I... don't think it was far. I was disoriented when he released me. Shaky. He hadn't fed me in a couple days and I was already weak. I wouldn't have been moving fast."

"And you probably took the path of least resistance." Shane nodded toward the mountain's summit, still soaring way above their heads. "So if you were uphill, you would've gone down."

"Okay," Zak said and called the team closer as he pulled out the map. "We'll start a new grid search here. Pierce and Raszta, take this field over here." He pointed to the open area to their left, then marked it with a square on the map in red marker. "Van, I know Spirit's still working on her SAR qualifications—"

Donovan rubbed his dog's head. "But if the fucker has any chemicals in his bunker, she'll be the one to find them."

"Right. So you guys take the area along this cliff face." He made another mark on the map. "It's the most likely place for a bunker, as far as I can tell. Ranger and I will start by the trees Alexis recognized here and work our way toward the cliff. We'll met back up here." He made a final mark. "Everyone clear on their search area?"

"Roger that," Donovan said, and Pierce gave a quick two-finger salute in agreement.

"Dante and I will stay with Alexis," Ash said, and for once, Shane was in complete agreement with the sheriff. If the killer was still up here, he wouldn't make an attempt at her with that big black hellhound by her side.

"We'll keep making our way south along this path," Shane added.

Donovan snorted. "He calls it a path, like it's all paved and shit."

"It's just another nature walk." Shane smothered a smirk. "But I get it. Even that's probably too hard for a crayon eater like you to understand."

Donovan's abrupt laugh sent a flock of birds into the air. He hooked a thumb over his shoulder at Shane and said to Zak, "The crazy frogman's over here firing shots."

Zak grinned. "Hey, he's got a point. Doesn't Marine stand for Muscle Always Required, Intelligence Not Essential?"

Pierce gave an exaggerated golf clap.

Donovan punched Zak's shoulder. "Aw, fuck you, Stumpy." Then Pierce's. "You, too, Mutezilla. You're both just ground pounders, so go pound ground and let us big boys handle the hard stuff."

"Okay," Ash said with barely restrained patience, like he was trying to corral a group of rowdy five-year-olds. "Enough fucking around. Game faces on."

And, like that, the mood shifted. The moment of levity was gone, and the men turned back to the warriors they all were.

"Everyone stay frosty. Radio if you find anything," Zak said, then called Ranger to his side before they disappeared over the ridge up ahead.

Alexis shook her head as she watched them all go. "What was that all about?"

"Branch rivalry." It had been a long time since he'd engaged in banter like that. It felt good. It felt... almost like he was a member of the team.

She slid him a sideways glance. "I've never seen you smile so much."

Shit. Shane felt his cheeks heat up. He hadn't even realized he was smiling. But he shouldn't be. This was serious business. He cleared his throat and forced himself to focus on the task at hand.

"Let's keep moving," he said, tugging her toward Ash and Dante, who were waiting a short ways up the path. And it was a path, despite what Donovan thought. Probably carved into the snow by wildlife to get to the stream they'd passed a few miles back.

Alexis fell into step beside him. "It's okay to smile. It's a good look on you. It's even okay to laugh and have a moment of fun. I don't mind."

When he didn't respond, she added, "You like them, don't you? You enjoyed feeling like part of their team."

He merely grunted in response.

"You could be, you know? Zak told me he invited you. He wants to test Clue for SAR when she's healthy enough, and he thinks you would be the best handler for her because you already have a bond."

He glanced over at her. "But she's your dog."

"Yes, she is. But I'm always working, and it's not fair to her." Suddenly, Alexis stopped walking and pointed. "There. That tree. I recognize it."

Shane followed her finger to a tall pine tree with a jagged scar running down its trunk. It looked like it had been struck by lightning.

Alexis turned a slow circle, scanning the world around them, as if searching for any other familiar landmarks. "I think we're close. Maybe just a little farther up this way. I was running downhill when I saw that tree. Running from..." She did another spin, then stopped and started walking toward a ridge of gray rock jutting out of the snowy landscape. "This way."

"Hang on." He pulled her back and called over his shoulder, "Ash, we might have something."

"All right. Coming to you."

As Ash approached, all of their radios crackled to life with Zak's voice: "Ranger has a scent." He rattled off his coordinates, and Shane did a quick check of his mental map.

"That's just over that ridge."

Ash was checking his physical map and nodded. "Sure is."

"We're close," Alexis said. She was buzzing with so much energy and anxiety, it charged the air around her. "I recognize all of this. I came up over those rocks and lost my footing. I slid down here..." She made a motion around the spot where they stood, then faced the split pine tree again. "And that's when I saw the lightning tree. I got up, took a few steps..." Blindly, she took a few steps downhill, back toward Ash. She wasn't in the present anymore. She was back there, terrified and fleeing for her life.

Shane moved to hold her, comfort her. He knew how terrifying flashbacks were, how disorientating. But Ash held up a hand to stop him and mouthed, "Wait."

She sucked in a sharp breath. "This is where he shot me. I didn't know what happened at first. I thought he missed. I ran, and then the pain hit." She doubled over as if she'd been shot again, and Shane's stomach twisted into a painful knot. He had heard the story before, but hearing it again, in this context, seeing her relive it, made it all too real.

After a long moment, Alexis straightened. "It's that way. I'm sure of it." She pointed up the hill in the same place Zak said Ranger had signaled.

Ranger, who was primarily a cadaver dog.

Ash motioned for the two of them to stay put and cautiously moved in the direction Alexis had indicated. Shane pulled his rifle off his back and held it ready, watching as Ash disappeared behind a cluster of boulders. Alexis was trembling beside him and he wanted to reach out, wrap her up in his arms and shield her from the world, but he didn't dare take his finger off the trigger.

"It's going to be okay," he said, not entirely sure if he believed it himself.

Ash's voice came over the radio again. "I found it. Area's clear."

Shane's heart rate spiked, but his hands remained steady on the rifle. He lowered it only a fraction so he could respond on the radio. "Copy that. We're coming to you." Then he raised the rifle again and held out a hand behind him for Alexis. "Lexi, stay close."

chapter
twenty-eight

ASH HAD SAID the area was clear, but Shane was acting like they were walking into a war zone. He kept one hand on her arm, keeping her tucked so closely behind him she was practically walking in his boots. He moved smoothly, confidently forward, his rifle held at the ready, sweeping the area for any potential threats.

There was the SEAL.

She'd known he'd been one, but hadn't seen it in him until that moment. It was in the way he moved, the way he held the gun as he led her over the ridge. Laser focused in a way that was both impressive and terrifying. A predator stalking his prey. Silent. Intense. But he was also a protector, a guardian.

She had never felt as safe as she did with him at that moment.

Ash and Zak stood by a pile of boulders up ahead and the sight of it made her blood run cold. She remembered this. She remembered emerging from the darkness into this small clearing, breathing in fresh air for the first time in a month.

For a split-second, she'd been free...

Then she'd heard the rifle cock behind her, the sound of it echoing up from underground. Sharp, decisive, and deadly.

And terror had flooded her every sense. She hadn't been human in that moment. She'd lost everything that made her Alexis as she'd scrambled to run in the too-big boots and bulky snow clothes. She'd been nothing but a frightened animal, just as the killer had wanted.

And now she was frightened all over again.

She hated she couldn't be stronger. That she couldn't push aside the fear and face this head on. But she was here. That was something. And last night, she'd used Shane to burn away the slimy memories of the Shadow Stalker's touch. She was taking back control of her life, step by step.

Shane must have sensed her fear because he squeezed her arm reassuringly and stepped forward, his gun trained on the bunker dug into the side of the hill.

As they drew closer, she could see a small opening in the rock pile. A rusted metal door, hanging wide open. Zak and Ash were already examining the entrance, but Pierce and Donovan were nowhere to be seen.

"Where are the others?" Shane asked, his voice low and tense.

"Securing the perimeter," Zak said, not looking up from his examination of the door. "He's not here, but that doesn't mean he's not watching from a distance. He left the door hanging open like he was in a hurry."

Ash turned to her and his blue eyes, usually so hard, were filled with compassion. "Do you recognize any of this?"

Alexis stared into the gaping mouth of the bunker. Her throat was dry. Her lungs didn't want to expand.

Shane was suddenly at her side again, sliding his arm around her waist. "You're okay. You're safe. Breathe, Alexis."

She exhaled a choppy breath. "Yes, I remember it all." Her voice was barely above a whisper, but it felt like a roar in her own head.

She swallowed, trying to calm her nerves. She couldn't let

her fear control her. Not now. Not when they were so close to finding the man who had tried to take everything from her.

"I want to go in," she said, her voice more steady than she felt.

Ash shook his head. "Not a good idea. Ranger signaled on it. Who knows what's down there?"

"I do. I know exactly what's down there."

Shane tightened his arm around her and looked at the sheriff. "She needs to do this. She needs to see it, and you need her to show it to you. Her insight could prove vital. She could spot something you'd miss."

"Shit," Ash said after a beat of silence, rubbing a hand over his ice-crusted beard. "Fuck. Okay. But don't touch anything. This is a crime scene."

Shane went in first, crouching low to enter the space, his rifle held out in front of him. Alexis followed, trying to make herself as small as possible. Ash brought up the rear while Zak stayed topside with the two dogs, guarding their exit.

As they descended the steps into the bunker, her stomach clenched with each step. It was dark. So dark. And cold.

She remembered this dark.

And this damp cold.

Both had nearly driven her to the brink of insanity.

The chill seeped into her bones, and the sound of her own breaths echoed. Even though the walls and ceiling were reinforced with concrete, she swore she could feel the weight of the dirt over their heads pressing down, trying to suffocate her.

But she kept moving forward.

She had to keep moving forward.

She had to face it. If she turned back now, she'd dwell on what happened forever and become a terrified recluse like Veronica. Then the Shadow Stalker would win, and she refused to let the bastard have that victory. He didn't kill her, but he could still steal her life if she let him. She wasn't about to let him.

When they reached the bottom of the steps, the stench of death and decay was overwhelming, making her gag. She could hear Ash cursing under his breath, and Shane's hand tightened around her arm, pulling her closer.

"Did it smell like this before?" Ash asked.

"No. It was damp and musty. And the bucket he gave me for a toilet stunk, but it never smelled this strongly of decay. Not like this."

Ash's flashlight bouncing off the walls, casting eerie shadows over the shelves lined with cans of food, bottles of water, and other supplies. There were also weapons— guns, knives, and ammunition piled up haphazardly. Enough to start a small war.

Ash stared at the munitions for a second, then flashed his beam at Shane. "A prepper friend of yours?"

Shane stiffened beside her, but he didn't take the bait. She hated that even the sheriff, supposedly his friend, didn't quite trust him because of the way he chose to live.

Instead, Shane swept his flashlight over the rest of the space, and her heart skipped a beat as the beam found a room off the main hallway, with a small bed pushed up against the far wall.

It was just like she remembered it, the thin mattress stained with blood and other bodily fluids, the chains hanging from the ceiling, the putrid bucket in the corner.

Except, now, there was a body on the mattress.

A woman.

She had to swallow down bile before she could speak. "He took another victim. I escaped, so he killed her instead."

Ash swung toward her, and then his flashlight beam joined Shane's, illuminating the poor dead woman.

The woman's mouth was covered in duct tape and her

dark hair hung in limp tangles over a once-pretty face now twisted in a final, grotesque expression of pain and terror. Her skin was mottled and bruised, and her eyes stared, glassy and lifeless, at the ceiling. She was young, no more than twenty-five.

So young.

Too young.

Alexis's chest tightened at the sight of her, and she had to fight back the tears that threatened to spill over. She had been that woman once, trapped and helpless in this cramped, dark space.

"Do you know her?" Ash asked.

"No, I don't recognize her." And a wave of guilt washed over Alexis for it. She had escaped, but this woman hadn't been so lucky. "She wasn't here when I was. I was alone. He took her—after. God. Did that sick fuck punish her for my escape?"

Shane's grip on her arm tightened, his voice low and rough. "This isn't your fault."

Ash cleared his throat, breaking the heavy silence. "Let's go back up. I need to call this in and somehow get the state forensics team here to process the scene."

When Shane tried to pull her back toward the door, she stood her ground. "Wait." She broke free of his grasp and picked her way closer to the body.

"Alexis," Ash said. "This is a crime scene."

"You're going to find my DNA all over here anyway." She waved his warning off and crouched down next to the mattress. The woman had track marks up both of her arms, some old and healed, some fresh.

Ash growled. "That's not how crime scenes work—"

"Look at her, Ash."

The sheriff snapped his mouth shut and turned his flashlight back to the dead woman. "What do you see?"

"She wasn't hunted. He brutalized her and left her here to die."

"Maybe he decided setting her loose was too much of a risk."

She nodded, conceding the point. That was entirely possible. But... she couldn't explain it, but it didn't feel right.

She pointed to the track marks. "This woman was a long-time drug user. She matches the profile I gave you when I was investigating."

Ash scowled. "Which I distinctly remember telling you not to do."

Yes, he'd told her not to investigate. And, yes, she'd paid in the worst possible way for ignoring him. But that wasn't the point.

She straightened and turned toward him, raising her arm to shield her eyes from the beam of his flashlight. "The binder I gave you was full of twenty-eight years' worth of missing woman that looked like her. Dark hair. Young. Vulnerable. We'll probably find out she has no close family in the area."

"Don't all serial killers have a type?" Shane asked.

She nodded and motioned back to the dead woman. "Except I'm not his type. I never was. And I can say with one-hundred percent certainty that unless the man who raped me started killing when he was a child, he wasn't responsible for those murders in the nineties."

"What are you saying?" Ash asked, his voice tight with dread. He knew exactly what she was getting at, but he didn't want to hear it.

And that was too damn bad.

"Sheriff Rawlings." She said his name slowly, making sure she had his full attention. Because the more she thought about it, the more sure she was that the man who released her and hunted her was not the same man who had raped her and delighted in causing her pain. "I think the Shadow

Stalker is more than one man. It's a team. One older, one younger."

Ash groaned. "Jesus fucking Christ. This is over my pay grade. I need to call in the feds."

Shane was shaking. He didn't realize it until they emerged back into the cold, fresh air and Ash filled the team in on what they'd found in the bunker.

It was bad enough when they thought they were dealing with one serial killer on his mountain, but two? That was a whole other level of fucked up.

He'd seen a lot of awful shit in his life. Hell, he'd done some pretty awful shit in Uncle Sam's name, and he knew better than most of the atrocities humans were capable of inflicting on each other. But what happened to that poor woman in the bowels of that bunker... it was a scene straight out of a horror movie. It was going to haunt him.

He should've known.

He knew everything about this mountain.

He should've stopped it, but instead he'd been too busy wallowing in his own mental muck, he never noticed this shit happening in his own goddamn backyard.

Alexis was ghostly pale, her green eyes huge behind her glasses as she sank to her knees in the snow and hugged Ranger. The dog endured the hug patiently, setting his wedge-shaped head on her shoulder.

Shane knew that look on her face all too well. It was the same one he'd seen in the mirror every morning before he stopped looking into mirrors. The look of someone who had seen too much, who had been through too much.

He knew she was strong, but this was a lot for anyone to handle. He wanted to wrap Alexis in his arms and shield her from all the darkness in the world, but he knew that wasn't possible. He couldn't even protect himself from his own demons, let alone someone else's.

Ash's radio crackled at his belt with a voice. "Sheriff, you copy?"

Ash grabbed the radio and thumbed the talk button. "I'm here. Go ahead, Sullivan."

There was a burst of static.

Ash glowered at the device, then said, "Say again?"

Another burst, followed by something that sounded suspiciously like, "There's been a murder."

Ash looked at the group, a line of confusion between his brows. He raised the satellite communicator again and pressed the talk button. "How the hell do you already know that?"

"What?" Undersheriff Jonah Sullivan said, his voice coming through loud and clear this time.

"How do you already know we have another victim?"

"What other victim?"

Ash pinched the bridge of his nose and took a deep breath. "All right, start again. What happened?"

A pause. "Twenty minutes ago, dispatch received a call from Hank Firestone. He just got home from a fishing trip and found his wife, Amelia, dead in their kitchen. I'm on scene now and…"

"What happened?" Ash asked after several beats of staticky silence.

Jonah sucked in an audible breath. "It's ugly, Sheriff. She's been stabbed multiple times. This was an act of rage."

"Fuck," Zak said softly.

Donovan, jaw hard, hands fisted, walked away from their little circle without a word.

Pierce blinked hard and looked up at the sky.

All three men looked like they'd just been punched in the stomach.

Dread crept up the back of Shane's neck as Alexis grasped his hand. This was bad.

"Listen, I can't come down," Ash said into the radio. "There's a body up here. Another victim of the Shadow Stalker, who I now believe to be two men working as a team. I need forensics here and we're gonna have to bring in the FBI."

"I'll contact the local satellite office and see if they can get an agent to you. Forensics is going to take a bit longer, unless the Feds want to share their guys."

"Do what you can. I'll stay here and—"

"I don't think that's a good idea, Sheriff. Assign some deputies to sit on the crime scene. We need you here in town. Hank's been going around telling anyone who will listen that the 'freak from the mountain'—his words, not mine—killed his wife. People are pissed and calling for Shane's head."

Ash's gaze snapped to him. "Impossible. Shane's been with me for the last two days."

"From the looks of things here, Dr. Firestone has been dead longer than that. Hank claims Shane attacked her in her office, frightened her pretty good just days before her death."

Shane closed his eyes for a moment, the dread along his spine coalescing into fear. "Ash, you know I didn't do it."

Ash gave him a long, hard stare, then nodded. "Yeah, I know." Then he said into the radio, "Keep the peace as best you can, Jonah." He squinted at the setting sun. "It's too late for me to make it off the mountain tonight. I'll come down first thing in the morning." His gaze flicked to Shane again. "With Shane."

Oh, fuck.

A cold sweat broke out on his forehead as Ash pocketed the radio. He'd never been one to fear much, but he'd also never been accused of murder before. Though he shouldn't be surprised. He'd always been an outsider in this town, feared and mistrusted. But he never thought it would come to this.

Alexis's grip on his hand tightened as the sheriff turned toward them.

"You have to come in for questioning," Ash said. "It's the only way to clear this mess up."

"I didn't hurt the doctor."

"I believe you, but we need to do everything by-the-book, get it all on record." He looked at the bunker, then turned to Zak. He barely opened his mouth before Zak was nodding.

"Yeah, go." His voice came out thick, and he cleared his throat. "Van, Pierce, and I got this place locked down."

The other two men nodded in agreement. Pierce signed something that no one bothered translating.

"Nobody's coming near the bunker until the feds get here," Donovan said. "Go take care of the doc, Ash. She deserves it."

In a rare show of emotion, Ash put a hand on Zak's shoulder and then one on Donovan's. He gave them both a quick squeeze. "We'll be at Shane's cabin tonight if you need us, then head to town at first light. I'll try to get someone back up here to relieve you before dark tomorrow."

chapter
twenty-nine

ELLIE ARRIVED at the Mad Dog Pub fifteen minutes before she and Cal were supposed to meet and chose one of the booths along the wall near the fireplace. The pub's owner, Rose—a stunning woman with the kind of body rich trophy wives paid good money for—waved at her as she entered. Ellie knew her by sight and name, but they'd never shared more than a few words in the month since she'd come to Steam Valley. And yet Rose greeted her like an old friend. It was nice. People weren't like that in Chicago.

Rose finished filling a drink order for the group of men at the bar, then came over to her table.

"Hi, Ellie." Rose's smile was as gorgeous as the rest of her. "Just you tonight?"

"Oh, uh... no." She fiddled with her earring, realized she was doing it, and made herself stop. "Cal's coming."

Why was she suddenly so self-conscious? She never before cared what she looked like. She'd always been the cute, quirky nerd girl, and she was fine with people thinking that about her. In fact, she'd embraced the image with her colorful wardrobe and funky glasses. But now she felt frumpy and a little pathetic, like she was trying too hard to be pretty— a wilted dandelion next to the stunning and seductively dangerous Rose. The mustard yellow sweater and green skirt she'd chosen after trying on everything in her suitcase twice didn't help the whole dandelion image.

Ugh. She should've worn something else.

Instead of taking her order and going back to the bar, Rose slid into the booth across from her. "Do you have a date with the pretty boy lawyer?"

"We're just friends."

Rose's bright blue eyes twinkled. "If I weren't married..."

Oh, great. And now she was jealous. Which was stupid because she and Cal were just friends and Rose was happily married to the grumpy sheriff. "He's not your type."

Rose laughed. "You're right. But he sure is pretty to look at." Her smile faded. "You do know his reputation, right? He's kind of the king of flings around here."

Her stomach twisted, but she shrugged like it was no big deal. "He can have all the flings he wants. We're friends. Nothing more." It sounded like she was trying to convince herself, so she changed the subject. "Have you talked to Sheriff Rawlings since they left?"

Rose shook her head. "I'm sorry. He called late yesterday morning to let me know he would be out of cell phone range soon and, if I needed him, to contact Jonah, the undersheriff."

"Did he... tell you what they're looking for?"

"If I ask, he'll tell me everything he can without compromising an open case, but I don't usually ask. But the local grapevine..." She tilted her head toward the men gathered around the bar. "Says they're looking for Shane."

"What?"

"They're convinced he's responsible for what happened to her."

"That's ridiculous. He saved her."

The bell over the door chimed and Cal rushed in, still

wearing his work suit and looking a bit harried. He spotted them and Rose slid from the booth as he crossed the room in long-flooring eating strides.

"Hey, sorry I'm late."

Rose offered him a sympathetic smile. "Long day?"

"The longest." He dropped into the seat she had vacated and rubbed a hand down his face. "I'm starving. Can I get—"

"Your usual?"

"Yeah. Thanks." When he turned to Ellie, his whole expression changed, softened, and the tension visibly eased out of his shoulders.

Rose noticed the change and lifted her perfect eyebrows as if to say, *Just friends, huh?*

"Did you order already?" he asked.

God, he was adorable, with his slightly too-long blond hair falling carelessly over his forehead and the knot of his tie hanging loose and crooked. "No, I was waiting for you." She looked up at Rose. "I'll have whatever he's having."

His eyes widened. "Uh... I haven't eaten all day."

"Neither have I." She'd been too worried for her sister, but she realized now the knot in her stomach had loosened when she saw Cal.

"I usually get a lot. A—"

"Cheeseburger with everything, double side of parmesan fries, chef's salad, and a beer," Rose recited with him, then added, "Burger, medium. Beer, the darker, the better."

"Like my soul," Cal said.

Rose scoffed. "You're so full of shit, Holden. Your soul is about as black as a puppy's."

Ellie wondered briefly what it would be like to frequent a place so often that the owner knew your order. Of course she had her favorite restaurants in Chicago, but the staff turnover was high and she was never more than an order number to them. "Sounds perfect."

"I'll have your beers and salads right out." Rose walked away, waving to another couple as they entered the pub.

Ellie watched her go. She didn't make it back to the bar without having three more conversations. "Does she know everyone?"

"Hard not to when you're born and raised and live in the same town your whole life."

She refocused on him. He really did look tired. "Were you born here, too?"

"Pretty much. Next town over, but I went to the high school here. It's the best one in the area, so my parents paid tuition to bus me in."

"And you never wanted to leave?"

"Are you kidding me?" He huffed a laugh. "I left as soon as I could. Went to law school thinking I'd make a career for myself as a big-time lawyer in LA… then somehow I ended up back here. Still not entirely sure how it happened, if I'm honest." He sat back in the booth and yanked at the knot of his tie, pulling it free. "I'm glad you could make it."

Ellie realized she was fiddling with her earring again and dropped her hand into her lap. "With Alexis on the mountain, I didn't have much else to do other than sit around and worry. Dinner and drinks with you sounded like a better plan."

"Anytime you need a distraction, I'm your guy." Cal grinned, flashing his dimples, but when she could only muster a wan smile in return, his faded. "How is your sister?"

She sighed. "I don't know. She's been focusing on Shane's problems—I think it's so she doesn't have to think about her own."

"Getting her back to Chicago should help."

"Yeah, that's the plan." Except why did her stomach twist at the thought of leaving? "It will be safer for her there."

"For you both." Cal reached across the table and squeezed her hand. "When are you leaving?"

"As soon as she's back." If she could convince Lexi of that fact. Her sister wasn't thinking clearly right now, hadn't even wanted to entertain the idea of leaving.

Cal nodded, his thumb rubbing soothing circles over the back of her hand. "You're a good sister."

She gave him a small smile, the knot in her stomach easing a bit more. "I try."

Their food arrived, and they ate in comfortable silence, the pub filling up around them with locals stopping in for dinner and drinks. Ellie couldn't help but notice the way people looked at her and Cal, the way they murmured and whispered as they passed their table. She couldn't blame them for being curious—not only was she an outsider, but she was also part of the podcast that had uncovered town secrets and poked at old wounds.

But the way they looked at her now made her skin crawl.

"Do you feel that?" she asked softly, leaning closer to Cal.

He followed her gaze, his expression darkening. "Yeah, I feel it."

"It's like they're blaming me for something."

"Probably because they think we're here to stir up trouble. Your podcast and all..." He trailed off, shaking his head.

A chill ran down her spine. "We never meant to cause trouble. All Alexis and I ever wanted was to just find the truth. That's the whole point of the podcast."

"I know," Cal said, his eyes softening. "But these people are scared, Ellie. They're scared of all the crazy that's been happening around here, and they're looking for someone to blame. You and Alexis are easy targets."

"And Shane."

Cal's eyes narrowed. "What about Shane?"

"Rose said—" She was cut off by the front door slamming open with enough force to dent the wall.

Ezra Jacoby stormed in, followed by an angry crowd of red-faced men.

"Ezra!" Rose snapped. "Get out. You're not welcome here anymore. And you're paying for my wall, asshole."

Ezra just sneered at her and turned to address everyone in the pub. "I'm here for volunteers."

Rose crossed her arms over her chest and glared at him. "Volunteers for what?"

"Amelia Firestone is dead."

Rose went white and her arms dropped to her sides like her hands suddenly weighed twenty pounds each. The room crashed into silence, the only sound Rose's softly exhaled, "What?"

"It was that freak from the mountain. We're going after him, since your husband has no interest in doing his job."

Color finally infused her cheeks again. "Ash lives for his job, asshole."

"Then why the fuck hasn't he arrested Shane Trevisano? I have it on good authority that Shane attacked Dr. Firestone in her office and scared the hell out of her. She told her husband she didn't want to treat him anymore and so he killed her for it."

Cal's expression darkened with anger as he pushed to his feet. "That's bullshit, Ezra. Shane may be a little rough around the edges, but he's not a killer."

Ellie's heart jumped into her throat as the crowd turned their attention to Cal. If the men decided to take their frustrations out on him, he was outnumbered and outmatched, but he was undaunted by the odds.

For the first time, she saw Cal, the defense attorney. He was intense and focused, his eyes locked onto Ezra as he stepped forward. "You have no proof. You're just spreading lies to rile up these people against Shane."

Ezra sneered. He was very obviously drunk, and maybe

also flying high with some chemical help. "Oh, that's right, you're his lawyer, aren't you? I bet you know every sick thing he does up on that mountain."

"No, but I do know accusing Shane—or anyone—without evidence is wrong."

"Wrong?" Ezra spat. "A woman is dead. Murdered in her own goddamn kitchen. And you're standing here defending the guy we all know did it?"

"Hell yeah, I am. Innocent until proven guilty."

"Bullshit," Ezra said. "Shane's not innocent. He's a psycho."

Ellie watched as the angry crowd advanced on Cal, their faces twisted with hatred. Oh, God. This was bad. Cal wouldn't back down—he was too principled and hardheaded for that—but he was no match for a mob.

Suddenly, a gunshot rang out, and the crowd scattered.

Ears ringing, Ellie looked around to see where the shot had come from, and she spotted Rose up on the bar, a rifle in her hands. There was a bullet hole in the ceiling and plaster had rained down like snow onto her sleek black hair.

"Everyone out! We're fucking closed." Rose herded the crowd to the door and flipped the lock as soon as the last person was outside. She turned back to Cal and Ellie, her eyes wide. Her hands, so steady on the gun moments before, now shook violently. "We need to warn Ash."

Cal stepped forward and gently removed the gun from her grasp. "Sawyer's staying up at the Rescue tonight. He should be in radio contact with the team. You two go up and let him know the shit's about to hit the fan. Rose, do you have more ammo for this?"

She nodded. "Behind the bar."

He found the box of ammo and stuffed it into his pocket.

Ellie caught his arm as he strode toward the door with the gun still in his hand. "Where are you going?"

"Sticking close to Ezra Jacoby. He's dangerous, and did you see that look in his eyes?"

"He's high," Rose said. "When I kicked him out last night, he dropped a baggie of something I think might be meth. He's been in here every night, high as a kite, saying this shit."

Cal nodded. "Yes, but now people are believing him, and he's relishing it. I don't think this is just about Dr. Firestone's murder for him. It's something more personal than that. He *wants* this mob to happen."

chapter
thirty

BY THE TIME they made it back to the cabin, it was already well after dark. Ash pitched his tent in the yard and said he was turning in. He didn't offer a space in his tent for Alexis like he had before. She wasn't sure if he was being nice by giving them privacy, or if he just needed the silence of his own company. The sheriff seemed like a man who valued his alone-time.

Without a word, she took Shane's hand in hers and led him inside. His eyes were dark and troubled. She knew he was scared, and she felt guilty for dragging him into this mess. If she'd never shown up in his cabin, bleeding and terrified, the townspeople wouldn't suspect him of murder now.

Inside, he broke away from her and turned on the camp lanterns, then lit the wood stove to ward off the chill in the air.

She stood in the middle of the cabin, arms wrapped around her middle, watching his mechanical movements. "I'm sorry."

He glanced at her, gave a tight smile. "It's not your fault. This was bound to happen sooner or later. I'm the 'freak from the mountain.' Of course they were going to blame me."

"Ash will prove your innocence."

"Even if he clears me, they won't believe it." He sat down

on the cot and rubbed his hands over his face. "This won't end well for me."

Alexis wanted to comfort him, to tell him that everything would be alright, but she knew that would be a lie. There was a very real chance that Shane would be taken away from her, and she didn't know what she would do without him. So, instead, she walked over to him, cupped his face in her hands, and dropped her mouth to his.

She tasted his sadness on his lips, sensed his resignation. She deepened the kiss, hoping to distract him.

After a moment's hesitation, Shane responded, wrapping his hands around her hips and pulling her close. His kiss changed—became desperate, hungry, with a bite of fear and uncertainty.

"Let me in, Shane," she whispered when they broke apart. "You don't have to be alone tonight."

Or ever again.

But she didn't say that out loud. Instinctively knew he wouldn't want to hear it.

Shane's eyes searched hers, and for a moment, she thought he was going to push her away, but then he nodded and stood up. He took her hand and led her over to the ladder that led to his loft. He boosted her up, then followed.

The loft was cozy, stuffed with blankets and an actual mattress that looked old, but not uncomfortable. She didn't know what she'd been expecting of his "bedroom"—had always kind of figured he slept on the floor covered in furs or something—but she was glad he'd allowed himself this one small slice of civilization.

She turned to tell him so, but never managed a word. He'd stripped out of his shirt and he looked... vulnerable. His hair was tousled and his face was pale. Her heart contracted, and she realized that she wanted to see him like this every day.

She went to him, skimming her palms up his arms, over his

shoulders, down his back. She kissed the thick, waxy scar that extended from his collar bone up his neck to his chin. He shivered beneath her touch, and she knew it wasn't from the cold. His eyes were closed, his breathing ragged, as she opened her mouth and traced the scar with her tongue. She wanted to show him that he was more than these marks on his skin, that he was more than what the townspeople thought of him.

His cock swelled against her belly, and she reached down to unfasten his pants. He was long and hard, with a thick vein pulsing down his length. He was scarred here, too, the skin smoother in places than it should be.

God, he'd experienced so much pain. Even the pain and humiliation she'd endured at the hands of the Shadow Stalker paled in comparison.

She stroked him, slow at first, tightening her grip and watching his face for that moment his breath hitched and his eyes rolled back in pleasure. She dropped to her knees in front of him.

"Alexis." His voice was strained. "You don't... have to do that."

"I want to." She took him in her mouth, relishing his sharp exhale as she licked him from root to tip. His fingers shook as he tangled them in her hair, holding her closer while she sucked and stroked and scraped her teeth down his shaft. He pulsed in her mouth. It wouldn't be long before he was at the edge, and she wanted to savor every moment of his release.

He was breathing faster now, his hips rocking up to meet her mouth, his fingers tight in her hair.

Groaning, he pulled her off him and lifted her up, all but tossing her down on the mattress. She laughed and wiggled out of her clothes as he kicked off his pants.

But her laughter melted into a moan as Shane crawled up her body, kissing and licking every inch of skin in his path, his body radiating heat.

She arched into his touch, savoring it. There was something primal about their connection, something that went beyond the physical. She wanted him with an intensity she had never felt before. But she knew it wasn't just about the physical desire. She wanted to protect him, to keep him safe from the townspeople, who were quick to judge and condemn. She wanted to show him that he wasn't alone and that he was worthy of love and acceptance.

Shane leaned in and captured her lips in a slow, deep kiss. She melted into the warmth of his embrace, her hands tangling in his hair. He tasted of wood smoke and something uniquely Shane.

His hand moved down her body, tracing the curve of her hip before slipping between her legs. He dipped his fingers into her and she gasped at the quick intrusion, her skin coming alive with sensation. He swirled her wetness around her clit, then dipped a second finger into her, driving her to the edge and holding her there while his tongue slid over hers. His hips surged reflexively against her thigh, and she reached down to stroke him as she rocked against his fingers.

"Shane, please..."

He shifted his hand out of the way and positioned himself at her entrance. With a push of his hips, he slid into her, stretching her wide. She gave a low whimper at the sensation of having him so deep inside her that they were nearly one being. There was something so raw about the moment, so real. It wasn't about the frantic need to reach satisfaction, but rather about the simple act of being together. Of loving one another.

His body was heavy against hers, pinning her to the mattress as he moved with a slow, rocking rhythm that made her feel completely surrounded. Completely claimed, but not trapped. With him, she only felt safe, cared for, protected. She wrapped her arms and legs around him, holding him closer as tension started coiling in her lower belly.

"Shane."

"I'm here," he whispered, kissing her neck. His lips found the sensitive spot behind her ear, kissing and sucking until she was writhing beneath him, drowning in sensation. His cock was so deliciously deep, stretching her. His rough chest scraping against her erect nipples with every thrust. His lips, his mouth, his scent, his taste...

Oh, God. She was almost there, so close to the peak, but the overwhelming rush of pleasure loomed just out of reach.

"Shane..."

"Let go, sweetheart," he murmured against her skin, his hand moving down between them to caress where they were connected.

She gasped as he brushed her clit with his thumb, then cried out as the orgasm ripped through her, sudden and violent. Her muscles contracted and relaxed as her inner walls clenched around him.

Shane groaned, his hips moving faster now, more erratic as he chased his own release. "Lexi..."

She wrapped her legs around his hips, drawing him closer, wanting to make him feel as good as she did. Another, softer orgasm rippled through her and his body went rigid. She felt his cock throbbing as he spilled into her, the force of his release leaving him gasping and shaking.

He collapsed on top of her, but only stayed there for a moment to catch his breath before rolling to the side and tucking her into the protective circle of his arms. She lay there, boneless, listening to the sound of his heart pounding against her ear. With each breath, she inhaled his woodsy scent, memorizing it. She felt safe and warm and loved— and this time, she allowed herself to acknowledge it.

She loved him.

And it wasn't just about the sex and the endorphins and the shared sense of danger. She really and truly loved him, with all of his demons and quirks and scars.

Shane's hand was warm on her back, his lips on her temple. She turned her head and kissed his chest, then rested her head back against it, closing her eyes and reveling in the closeness. Trying to commit the moment to memory. Her mind spun in circles with all the reasons why she shouldn't be falling for him, why it was a terrible idea to fall for a former SEAL with as many mental scars as physical, how the entire world would be against them, how she'd never fit into his world on the mountain, how he would never fit into hers in Chicago.

That was when the fear hit. Fear that she might never be able to experience moments like this again after tonight. Fear that she might lose him.

She struggled to push it aside. She refused to imagine a future without him. She couldn't. Instead, she focused on the present. On the way he was stroking her back. On how his every exhaled breath tickled her ear. On the warmth of his body.

"Shane." She looked up at him, waiting until his gaze met hers. "They won't take you away from me. I'll fight for you. I'll do whatever it takes."

He studied her for a moment before the hard line of his mouth curved into a smile. He tucked a strand of hair behind her ear and kissed her forehead. "I know you will."

chapter
thirty-one

"THIS IS FUCKING CREEPY," Donovan said, breaking a long silence.

Zak glanced over at the guy. He sat against a rock with Spirit tucked under one arm, staring into the mouth of the bunker that Ash had taped off before he left. Pierce formed the other point of their little triangle, with Raszta asleep on his lap. Both men looked haunted, but maybe that was a trick of the firelight. Of maybe it was the news they'd received.

Dr. Firestone. She had helped them all through so much. She'd played just a big a part in his recovery as Anna and Ranger.

And now she was gone.

Murdered.

Jesus.

What were they going to do without her?

Zak casually swiped at his eyes. Damn things kept tearing up.

"Knowing a dead girl is down there," Donovan continued, his tone hollow. "Alone in the dark. Brutalized. And now the doc..." The words wavered as he shook his head. "What the fuck is wrong with people? Why is the world like this? Has it always been this fucked up, or is it getting worse? What kind of world are we leaving the next generation?"

"Whoa, man. Why are you getting philosophical on us?" Pierce signed. *"That's usually Sawyer's territory."*

"Well, he's not here, is he?"

"So you thought you'd take up his mantel as therapy group philosopher?" Zak asked, glad to latch on to a topic other than murder.

"Do we even have a group anymore?" Donovan grumbled. "The doc was our heart and soul."

"Of course we do." Pierce's hands and expression both said he was certain of it. *"The VA will send us a new doctor."*

"But it won't be our doctor. Fuck." He pressed his fingers into his eyes and Spirit, sensing his distress, nuzzled closer. "I wish I was home with Sasha right now. I want to run down this damn mountain and check on her, make sure she's safe."

Zak studied his best friend. Van was always intense, but there was something different about him tonight. He seemed... genuinely afraid, and Donovan Scott wasn't a man who frightened easily. Zak glanced over at the mouth of the bunker and a chill raced down his spine. Yeah, he wasn't easily scared either, but Van was right. This place was creepy. Knowing what happened down there. Knowing that poor girl's last moments were a horror show. Knowing the killer could come back at any moment.

He looked away from the hole and focused on the dancing flames of their campfire. "Sasha's okay. She's with Anna. They're safe." Except even as he said the words, he wasn't convinced by them. His wife was more than capable of taking care of herself, and she wasn't the killer's type... but neither was Alexis. This asshole already proved he was willing to hurt whoever got in his way.

But the women were home.

They weren't in the way. The killer shouldn't even know about them.

"They're safe," he said again, infusing his voice with more confidence.

"And Sawyer's staying at the Rescue until we get back," Pierce added.

Donovan sent him a droll stare. "No offense, but how is a blind man supposed to protect my pregnant wife?"

Pierce's eyes bugged.

Zak nearly choked on the drink of water he'd taken. "Hold on, back up. Sasha's pregnant?"

Donovan nodded, but he didn't look happy about it. "We found out a couple of days ago. I was going to mention it at group."

Pierce made a *WTF?* gesture, then signed, *"Is this not a good thing?"*

Donovan stared at him for a solid minute, then pointed at the gaping mouth of the bunker. "How am I supposed to be excited about bringing a kid—which might be a girl—into a world where shit like this happens? That's someone's *daughter* down there. How can I bring a kid into a world where good people like Dr. Firestone are murdered in their own kitchen?"

The man had a point. How many nights had Zak himself sat awake, worrying about his daughters? How often did he get physically sick to his stomach when he thought about Bella, almost eighteen years old, heading out into the world as a mixed-race lesbian? Or sweet Poppy, who had the biggest heart and trusted everyone? Despite her tragic life before coming to live with him and Anna, she had no concept of the evils of the world because Bella had shielded her from them all.

"Okay," Zak finally said on an explosive exhale. "Fuck. Point taken." He leaned forward, waiting until Donovan met his gaze. "We can't control the world, Van. But we can control how we respond to it. We can choose to be good people and raise good kids. That's the best we can do."

Donovan grunted, but Zak could see the wheels turning in his head. Pierce, meanwhile, looked like he was about to burst.

"Can we focus on the fact that Sasha is pregnant?" he signed excitedly. *"This is amazing news!"*

Donovan rolled his eyes, but Zak could see a smile tugging at the corner of his mouth. Spirit wagged her tail, sensing the shift in mood.

"I'm going to be a dad," Donovan said, his voice laced with disbelief. "Holy hell. I don't know how to be a good dad."

"Yeah, you do. Just be you. You'll make an awesome dad."

Donovan groaned. "Ugh, now he's getting all mushy on us."

Pierce flipped him off.

A comfortable silence fell over them for several moments, but Zak again found his gaze wandering back to the bunker. Donovan was right. This world was a horrible place to bring a child into, and he suddenly wanted to go home and hold his girls more than anything.

"Fucking creepy," Donovan repeated under his breath.

Zak stood up and stretched his legs, trying to shake off the darkness that seemed to be settling over them all. He looked out at the trees, the stars winking between their branches, and tried to focus on something positive. Anything positive.

And then he saw it.

Movement in the distance, a flicker of light.

"Hey," he said, pointing. "What's that?"

Both Pierce and Donovan looked up, squinting against the darkness.

"Looks like a fire," Pierce signed.

"Out here?" Donovan asked, incredulous.

Zak didn't answer. Instead, he grabbed his binoculars

from his backpack and trained them on the distant flames. It was hard to tell, but it looked like they were coming from a clearing...

Near Shane's cabin.

No.

Not near.

It *was* Shane's cabin.

And there was a mob of people surrounding it.

"*Go,*" Pierce signed. "*Help them! I'll stay here and guard the bunker.*"

chapter
thirty-two

SHANE WOKE WITH A START. He sat up, heart pounding, eyes wide, tension coiling in his muscles. The loft was dark, the only light coming from moonlight streaming in through the window. His fingers grazed the floor where his knife should be. It wasn't there. He searched the shadows, but saw nothing.

Alexis was still sound asleep, curled up against him.

He swallowed hard, willing his heartbeat to slow. It wasn't the first time a nightmare had woken him in a cold sweat. It wouldn't be the last.

But...

This hadn't been his usual nightmare. In fact, he didn't remember having a nightmare at all. So what had awakened him?

He scanned the room, searching for any movement out of the ordinary. Behind him, Alexis gave a soft moan and turned over. He watched as she stretched, hugged the pillow closer, and settled again. She took a deep breath and let it out with a sigh.

It was only the sound of her breathing. He just wasn't used to sharing his bed, that was all.

He frowned. Except her breathing was the last thing he would have expected to wake him up. He liked having her here with him. He found her presence a comfort. So why would she cause the cold sweat and snaking feeling of unease?

He swung his legs to the side of the bed, keeping his movements slow and silent. He could hear the faintest sound coming from outside. Snow falling off a tree, maybe. Or was it...

A footstep.

Snow crunched beneath a boot.

Probably just Ash, he told himself. The sheriff had wanted to get an early start this morning, and even though it wasn't yet dawn, he was probably already up and about, packing up his campsite.

Nothing to worry about.

He dressed quickly, checked to make sure Alexis was still asleep, and then climbed down the ladder to the cabin's main floor. The wood stove had burned down, and the floor was cold under his bare feet as he crossed the small space. He stuffed his feet into his boots and grabbed his rifle before easing open the door.

The cool night air hit him like a punch to the gut, and he took a sharp breath, drawing in the scents of the forest. Pine and snow and crisp, clean air. He breathed deeply, letting the crispness clear his head. Then he scanned the trees, trying to pinpoint his unease.

Ash was up. He could hear the sheriff talking in a low voice like he was on the phone. Shane couldn't hear what he was saying, but a sliver of worry wormed through his gut. Something wasn't right here. The sheriff should be talking on the radio, not on his phone. There wasn't a signal all the way up here.

Wait.

Ash's tent was still zipped up and quiet.

There.

Movement in the shadows, coming up the path toward his cabin. He saw a flicker of fire among the trees, and then another.

Holy hell.

Those were torches.

Carried by at least a dozen men.

So, this was it. They weren't even going to let the sheriff bring him into town for questioning. They'd already decided he was guilty. Of course he had to be—he was a freak with a melted face, a monster who chose to live in the woods instead of in civilization. He wasn't like the good, upstanding people of Steam Valley, so he must be evil. He threatened their little community and needed to be taken care of.

He could fight them off—he'd been trained for this—but he'd have to do it one man at a time. And there were a hell of a lot of them. And, dammit, they weren't actually the enemy. They were scared, small-town folks hurting from their recent losses and needing someone to blame. He couldn't fight them.

Shane quickly closed the door and latched it, hoping it would slow them down enough for him to prepare. Maybe Ash would be able to talk some sense into them, but he wasn't going to rely on it. He grabbed his backpack and started shoving essentials into it—a few changes of clothes, extra ammunition, a first aid kit, and a map of the surrounding area. He knew he couldn't stay here. Not with the townspeople coming for him.

Alexis stirred in the loft, and he cursed under his breath. He hadn't wanted to wake her, but couldn't leave her behind. She was the only one who truly believed he was innocent. He climbed back up the ladder and shook her gently.

"Alexis, wake up," he whispered. "We have to go."

She blinked sleepily, then sat up with a start as the sound of angry voices grew louder outside.

If that was the sheriff trying to get them to stand them down, it wasn't going well.

"What's that noise?"

"Looks like some of the men in town decided they didn't want to wait until Ash brought me in for questioning. They're coming up the path with torches."

"Holy shit." She swung her legs off the mattress and started pulling on her clothes. "Where's Ash?"

"I imagine trying to talk sense into them—"

Glass shattered.

He looked over the edge of the loft platform as a rock came to a rolling halt beside the wood stove. "Which doesn't appear to be going well."

Alexis stared down at the rock, then looked at him with impossibly wide eyes. "How can you be so calm?"

That was the question, wasn't it? How could he freak out in a grocery store, but his heart rate wasn't even elevated now with an angry mob at his front door?

He was a really fucked up guy.

"No easy day," he muttered.

"What?"

"Nothing." Instead of helping her down the ladder, he took her hand and led her to the back of the loft. He pushed the crates he used for a dresser out of the way and dug his fingers into a panel in the wall behind. It popped open easily, and for once, he was glad for being a paranoid bastard who tested his many escape routes weekly. "You need to get out of here. Go find Ash and get off the mountain."

"What about you?"

He grabbed a rope ladder from the nearest crate and secured it to the D-rings installed on the floor. "I'm staying until I know you're safe."

She watched as he pushed the ladder out into the night. "You can't be serious."

"I am. Mob mentality, Lexi. You can't reason with them." He reached out and traced his finger down the curve of her cheek. "They won't stop until they have me, and they won't hesitate to hurt you. I want you as far away from here as possible."

"I can't leave you here to face them alone."

"Yes, you will."

She shook her head, her eyes filling with tears. "They'll kill you."

"I'm hard to kill." He gave her a gentle push toward the ladder. "Now go."

She hesitated for a moment, then grabbed his face and kissed him hard on the lips. "Don't die, or I'll be really pissed at you."

With that, she lowered herself to the ladder's first rung and started climbing down. He watched her descend, his heart heavy with the knowledge that he might never see her again.

But she was safe.

And that was all that mattered to him.

As soon as she was out of sight, he closed the panel and returned to the front of the cabin. The mob was pounding on the door, their angry voices calling for him to come out and face them. He took a deep breath, grabbed his rifle, and headed for the window.

He had already made up his mind. He wasn't going to let them take him without a fight. If they were going to kill him, they were going to have to work for it.

This was his goddamn home, and he had every right to defend it.

He peeked through the window and saw at least fifteen men, their torches casting flickering shadows across their faces. They looked like a pack of rabid wolves thirsting for his blood.

And yet, somehow, he was considered the crazy one in this scenario?

His hand tightened around the rifle as he aimed at the door. He couldn't take them all out, but he could make them think twice about coming in.

With a deep breath, he steadied his aim and fired a warning shot through the top of the door, far over their heads. The sharp crack echoed through the forest, and the mob fell silent. For a moment, nobody moved. Then another rock sailed through the window, missing him by inches as he lunged out of the way.

"Come on out, you freak!" someone yelled.

Shane didn't respond. He didn't want to give them the satisfaction. Instead, he took up his position by the window again and waited, his finger on the trigger, ready to fire again if necessary.

"Burn him out!" someone else shouted, and a chill of fear scraped down his spine.

He looked around his cabin. His home. His sanctuary for nearly ten years. The place where he had found solace and peace of mind. It was all going to be gone if they set fire to it. He couldn't let that happen. Couldn't let them destroy everything he had built for himself. But a fire was not something he could fight off, and he had no interest in ever getting up close and personal with it again.

Shane looked around the room, scanning for something he could use to put out a fire. His gaze landed on the three-hundred-gallon water tank beside the wood stove. He'd rigged it to catch rainwater from a spout in the roof, but it was only half full now, drained by the dry, cold winter. It was also his only chance to save his home. He opened the valve, and water gushed out, drenching the area beneath the window and the door. He grabbed a bucket and started splashing it on the walls, the door...

But then a familiar scent reached his nose.

Smoke.

They had already started the fire.

Shane quickly finished splashing the water around and took one last look around his home. Memories of the past decade flashed through his mind. The lonely times. The times his PTSD was so bad he could barely function. The pain as his scars healed and hardened. The anger.

So much anger...

But there had also been good times. Sunsets and sunrises so dazzling there were no earthly words to describe their beauty. Quiet, misty mornings listening to the world wake up around him. Cool spring afternoons, watching a mama bear and her cubs emerge from their den. Hot summer days, witnessing the wildflowers coat the mountainside in a riot of unimaginable colors...

He had thought he could hide away from the world here, and for a long time, he had. But the world had finally caught up to him, so it was time to face it again.

Time to move on.

And with sudden, startling clarity, he knew that he wouldn't come back even if his cabin survived tonight.

He touched the cold wood stove, offering a silent thank you for all of its years of service, then grabbed his backpack, slung his rifle over his shoulder, and climbed up to the loft. He pulled the panel out of the wall again. The rope ladder still hung down the back of his cabin, and he tossed his bag to the ground before swinging out onto the first rung.

The smoke was getting thicker, stinging his eyes, burning his throat. He couldn't afford to waste any more time. With a deep breath, he started climbing down the ladder, the sound of the mob out in front of the cabin growing louder with every rung he descended. He hit the ground running and took off into the forest, scanning his surroundings for any sign of Alexis.

The smoke was making it difficult to breathe, and dangerous memories pushed at the edges of his consciousness.

Jax.

Fuse.

Mack.

Alejandro.

Rylan's arm, reaching toward him as if the kid had been asking for help when the limb was blown off...

He blinked the memories back, even as tears streamed down his cheeks. He'd lived for years with the knowledge he'd failed his men. He'd made mistakes during that mission. He'd forged ahead when every instinct had insisted he scrap it...

But none of his men had raised concerns, either. At least not until after, when Jax came to his hospital room and accused him of forcing the mission when nobody else felt good about it. He'd changed the mission last minute, and it had fucked them.

And for a long time, he'd believed that. He'd hated himself because of it, had thought he wasn't worth saving...

But he'd been wrong.

Alexis had shown him just how wrong. So had Zak and Redwood Coast Rescue. Ash and Dr. Firestone. And even Clue, with her brown ears and stubborn eyes, who had trusted him with her whole heart when she was at her most vulnerable. Would the dog have trusted him like that if he were such a monster?

No.

And with that trust, she'd put the first crack in the wall he'd spent the last decade building between him and the world. Then Alexis came along and blew the wall apart, exposing his isolation for what it was—fear.

All of them had forced him to examine the past more closely, and the more he thought back to those dark days, the more he realized that they'd all made mistakes. Fuse had been too cocky, taking the mission too lightly, and Jax had been mutinous from the start. Mack had warned of the incoming fire too late. Alejandro's grenade had set off the protective charges laid by Al-Mansoor's men, causing Fuse's door charge to blow the whole side of the building off. Rylan, still as green as a tadpole, had lost his nerve and broke formation.

The mission had been a complete clusterfuck, but he wasn't solely to blame. Even if they had done everything perfectly and executed the mission as planned, they still wouldn't have walked out of there in one piece. Al-Mansoor had made damn sure of it.

And with that realization, a weight lifted off Shane's shoulders. He was leaving behind his old life, his old demons. It was time to start fresh.

And he knew exactly where he was going to start.

Alexis.

He would find her, and together they would start a new life. They would leave behind the pain, the memories, and the fear. He would be her protector, her provider, and her lover. He would make up for all the years he had spent isolating himself from the world. And he would make sure that she knew just how much he loved her.

As he pushed through the dense trees, his eyes stinging from the billowing smoke, he caught a glimpse of her blonde hair in the distance. She was running towards him, and he had never been more grateful for anything in his life.

"Shane! Oh my God. You're okay!"

He opened his arms, ready to catch her. "Lexi—"

A shadow stepped out into her path and grabbed her by the hair, pulling her back so hard her scream of surprise was cut short. A knife flashed against the pale skin of her neck.

Shane's heart plummeted. He'd seen that bulky white coat, scarf, and goggles before when Alexis first ran from his cabin, and he'd gone after her. Only now, there was a brownish stain on the white from where Shane had stabbed him.

The Shadow Stalker.

He raised his rifle, aiming for the man's head. His finger twitched against the trigger, ready to fire. "Let her go. We found your bunker. It's over."

The man laughed. A cold and heartless sound that made Shane's skin crawl. Then he pulled off his hood and goggles, and Shane's heart stopped.

He knew that face.

He'd seen it before in town. At the grocery store. At the pub— the bearded man in the 49ers ball cap. That face. He hadn't recognized it then, but it was clean-shaven now. Leaner, with more scars and lines, the brown eyes sunken and too bright in the flickering light thrown by his burning cabin.

Recognition struck like a lightning bolt, an electric charge sizzling over his dulled nerve endings, raising the remaining hair on his arms into goosebumps.

He. Knew. That. Face.

He lowered the rifle. "Jax?"

chapter
thirty-three

JAX GRINNED, the expression twisted into something almost feral. "Long time no see, Shane. You're looking... well, like shit, actually."

Shane's mind reeled. It couldn't be Jax. His best friend and teammate, the man he'd considered a brother, who was always quick with a laugh and a dirty joke... he couldn't be capable of all the atrocities the Shadow Stalker had committed.

But here he was, standing in front of Shane, holding Alexis captive. It didn't make any sense.

"What the fuck, Jax? You're not a killer."

Jax's grin only widened. "What? You're surprised I'm doing exactly what the government trained me to do?"

"I don't remember rape and murder as part of our training."

Jax's grin faltered slightly, but then he straightened up and shrugged. "We always did what we had to do for the mission. You know that. And I'm still doing what I have to do."

Shane's heart banged around in his chest like it was trying to jump out from between his ribs. He'd never been so terrified in his life, and his hands shook on his rifle. He couldn't risk a shot, but he couldn't let Jax hurt her. Not again.

"C'mon, man. Let Alexis go. She has nothing to do with this."

Jax raised an eyebrow. "Oh, I think she has everything to do with it. You care about her." He tightened his grip on Alexis's hair, causing her to whimper in pain. "I've been watching you for years. Watching you hide away in your little cabin, thinking you could escape the world."

"If you've been here for years, why didn't you come talk to me?" He knew it wouldn't have mattered if Jax had. He'd had no interest in talking to anyone until Alexis came into his life. But now he needed to keep Jax talking and hope someone—preferably Ash—noticed them. "What happened to us was bullshit, but we could've figured it out together, helped each other and—"

"I don't want to figure it out with you. There's nothing to figure out. I don't want your help."

"Then what do you want?"

Jax's grin turned into a sneer. "What do I want? I want you to suffer. You led us to our deaths in Afghanistan."

"Jax, you survived."

"No, I didn't!" His face flushed red, and spittle flew from his mouth as he yanked on Alexis's hair again and forced her to her knees. "My wife left me while I was in the hospital. I lost my career, my goddamn sanity. I can't sleep without a downer. I can't get out of bed without an upper. I can't get the fucking images out of my head. Alejandro was fucking vaporized. Right there in front of my eyes, and I couldn't do a goddamn thing to stop it."

"I saw it, too, Jax," Shane murmured and slid a step closer. "I saw his face right before it happened. Saw his fear. He haunts me, too. Every night. You all do."

"And you call that surviving?"

"No. You're right. We didn't survive. Not the men we used

to be. We're ghosts of those men, but that's our own doing. Our choices when we got home made us this way."

Jax let out a bitter laugh. "*Your* choices made us this way. I told you the mission was fucked, but you didn't listen. You never fucking listened. The esteemed Echo One always knew what was best for Echo Team. But you led us into a massacre. You killed us!"

Guilt and shame twisted into a messy mix in his gut. Jax was right. He had been the leader of Echo Team, and he had made the call that day. The call that had resulted in the deaths of three of his teammates. The call that had blown his face off and twisted Jax into... this.

A monster.

"Jesus, I'm so sorry, Jax. I truly am, but I was just doing the job. I brought up my concerns with command before we even set foot in country, and they told me to shut up and follow orders. So, I followed orders. We were working off bad intel, and no matter what calls I made, we were never going to come out of that mission in one piece. We just weren't."

"Save it. Your apologies and excuses mean nothing to me." Jax's grip on Alexis tightened, and the knife blade pressed against her throat, drawing a bead of blood.

Tears streamed from her eyes, but she didn't make a sound.

Shane's mind raced. He had to find a way to diffuse the situation, to get Alexis out of Jax's grasp. But he couldn't think straight with the memories of that day flooding his mind. The sound of gunfire and screams, the smell of blood and burning flesh. *His* flesh.

The pain...

"But I'll tell you what does mean something to me," Jax continued. "Watching you suffer like I've suffered. Watching you lose everything you care about. I've waited years for this day. You didn't care about any-fucking-thing for so long. I thought I would just have to kill you, but I hated the thought of putting you out of your misery."

Shane clenched his fists and took a step closer, ignoring the warning glint in Jax's eyes. "You don't have to do this. We can fix this. You're still my brother, and I still love you."

Jax barked out a laugh. "You think this is about brother-hood? You think I'm even the same person I was when we were brothers? You think I don't enjoy what I do, killing all those people? I love it. It's the only thing that makes me feel alive anymore."

Shane's stomach turned at the words. He took another step forward, his finger moving from the rifle's trigger guard to the trigger.

But Jax was too quick. He grabbed a fistful of Alexis's hair and yanked her head back, exposing her neck. "Don't even think about it, Shane. One move, and she's dead."

"Jax, she's innocent."

"Innocent? She's a nosy bitch, always digging around in other people's business. She deserves this as much as you do."

"I love you," Alexis said, her voice shaking, her gaze locked on his as tears spilled down her cheeks. Her eyes had gone wide, showing too much white. Her neck bobbed against the knife as she swallowed.

He'd seen that look in men's eyes before. He'd seen that fear and resignation in Alejandro's eyes before the RPG exploded at his feet—that knowledge of impending death.

No. He couldn't lose her. He wasn't strong enough to survive it.

"Please, Jax. This doesn't have to end badly."

But Jax only sneered, his eyes glinting with a twisted plea-sure. "It's already ended badly."

With a sudden movement, Jax dragged the blade across Alexis's throat, cutting off her scream.

Shane felt as if his heart had been ripped out of his chest as he watched Alexis drop to the ground. Blood gushed from her throat, staining the muddy snow a deep, scarlet red.

So much blood.

He raised his rifle and aimed at Jax's head. Brother or not, he was going to kill this fucker. He was going to pump him full of bullets and stand over him, watching him bleed out.

Jax held out his arms as if welcoming the bullets. "Do it."

"Shane!" Ash's voice boomeranged through the trees. "Don't."

He glanced to his left. Ash was there, his clothes coated in mud, one of his eyes swollen shut, his gun out and aimed at Jax. He was limping slightly. His big black dog appeared from the shadows next to him, its lips peeled up in a snarl, showing a row of blood-stained teeth. He held the animal back with a hand signal.

Cal appeared at Ash's other side, looking just as ragged, his lip split and bleeding down the front of his dirty dress shirt. "Killing him won't bring her back, Shane."

"He wants you to kill him," Zak said, appearing from the woods with his gun raised and Ranger snarling at his side. "Don't give him that satisfaction."

"He needs to pay for his crimes," Donovan added, approaching from the right, his gun also pointed at Jax. "If he killed Dr. Firestone, death is too easy for him."

Donovan's border collie, Spirit, usually so happy-go-lucky, took a slow step forward, stalking Jax, head down, eyes blazing. She wasn't growling like Ranger or Dante, but she looked like she was contemplating eviscerating him.

Jax dropped his arms, and his grin faded into panic. "What are you waiting for? Just shoot me already."

Shane lowered his rifle. "Ranger," he said softly, and the dog's radar dish ears perked. "Attack."

Ranger looked up at his person for confirmation of the order. When Zak nodded, the dog launched forward in a lightning-fast strike and dragged Jax, screaming, to the ground. The men and dogs surrounded him, subduing him while Ash cuffed him and read him his rights.

Shane ignored it all and rushed Alexis, scooping her lifeless body up in his arms. He held her close to his chest, buried his face in her hair, and rocked her. "I'm sorry. I'm so sorry, sweetheart. I love you, too. Jesus, I should've told you. I was scared. So scared that you didn't mean it or I couldn't be what you deserve. I should've—"

Her cold hand tightened around his.

He sucked in a sharp breath and drew back, watching in shock as her eyes flickered open. Those beautiful green eyes, full of pain and love. Her lips moved, but no sound came out. More blood bubbled from her throat.

"Shh. Don't talk. Don't talk, Lexi." He pressed his hand over the wound. "She's alive! Ash—" His voice caught on the ball of emotion in his throat. "She's alive!"

thirty-four

Three Weeks Later

"I HATE THIS."

Alexis smiled at Ellie's vehement statement and let her sister fuss around her as they walked toward the front door of the Lost County Sheriff's Department. Ellie still acted like she was as fragile as an egg, even though she was all but healed.

She'd been in the hospital for only a week, intubated in the ICU for two of those days due to her throat swelling and closing off her airway. The blade had nicked her carotid artery, but there had been no other major damage done to her jugular, windpipe, or the muscles in her neck. All in all, the doctors agreed she was incredibly lucky.

Lucky she had instinctively pressed a hand to her throat when she fell, pinching off the ruptured artery and slowing her bleeding.

Lucky the sheriff had been right there to call in a Life Flight.

Lucky a former SEAL with extensive medic training stayed right by her side through the whole thing.

A former SEAL she hadn't seen since she lost consciousness in the helicopter.

At first, she wondered why Shane had stayed away. The fact he was not there had hurt. She'd hated him, then mourned the loss of their relationship. Then, slowly, she realized why he hadn't come to her...

Guilt.

He thought what happened to her was his fault.

But Alexis knew better. She had seen the way Jax had looked at her in that final moment, the look of satisfaction in his eyes as he slid the blade across her throat. She knew that Shane had done everything he could to protect her, just as he had always done in their time together.

As they walked into the department, Ellie's grip on her arm tightened. "I hate this," she said again. "Why do they need another statement from you? They already got one at the hospital, and there were witnesses. You shouldn't need to come here."

It had been her idea, her request, but she decided not to tell Ellie that. "They need a formal statement for the record."

"You should be resting. Or better yet, we should go back to Chicago, where it's safe."

Alexis smothered a laugh behind her hand. Chicago had never been considered a safe city, and Ellie knew that. Hell, they'd done an entire podcast on Chicago's murder problem when they were just starting out and hadn't decided on the right direction for the show yet.

Ellie scowled at her. "You know what I mean. I want to go home."

She gave Ellie's arm a reassuring squeeze back. "I'm just as safe here now as anywhere else. And we need to stay, at least for a bit longer."

Ellie turned to her, pulling her to a stop. "A week," she said, her eyes pleading. "Then we'll go home. Please."

"I thought you wanted to stay because of a certain sexy lawyer..."

Ellie's expression darkened like a storm cloud. "I don't want to talk about him."

"Oh. Wow. Okay. That bad?"

"Worse. I said I don't want to talk about it. One more week, Lexi, then we go home. Promise me."

"Okay," she said after a beat of hesitation. In truth, she didn't know why she was hesitating. If Shane didn't want to see her anymore, there was nothing keeping her here. "Go ahead and make the travel arrangements. I know you're dying to."

Ellie winced. "Let's... not use that phrase anymore, okay? Nobody's dying for anything."

Ash waited in the lobby and greeted them with his characteristic tight smile. "Ellie. Alexis." He eyed her up and down, his gaze finally landing on the bandage at her neck. He must have decided she was okay, because he didn't ask.

Instead, he held out an arm, motioning them down a nearby hallway. "Are you ready for this?"

Alexis drew a breath. It hurt. Breathing still hurt sometimes. So did swallowing. And talking. But she was still doing all three, so she couldn't be anything but grateful for the pain. "As ready as I'll ever be."

Ash led them into the same room where she gave her initial statement about her abduction. He waited until they sat on one of the couches and, just like before, pulled over a chair from the table.

He set a recording device on the coffee table in front of them and went through the now-familiar spiel of his name, rank, their names, and case number.

"Okay, Alexis," he finally said and pulled out his battered green notebook. "I'm going to record this and take notes, then I'll need you to write it all out. I know it's tedious, but we can take a break whenever you need. Just start at the top and tell me everything you remember."

It wasn't much. Most of that night on the mountain was a black hole in her memory, but she could pinpoint Jax as the man who slit her throat.

Ash confirmed it with a photo lineup. She was surprised at how Jax looked in the mug shot. She remembered him as something twisted and evil, like the supernatural villain from a horror movie. But he was just a man—gaunt, with limp hair and glassy, haunted eyes.

And seeing him like that jarred another memory loose. She pointed at his photo again before Ash could close the book of mug shots. "He's the man I saw at the coffee shop before I was abducted. The angry one I told you about. But he had a beard then."

Ash nodded. "We were able to get the security video from an ATM down the street and can confirm he followed you from the shop to your motel. There's no footage of him abducting you, unfortunately."

She sat back in her seat. She didn't know why that news shocked her. "So he is the Shadow Stalker."

"There's no such thing," Ash said. "At least, not the Stalker of legend. But, yes, we have a strong case against Jax as the man who abducted you and murdered those other women. The blood on Shane's furs, from when he brought you off the mountain, matches Jax, and there's a corresponding wound on Jax's side where Shane stabbed him during that encounter. The blood on the coat you gave us matches two women who went missing in 2019 and 2021. Jax has lived here in town under an assumed name, Ezra Jacoby, for over six years. And he was seen with the final victim, Kelly Harris, just hours before she was reported missing by her roommate."

Jaxon Thorne, a.k.a. Ezra Jacoby. It was strange to have a name for her personal bogeyman after all this time.

But... something still wasn't sitting right with her. It wasn't adding up.

She shook her head. "But he couldn't have killed them all. From my research, the earliest victim was Maria Socktish, and she disappeared in the late nineties. Ninety-seven or eight. I can't remember. But Jax would've been... what? Five or six?"

"We don't believe they're connected."

"What?"

Ash's expression was grim. "I know you were convinced there's a serial killer in town. And, yes, technically, you were right. Jaxon Thorne is one, but he's not the Shadow Stalker."

She blinked at him in shock. "But all those disappearances and murders... they're all so similar. Victim type, M.O." Including that of her sister, Hope. She'd been so sure Hope had been a Shadow Stalker victim. It was why she'd been so determined to investigate in the first place.

But now he was telling her they weren't connected?

"They have to be connected," she said, more to herself than the sheriff. "They have to be."

"I'm sorry. They're just not."

"But what about the FBI? You said—"

"I sent them everything you gave me, and they agree. There is no Shadow Stalker, but Jax confessed to the most recent murder— Kelly Harris— and to the murder of a woman in San Diego. We're still trying to verify that one, and we believe we will uncover more victims the more we dig. He also confessed to attacking you, but he flatly refuses to admit that he had a partner." Ash held up a hand, stopping her protest. "Listen, this doesn't mean I'm not still investigating Maria Socktish and all the others. I am. But the evidence is pointing toward them having nothing to do with Jax, or even each other."

"What about Dr. Firestone?"

Ash exhaled, long and slow. "He confessed to her murder, too. He overheard Hank Firestone complaining at the Mad Dog about how Shane scared his wife and decided she was the perfect victim to frame him for."

"But if this was all just to hurt Shane, why did he abduct me at all? I didn't know Shane until after I escaped the bunker."

"At this point, we can only speculate. He won't admit to abducting you."

"That doesn't make sense."

"In my experience, men like him rarely do." Ash closed the binder of mug shots, and the sound of the heavy book closing was like a period on the conversation.

Alexis opened her mouth to ask another question, but Ellie gave her hand a quick squeeze. "Lexi, it's over. Please just drop it."

But she couldn't. Not when things weren't making sense.

She stood up. "I want to talk to Jax."

Ash shut his eyes for a moment and pinched the bridge of his nose. "I don't think—"

"Lexi..." Ellie began, but she cut her sister off.

"I have a right to face him."

"And he has the right to refuse," Ash pointed out.

"He won't."

Ash shook his head and stood. "He's with his lawyer now. If you're serious about it, I can make the request."

"I'm serious. Who is his lawyer?"

Ellie made a disgruntled sound, a cross between a disgusted sigh and a growl of annoyance.

Ash raised a brow at her, then turned back to Alexis. "Cal Holden."

Ah. That explained so much about Ellie's sudden interest in leaving.

She nodded. "Please make the request."

It didn't take long.

Barely ten minutes after Ash left the room, the door opened again, and there stood Cal. His gaze strayed momentarily to Ellie, and he opened his mouth like he wanted to say something to her, but he closed it again without uttering a sound.

He refocused on Alexis. "I'm told you want to speak to my client."

Ellie harrumphed and crossed her arms over her chest. "This isn't a good idea."

Alexis ignored her. "Yes. I have questions."

"He's..." Cal trailed off, then sighed. "He's not in good shape. He had so many drugs in his system that night it's amazing he didn't overdose. He's going through withdrawal now and is not entirely coherent. I don't know if he can answer your questions, but he said he's willing to try."

"Thank you."

Cal gave a small nod and gestured for her to follow him. She stood and walked past him, feeling Ellie glowering at her back. She didn't care. She needed to do this.

The county jail was next door, connected to the Sheriff's Department by a breezeway. She followed Cal through the lobby and admin officers, then through the metal detectors. From there, a guard escorted them into the prison itself.

As they reached the visitation room, she was surprised to see two men step out. One was a handsome man no older than thirty with a movie star's square jaw and hair that wasn't blonde but wasn't quite brown either. It was a glorious mix of all the colors, thick and wavy and artfully tousled. His eyes were also not quite one color—a little gray, some green, a bit golden brown. Bright tattoos peeked out from under his shirt on his left arm. His right arm was a prosthetic from the elbow down. Alexis didn't recognize him, but he carried himself like Shane did. They moved the same way— decisive, practical, no wasted movements.

The man a step behind him was Shane. He stopped short when he saw her, and she watched the shutter fall over his expression. He was closing himself up, locking down tight as if he expected a storm. She wanted to reach for him, to wrap her arms around him, but she knew it was a bad idea. Shane was not the same man she had fallen in love with. He had retreated back into himself, back to the man she had first met on the mountain, guarded and impenetrable.

The handsome man stepped forward. "You must be Alexis Summers." His voice was warm and friendly, with a trace of an accent she couldn't place. "I'm Rylan. Rylan Cross." He held out his non-plastic hand, and she shook it.

"Nice to meet you, Rylan. Are you... friends with Jax?" It made her stomach twist to think of Jax having friends or family. But of course he did. He'd been a normal man once.

Rylan slid a glance at Shane before answering. "We worked together."

Oh. He was a SEAL, too. That explained a lot.

Shane scowled at their small talk. "What are you doing here, Alexis?"

A little piece of her heart withered and died at his use of her full name.

Not Lexi.

Not sweetheart.

God, it really was over between them, and she didn't even know why. She could only guess it was because he felt guilty for what happened to her. Felt responsible for the horrors she'd faced at the hands of his teammate, his brother. Felt like he'd failed at protecting her and was no longer worthy of her love. Maybe he even felt like he had to choose between helping his damaged teammate and loving her.

She opened her mouth to tell him none of it was true. It wasn't his fault, he was worthy, and if he wanted to help Jax, she wouldn't make him feel guilty for his loyalty. But she never got the chance to say any of that because Cal answered for her.

"She requested to talk to Jax."

Shane's jaw clenched, and he glared at Cal. "I don't think that's a good idea."

Cal shrugged. "It's her right, and Jax agreed to this meeting. I can't stop them. And maybe they both need this closure."

"Fine," Shane said after a moment thick with tension, his voice oddly flat. "We're leaving."

Before she could say anything else, he turned and walked away, Rylan following close behind. She was left standing there in the austere hallway, empty and alone.

Cal cleared his throat, breaking the silence. "Shall we?"

She nodded and followed him into the visitation room.

Jax Thorne sat at the table, his hands shackled to the metal surface. He looked up as they entered, his eyes meeting Alexis's in a brief moment of recognition before he glanced away. His hands trembled, jangling the chains, and sweat beaded on his forehead. He was thinner than she remembered, his skin sallow and his eyes sunken in.

Did it make her an awful person that she felt a spark of satisfaction at his pain?

Probably.

Especially considering why she'd requested this meeting.

Cal pulled out one of the chairs for Alexis and gestured for her to sit. "I'm going to record this, if that's okay with you?"

She nodded.

"Okay. I'll be right here," he said before melting back against the wall, making himself unobtrusive.

For several long moments, she and Jax just stared at each other. She tried to see the man who had been Shane's teammate, the man who had inspired such loyalty from his former friends, but all she saw was the monster who had tried to kill her.

Finally, she spoke. "Why?"

Jax's eyes flicked up to and landed on the bandage at her neck. "Why what?" His voice was dry, raspy.

He knew exactly what she was asking, but she spelled it out for him anyway. "Why did you do it? Why did you hurt all those women?"

"I'm not right. I'm—" He stopped short.

"Tell her what you told me," Cal prompted from his spot against the wall.

Jax curled in on himself, his thin shoulders hunching forward. "I'm so fucking angry all the time. And I somehow convinced myself that everything wrong with me was all Shane's fault..."

When he trailed off, she nodded for him to continue. "I'm listening."

"I held on to that anger and hatred and fed it with drugs because it made me feel alive again. I didn't mean to hurt those women— I hired the first one in San Diego for sex, but then something just... snapped. Next thing I knew, she was dead." He drew in a shuddering breath before continuing. "I decided I needed to find Shane and make him pay for everything. I knew where he'd gone. He talked about the mountain all the time, said it was the most beautiful place in the world. He and his dad used to come camping here when he was a kid. So, I came to find him. It took years... I kept my darker urges in check, but when I finally saw him in town, I knew exactly how to punish him. I knew that if I kept killing and riled up enough people about it, they would blame him instead of me."

She shook her head slowly in disbelief. "But then, why abduct me? I didn't know Shane until after I escaped the bunker. I meant nothing to him, so it couldn't have been to hurt him."

He straightened in his seat and met her gaze. "I swear I didn't abduct you, Alexis. I didn't rape you. I found the bunker last summer while I was looking for Shane's hideaway, but I've only been there twice— once when I found it and again when I planted Kelly's body there. I'd planned to use her as proof that Shane was the killer."

"You expect me to believe that you just stumbled on the bunker and decided to use it for yourself? That you didn't know what was happening down there?"

He closed his eyes for a moment. He looked defeated, exhausted. "Whether you believe me or not, it's the truth. I didn't know you until I saw you leave his cabin. I figured for you to be there during a snowstorm, you must have meant something to him, so I tried to grab you."

She couldn't tell if she believed him or not, but the sorrow in his eyes made her think it might be at least partially true.

This was not the same man who slit her throat.

She touched her throat at the thought.

Again, his eyes went to the bandage. "I'm sorry."

She dropped her hand. She didn't want his apology. She wanted answers. "You said you didn't know me, but the police have video footage of you following me from the coffee shop the day I was abducted."

He exhaled, and she could smell the reek of his breath from across the table. "Yeah, okay. I did know you. At least, knew of you from that whole Darcy Cantrell case. Everyone in town knew you, and there were rumors you'd been poking around about that Shadow Stalker legend. I thought I could point you toward Shane. Yes, I followed you that day."

"Did you see who abducted me?"

He shook his head. And, yes, she believed him more with each passing minute.

But there was one sure-fire way to know for sure, something she hadn't even told the sheriff because every time she thought about it, bile surged into her throat.

She moistened her lips, taking a moment to steel herself against this next question. "The man who—" She found she couldn't say the word and broke off. Her throat burned, and it wasn't from her wound. She swallowed back the rising bile and started again. "The man who raped me had a birthmark or tattoo or something on his pelvis. Do you have anything like that?"

Cal pushed away from the wall. "Whoa, whoa. I think we've—"

But Jax stood, his chains rattling as he dropped his pants.

She quickly looked down at the table as tears flooded her eyes. "Cal, can you please tell me... is there anything there?"

There was a moment of silence.

Then, on a surprised exhale, Cal said, "No."

"I told you," Jax said. "I've done a lot of horrible shit, but I've never raped anyone. And I am sorry for trying to kill you, Alexis. I wasn't thinking clearly."

She nodded and pushed to her feet. "He didn't abduct me. The Shadow Stalker is still out there."

Then she fled toward the door without looking back.

chapter
thirty-five

A WEEK HAD PASSED since Shane ran into Alexis at the prison, and his stomach hardened into knots every time he thought of her there, sitting across the table from Jax.

He was so fucking conflicted.

Part of him wanted to go back to the prison and rip out Jax's throat for even daring to look at her after what he did. But the other part, the part that still saw Jax as a brother, wanted to believe that he was telling the truth and that he didn't abduct and assault Alexis.

So, as much as it hurt, he'd stayed away from both of them. He needed to think.

Zak said his room at RWCR was open for as long as he wanted it—which, given that his cabin was a pile of muddy ashes, might be a while. Weirdly, though, he wasn't mad about it. He liked the dogs. He liked Zak and Anna, Donovan and Sasha, Pierce and Sawyer. He liked feeling like part of a team again.

He also enjoyed having Rylan around. They'd spent a lot of time talking after visiting Jax together, and the chats had eased the tension he'd been carrying around for years. Rylan didn't blame him. He blamed the Navy, the shitty intel, Al-Mansoor.

"And I blamed myself for a long time," he confessed as they sat together at a table in the Rescue's common room, drinking coffee. "In those seconds, when everything went sideways on us, I got scared. I froze. All that training, all of that work, just went out of my head."

"You were a kid, Ry."

He gave a grim smile. "No, I was a SEAL. I should've done better, been better. For a long time, I blamed myself for what happened. I hated myself. I'd get wasted and punish myself by saying your names before I passed out every night. Mack, Fuse, Alejandro—"

"Ezra," Shane muttered and set down his coffee at the sudden realization.

Rylan tilted his head much like the dogs did when they were confused. "Uh, pretty sure we didn't have a guy name Ezra."

"No, Jax's alias here in town was Ezra Jacoby, and I just got why he chose that. Mack's first name was Ethan, Fuse's was Zeke. Ethan, Zeke, Rylan, Alejandro. E. Z. R. A. Fuck." He shook his head, and a lump rose into his throat. "He really does hate me."

"Nah, man. He hates himself. He just can't admit it, so he blames you."

Shane grunted. "When did you become a shrink?"

"About three years ago."

Shane nearly choked on his next swallow of coffee. "No shit?"

Rylan nodded. "I was so fucked up after that last mission that I was nearly catatonic for a year—"

"I'd heard that. I thought you still were."

"Nah, I eventually came out of it and then spent another

year trying to off myself. But I was lucky. I had a strong support network and a good therapist who talked me down from the ledge. And, because of them, I pulled my act together, went back to school, got a master's in psychotherapy, and became a certified trauma counselor." He set down his mug and met Shane's gaze. "You should be the first to know I asked the VA to transfer me here, and the paperwork just went through. Your group lost your doctor in a very traumatic way, and I want to help."

"It's not my group."

"It should be." Rylan glanced around the room and smiled. "They got a good thing going here, Master Chief."

He flinched at the sound of his rank. It had been a long time since anyone used it. "It's just Shane now."

Rylan gave a self-deprecating laugh. "Sorry. Force of habit."

"Nah, it's okay." He waved it off. "It's just been a long fucking time since I've been around people who knew me before. Sometimes even I forget who I used to be."

"I hear that," Rylan said. "But to me, you'll always be Master Chief Shane Trevisano, Echo One. You're still a badass SEAL who survived some of the worst shit imaginable."

Shane snorted. "Survived, sure. But at what cost?"

"That's the question we all ask ourselves, man." Rylan leaned forward, his expression serious, and Shane already knew what was coming next. "You know, I can help you, too. With the PTSD."

"I don't need help. I'm fine."

"You're not fine, Shane. You're isolating yourself from the people who love you." He paused for a long, meaningful moment. "From the woman who loves you."

The mention of Alexis drove a spike of anger and regret through him, and his jaw tightened reflexively. "I said I'm fine."

Rylan didn't budge. "You're not fine. With what Jax did

stirring up all this nasty shit again, nobody expects you to be. Hell, I'd be fucking worried if you were. It's okay not to be fine. It's okay to ask for help—you taught me that during our first deployment together, before Operation Ember Storm." He stood and squeezed Shane's shoulder as he went to the door. "Come to the group therapy session today at one-thirty. Just try it out."

"I'd rather go through Hell Week again."

Rylan's eyes glinted with a mischievous spark. "Well, if you're feeling nostalgic, I could always put the group through some SEAL drills. Make you feel more at home."

Shane snorted. "I think I've had enough of that for one lifetime."

Rylan shrugged. "Offers stands—without the drills because, yeah, I'm not doing that shit again either."

Despite his protests, when one-thirty rolled around, Shane wandered away from his work in the dog yard, where he'd been practicing hide-and-seek games with Clue to prepare for her SAR candidate test. And before he realized where he was going, he was standing at the door of the community room.

But he couldn't reach for the handle and go in.

At his hesitation, Clue sat down next to his boot and looked up with those trusting brown eyes, her ears flopping back. He stared down at the dog and couldn't help the smile twitching at the corner of his mouth. Her tail wagged, swishing across the floor.

He took a deep breath and crouched to scratch behind her ears. "You don't think less of me, do you, girl?" he murmured. "For needing help?"

Clue licked his hand and nuzzled her nose under his palm as if to say she didn't care about that.

Shane straightened and squared his shoulders. He had nothing to lose by trying, right?

He pushed open the door to the community room and stepped inside.

The room was filled with familiar faces—Zak, Donovan, Pierce, Sawyer—but they all turned to look at him as he entered. It was like a spotlight was shining down on him, highlighting every flaw and insecurity he had. He felt exposed and vulnerable, like he was back in the desert, surrounded by enemies. But he knew how to handle the desert.

This?

He had no fucking idea.

But then Rylan appeared at his side, clapping him on his shoulder and wordlessly guiding him to an empty seat before turning to address the room.

"Hi. I'm Rylan. I was a SEAL, and then I lost my arm." He lifted his prosthetic. "And then I was an alcoholic and a drug addict, and all I could think about was ending my miserable life... until I found a group like this one. They helped me, and now I want to help you if you'll have me."

Donovan growled low in his throat, but there was no other sound from the men.

Rylan nodded. "Yeah, I know this sucks. I'm not Dr. Firestone, and I have no intention of replacing her in your hearts. I'm only here to help."

Shane's gaze flickered around the room, taking in the tense postures and wary expressions of the other men. He saw fragments of himself in each of them—pain, fear, anger, guilt—but he also knew they were all courageous, resilient men. They were all survivors in their own ways.

But they were struggling with this change.

And Rylan needed his help. His teammate needed his help.

Shane took a deep breath and tried to relax his grip on the arms of the chair. It was a struggle, but he forced himself to let go. "I'm Shane," he said, breaking the silence. "I was a SEAL, and I loved my job. It was my life until an RPG exploded next to me, and I was burned over seventy percent of my body. And then I was lost for a long time…"

Clue leaned against his leg, and he reached down to pet her head.

"Until I found this dog, and she taught me about trust. Then a wounded, terrified woman found me, and she taught me that love—" His voice cracked on the word. "That love is healing. And they both made me realize I don't want to be lost anymore."

Nobody said anything for a solid minute.

Then Zak gave Shane a slight nod and spoke. "I'm Zak. I was Army black ops and a POW. I lost my leg and my sanity in Afghanistan but found love and purpose here, with my wife and girls and this team." He chuckled when Ranger bumped his elbow with his nose. "And this crazy dog who never lets me forget he exists." He glanced at Donovan, passing the conversational ball.

Donovan growled softly but, after a stubborn moment of silence, also relented. "I'm Donovan. I was a Marine. EOD. But I got blown up one too many times and scrambled my brain. Turned out okay, though. Still scrambled, but I'm managing. I like the work I do now, and I have the best partner for it." He smiled down at his border collie, asleep with her head resting on his boot, and the tension eased out of his spine. His smile brightened into a grin. "And in seven months, my beautiful wife is going to give me the family I always wanted."

"Congratulations," Rylan said, and sounded like he meant it. "That's awesome news. I bet you're excited."

"I wasn't at first," Donovan admitted. "I was terrified." He gave a short laugh. "Still am, because what do I know about being a dad? But I actually think I'll be pretty kickass at it." He glanced around the group. "And my kid's going to be surrounded by a shit-ton of 'uncles' who will die for him or her, so, yeah, I'm excited."

Hearty agreements sounded from all the men.

Donovan blinked like he was getting emotional and wiped a hand over his face. "Yeah, enough about my shit. Sawyer, you're up. Tell the new doc about your superpower."

"It's not a superpower," Sawyer hedged. "I was a Marine, too. A sniper bullet blinded me. Well..." He tilted his head from side to side. "Kind of. I can still see movement. I struggled with my disability for a long time until Zelda came into my life."

At the sound of her name, the chocolate lab beside his chair gave a lazy tail wag.

Pierce scowled and signed something.

"He said his name is Pierce, and he wants to know how he can participate in group when you don't sign," Donovan translated. "He doesn't want to type everything out on his phone and doesn't want us to have to translate. Dr. Firestone knew ASL."

To everyone's surprise, Rylan signed back with his good hand as he answered out loud, "Hi, Pierce. My sister is hard of hearing and uses ASL. I'm still learning to do it one-handed, but if that's what you're comfortable with, we can stick to it."

Pierce's eyes widened, and then the two of them carried on several seconds of silent conversation in sign language.

Well, shit, Shane thought. Now he really had to learn it, too.

The session wasn't as bad as he'd feared it would be. It

wasn't as claustrophobic as that disastrous session with Dr. Firestone all those weeks ago.

He could handle this.

When the session broke up, there was a man waiting outside the doors. He pushed away from the wall, his face full of hope.

It was the man from the pub with the computer, the one Shane mistakenly attacked. The writer. Connelly.

"She didn't come," Zak told the guy.

"Fuck," Connelly muttered and rubbed a hand over a jaw that hadn't seen a razor in a few weeks. "I really thought she would."

"Still can't get Veronica out of her house?" Sawyer asked, and Connelly shook his head.

"Not since Dr. Firestone died. She won't even talk to me through the door anymore. She's completely shut down."

"Is there anything we can do to help?"

Connelly lifted a shoulder. "I'm out of ideas."

"Is this about Veronica Martens?" Rylan asked as he approached their loose circle just outside the door. "I know she needs a female counselor, and I've asked a friend to come help."

Connelly eyed him suspiciously. "So you're the new doctor?"

"Not a doctor." Rylan flashed a grin. "Yet. But my friend is, and if anyone can help Veronica, it will be her."

Connelly sighed. "I'm willing to try anything at this point. She was doing so good, but Dr. Firestone's murder traumatized her all over again."

"Are you family?" Rylan asked.

"Friend. We grew up together. Her dad sent me. He's sick —cancer—and wants to make sure she's going to be okay when he's gone. But right now... I don't even know what to tell him."

Rylan nodded. "All right. Let me think on it, consult with some colleagues, and see what plan of action we can come up with."

Shane decided that was his cue to slip away. He felt like a voyeur, listening in on the problems of a woman he barely knew.

But Zak caught him before he could vanish into his room. "Do you think Clue's ready for her SAR candidate test?"

Shane looked down at the dog. Once again, she stared up at him with trusting adoration. With his determination to stay away from Alexis, Clue was the only thing that had been keeping him going these past few weeks. She'd been his constant companion as he helped train her for the test. "I don't think she can get more ready."

Zak grinned. "Good. We'll test you both tomorrow."

"Wait. Us both?"

"You want to be her handler, don't you?"

He opened his mouth. Closed it again without making a sound. He couldn't seem to find any words. "What about Alexis? Clue's her dog."

Zak's smile dimmed. "She made the difficult decision to sign Clue over to the Rescue. She doesn't think it'll be fair to confine her to a small apartment in Chicago when she's had a taste of the great outdoors."

All the air left Shane's lungs. "Alexis is leaving?"

"Tomorrow." Zak stared at him with narrowed eyes. "Shit, you didn't know. Why the fuck didn't you know? I thought you'd have been the first person she told."

"No, I… I haven't spoken with her."

To his complete shock, Zak smacked him upside the head.

"Jesus. Fuck. Ow. What was that for?"

"Because you're a dumbass." Zak hooked his thumb over his shoulder toward the now-empty community room. "After everything you said in there about love and healing, you're really just going to walk away from her?"

"She deserves better."

"Maybe let her make that decision."

"She almost died because of me."

"And she's alive because of you, too. You saved her life, Shane. Twice."

When Shane didn't respond—couldn't respond because he didn't have the words—Zak sighed. "Look, I get it. You're scared. Afraid she'll get hurt again because of you. But you're not the only one with scars, Shane. We all have them, but we don't let them dictate our lives. We push through the pain and live anyway." He gestured toward his metal leg. "I'm doing it. Donovan, Sawyer, and Pierce are, too, in their own ways. Even your friend Rylan's doing it. I like him, by the way."

"Yeah, he's a good man."

"He can help you if you let him. We all can if you let us in."

A heavy weight settled in his chest, and he suddenly couldn't draw a full breath. "I don't know if I can."

"You won't know until you try. And you owe it to yourself to try." Zak clapped him on the shoulder, then turned away. "But if you insist on continuing to be a dumbass, at the very least, you owe Alexis an explanation."

TODAY WAS THE DAY.

Time to leave Steam Valley and California and get on with her life. It was the right thing to do. The logical thing.

So why did it feel like her heart was cracking in two?

Alexis rubbed her chest as she watched the scenery pass in a blur out the passenger side of Ellie's rental car. This really was a beautiful place—the jagged coastline with cliffs that plunged into the churning Pacific, the towering redwood forests that cloaked the land in a serene, almost mystical aura, and the mountain standing in silent sentinel over it all. There wasn't another place like it. She could see why Shane had been drawn here.

Shane.

And there it was.

The real reason for the heaviness in her chest.

Would she ever see him again?

Probably not after she left here. She couldn't imagine him anywhere else but in this rugged place.

She'd heard through the town's ever-churning rumor mill that Shane was living at Redwood Coast Rescue. Even after the events on the mountain led to eight arrests of men from town for participating in a riot and destroying public property, the townspeople still spoke of Shane like he was the bogeyman in the woods.

Maybe they always would. Maybe he would go down in legend like the Shadow Stalker, and children would scare each other with mildly grotesque nursery rhymes about him on the playground.

For his sake, she hoped not. She hoped he could heal and the town would eventually see what she saw in him—a broken man trying to find his way in a world that had been unkind to him. A man who, despite his rough exterior, had a heart that was capable of great love and tenderness.

Alexis closed her eyes and leaned her head back against the seat, drawing in a deep, slow breath, trying to push away the memories of Shane that flooded her mind. Memories of his strong arms wrapped around her, his rough hands running over her skin, and the way he whispered her name like a prayer.

It was over now.

She had to move on.

But could she?

Ellie's voice broke through her thoughts. "Hey, are you okay?"

Alexis opened her eyes and nodded, plastering on a fake smile. "Yeah. Just... lost in thought."

As the car rounded a bend in the road, Alexis caught sight of Redwood Coast Rescue on a hill in the distance, and her heart quickened at the thought of seeing Shane one last time. She knew she shouldn't. It would only make things harder, but she couldn't resist the pull of him.

Ellie guided the car up the gravel drive and parked near the rescue's entrance. But when she killed the engine, she didn't move to get out. "Are you sure you want to leave Clue here?"

Clue.

That was why they were really here. Not to see Shane—for

all she knew, he might not even be here right now—but to say goodbye to the puppy she'd rescued from a kill shelter in Chicago, who had then tried to follow her up a mountain to rescue her.

Her throat closed up. She'd been trying not to think of this moment since she decided to sign her dog over to Zak. "This place is better for her than the city."

"Okay, but—"

"I've already made the decision, Elle. She's staying here." Alexis took a deep breath to ease that tightness from her throat and got out of the car, her eyes fixed on the building. As she approached the entrance, her pulse pounded in her ears.

She pushed open the door and was immediately hit with the familiar smell of antiseptic and animal musk. A man sat at a table in the common area, sipping a mug of coffee as he worked on a laptop. She recognized him from the prison.

Rylan Cross.

"Oh." She stopped short. She'd expected to see Zak, his wife, or one of the other guys on the SAR team, not Shane's former teammate. "Sorry to interrupt."

Rylan looked up and smiled. "No worries. I was just working." He laughed softly. "Which I do way too much, so it's a welcome interruption." He turned that kind smile on Ellie. "Hi, I'm Rylan."

"Uh, hi." Ellie's cheeks flushed pink as Rylan got up from the table and extended his good hand to her. "Ellie. I'm Alexis's sister."

"Nice to meet you, Ellie." Rylan's gaze flickered to Alexis. "What brings you two by?"

Alexis swallowed hard. "I'm here to say goodbye to my dog, Clue. I'm leaving California and can't take her with me."

Rylan's expression softened. "For what it's worth, she's very happy and loved here."

"I know."

Rylan closed his laptop and nodded toward the back of the building. "She's in the agility yard. They're testing her candidacy for SAR training today. You can go watch if you want."

As he led the way, Ellie leaned in and whispered, "He's handsome."

He was. And also kind, but he didn't do anything for her. And, she knew, he wasn't Ellie's type, either. "I thought you were laying off men after the disaster with Cal."

Ellie grumbled as she always did when she heard the lawyer's name.

"Are you ever going to tell me what happened between you two?"

"Nope."

The Rescue was quiet, but as they moved deeper into the building, she heard Clue barking excitedly from somewhere out back. Rylan opened a door and motioned them into the agility yard.

And there he was.

There they both were.

Shane was working with Clue, guiding her to find objects hidden throughout the yard as Zak watched from the sidelines without comment.

They were magnificent together, moving like a team. And Shane was grinning as the clever animal nailed one test after another. Alexis couldn't take her eyes off him. The way he moved with Clue, the joy on his face—it was like watching a man come alive. She knew he had demons, knew he was struggling to find his way, but in this moment, all of that was forgotten.

Everything in Alexis settled. Leaving Clue here was the right call. They belonged together.

Rylan stepped up beside her. "He's a good man. The best I've ever known. Stubborn as hell, though, and he doesn't always know what's good for him." The way he said it, she almost thought he was talking to himself, but then he slid her a sly sideways smile. "You're good for him."

He didn't give her a chance to respond. He just walked over to join Ellie, where she was chatting with Zak and the rest of the guys.

Shane and Clue finished up the test, and there was a burst of applause and congratulations from the team. Alexis clapped, too, even as her heart twisted painfully. She wanted to go to him, celebrate with him, but she knew it was better if she didn't. It would only make things harder for both of them.

As Clue had a burst of excited zoomies, Alexis took a step back, ready to leave. But before she could turn away, Shane looked over at her. He caught her gaze and held it, and her whole body tingled in response. Would she ever feel that sizzle, that spark, that connection with anyone else?

Probably not. She'd never felt it before him. She doubted she'd ever experience it again after she left.

Shane approached her slowly, his eyes never leaving hers. "Alexis," he said softly, his voice rough with emotion. "I didn't expect to see you here."

She swallowed hard. "I... I had to say goodbye to Clue."

His gaze went to the dog for a moment before returning to her. "You're leaving?"

Alexis nodded. "It's long past time I go home."

Something flickered across Shane's face, but he quickly hid it. "When are you going?"

She tilted her head toward the group as her sister's full-belly laugh filled the air. "We're on our way now. We need to be at the airport in an hour."

"Oh."

A beat of awkward silence.

"Are you, uh, going back to the mountain?" she asked.

Shane looked up at the mountain he'd called home for the

better part of the last decade and said nothing for a long moment. She studied his profile, trying to gauge what he was thinking.

Finally, he swallowed hard and looked back at her. "I don't want to."

Her breath caught in her throat. "Then what do you want?"

"You." Before she could form a reply, he reached out, stopping just short of touching her. "You're good for me, Lexi."

She blinked back tears. "That's what Rylan just said."

"Yeah, he'd know. He knows me better than anyone." Shane acted like he wanted to say more but seemed to struggle for the right words. "You... make me feel whole again, and I didn't think that was possible. You make me feel human."

"Oh, Shane." She stepped closer to him and rested her hand on his cheek. "You are human."

He leaned into her touch, his eyes closing as if he savored the feel of her skin against his. "Yeah, but I forgot that. I spent so many years hiding behind my scars, rejecting people before they could reject me. But you... you saw past them." His hand covered hers. "You never saw me as the monster I thought I was. You saw me as a man."

"Because I know what real monsters look like, and it's not you, Shane."

"I'm sorry I ghosted you these last few weeks. I wanted to see you so much it hurt, but I needed to figure some shit out first." He opened his eyes and looked at her with a desperate intensity that made her heart ache. "I love you. I want to be whole again for you. I want to heal for you."

"You should want that for yourself," she whispered around the lump growing in her throat.

"I do. Now, I do. Even if you don't feel the same way about me, I need you to know what you've done for me. I'm getting help, meeting with a therapist weekly to deal with my fucked up head. And I reached out to my doctor at the VA about my scars." His mouth tipped up at the corner. "To say he was surprised to hear from me is an understatement, but he's optimistic. I'll never look like my old self again, but he thinks we can make me look less..." He motioned to his face. "Horrifying."

Alexis stared at him with wonder. She had never known anyone so brave and yet so deeply self-effacing. She wanted to tell him she loved him too, but something kept her from saying those words again. So, instead, she leaned in and kissed him, her lips soft on his. He tasted like the wilderness he had made his home. She wrapped her arms around him and pulled him close, reveling in his warmth against her.

"I'm proud of you," she whispered when they parted. "But I never thought you were a monster."

"Lexi?" Ellie called. "We have to go if we're going to make our flight."

At her sister's voice, she closed her eyes and leaned into him, her hand sliding down his neck to rest on his chest. "I don't want to go."

"Then don't," Shane whispered against the top of her head.

"But I have a life in Chicago. A job I love. I need to go back to it."

"Take me with you." The words tumbled out of him in a rush. "I know I'm not... normal. But I can learn. I can try. And I'll be better with you by my side."

Tears pricked at the corners of her eyes. She had never expected to find love in such a dark place with a man who had been so broken by life. But here they were, two damaged souls finding solace in each other's arms.

"I can't ask you to move to Chicago. You'd hate it."

Shane's eyes darkened, his jaw tightening with determination. "I'll go anywhere with you. I don't care if it's the city or the wilderness. As long as you're with me, I'll be okay."

God. He was willing to take such a massive step for her, leaving behind everything he knew and facing the unknown. If nothing else, that told her exactly how serious he was...

But he couldn't go with her.

Shane's deep-seated issues couldn't be solved simply by moving to a new place. He needed therapy, support, and time to heal. And he had all of that here at Redwood Coast Rescue.

She took his face in her hands and kissed him softly. "Shane, I love you, too. But we have to take this slow. You need to focus on your therapy and your healing. Moving to Chicago won't fix everything."

"I know I have a lot of work to do on myself, but I'll do it. For you, Lexi. I've never felt this way before. I didn't think I could, and now I can't imagine my life without you in it. So, I go where you go."

Alexis felt the weight of his words in her chest. She had never been one to believe in fairy tales, but this felt like one. A story of two people finding each other in the darkness and, slowly but surely, finding their way into the light.

She looked up at the mountain again. It stood tall and proud against the bright blue sky. So much bad had happened here. So much ugly.

And the Shadow Stalker was still out there.

But there was so much beauty here, too. She had friends here, a community unlike anything she'd ever had in Chicago. And if she left now, would she forget all the good over time? Would this place become the place she only visited in her nightmares?

She didn't want that.

"Lexi?" Ellie stumbled to a halt when she spotted Alexis tucked into Shane's arms. "Oh. Uh, sorry. Take your time. I'll be in the car."

"Wait." Alexis broke from Shane's grasp and spun toward her sister. "Elle, I can't go."

Ellie's eyes widened. "What do you mean you can't go? We have to get back to work. The podcast isn't going to produce itself."

"We can do that from here. The story is still here. Hope is still here, somewhere. We could finally find her."

"Oh, Lexi..."

"Come on. What's waiting for us in Chicago? Long hours and takeout in a co-working space? Quiet, empty apartments? All of our old friends have married, had kids, or moved away. We never see them. We never date. Mom and Dad are in Florida. There's nothing there for us anymore, and I know for a fact you don't really want to leave either." She smiled as Cal Holden appeared in the doorway behind her sister, wearing one of his rumpled suits, looking even more harried and frazzled than usual.

"Ellie?" Cal said softly, a note of desperation in his voice.

Ellie's spine snapped straight. Her cheeks flushed as bright red as the rims of her glasses. "I have nothing to say to you, Callum."

"I know, but... I couldn't stay away, knowing you're leaving. I had to come say goodbye."

Alexis didn't think it was possible, but her sister turned even redder. She smiled conspiratorially up at Shane, then took his hand. "I don't know about Ellie, but I'm not going anywhere."

Cal's eyes widened, and he shifted his hopeful focus back to Ellie. "Are you staying?"

"Uh, well...." Ellie fumbled. "I mean, I never really considered it."

Cal tentatively reached out and took her hand in his. "I'd like it if you stayed."

"Oh." Ellie stared down at their joined hands and all but

melted before her stubbornness kicked back in. She yanked her hand away. As soon as the connection broke, she shook herself as if waking out of a trace and pushed her slipping glasses back up on her nose with a hand that trembled ever so slightly. "If I decide to stay, it won't be for you." Her eyes flickered over to Shane, then back to Alexis. "You're sure about this, Lexi?"

"Never been more sure. But you can go back to Chicago if you want."

Ellie grumbled, but then shook her head. "No, I'm with you. Always. Okay, then. We'll stay, but we need to talk about logistics. We'll need to set up a studio, get equipment, see about breaking our contract with the co-working space and subletting our apartments, and— we need a place to live. We're homeless!"

Alexis laughed. "Elle, take a breath. We'll figure it out. We'll make it work."

Ellie pushed back her shoulders as a look of stubborn determination came over her face. "Leave it to me." She turned to go back into the building. "Cal, do you know any real estate agents?"

Cal flashed a quicksilver grin, then followed her. "As a matter of fact..."

A weight lifted off Alexis's shoulders as she watched them go.

This was the right decision.

She'd felt connected to this place even before she met Shane. Now she felt anchored, and she wasn't about to let the Shadow Stalker scare her away. She was still going to tell the story of his victims.

Shane slipped his hand into hers, his fingers warm and strong. She sent him a sidelong glance and caught the flash of relief on his face before he hid it.

She chuckled and leaned into his side. "You really didn't want to go to Chicago, did you?"

"No," he said after a beat of hesitation and exhaled a short laugh. "I didn't. But I was serious about it. From now on, I go where you go." He turned his head to capture her lips in a searing kiss. His hand slid down her back, pulling her closer to his hard body.

Heat pooled between her legs, the desire thrumming like an electric current through her veins. She moaned into his mouth, her body responding to his touch with a hunger she couldn't contain. She threaded her fingers through his hair, tugging him impossibly closer, wanting to feel every inch of him against her. She didn't care that they were still standing in the middle of the agility yard with an audience. All she knew was that she needed him.

Shane pulled away, breathing heavily. "Not here," he whispered against her lips. "I want you, but not with an audience." He sent a dry look toward his new teammates. Zak and Sawyer were grinning. Donovan gave them a wolf whistle. Pierce gave two thumbs up in approval.

Heat stung her cheeks. She took a deep breath and leaned her forehead against his chest, trying to steady herself. "Oh my God."

Shane kissed the top of her head, his arms still wrapped tightly around her. "We should go inside," he said. "We can talk about everything. And maybe..." He grinned wickedly. "We can find a more private place to continue this—"

Clue came running over to them and weaseled between their legs, forcing them apart.

Alexis let out a breathless laugh as Clue bounced around their feet, wagging her tail. "Looks like we're not getting any alone time."

He kissed her again. "Later." The heated promise in that one word had her legs turning to jelly and her nipples puckering inside her bra. She had no doubt he'd fulfill that promise tonight and then some.

She glanced back at the Redwood Coast Rescue team as Clue raced to join their dogs in a play session. "So, what do we do now?"

Shane looped an arm around her, and together, they started walking toward the group. "Now? I have a dog to train, and you..." He pressed a kiss to the side of her head. "You have a serial killer to catch."

epilogue

SHE WAS PERFECT.

Long dark hair.

Big, sad eyes.

Damaged.

Alone.

He watched from the shadows as a light flicked on in her kitchen.

It had been so long since he'd let himself play.

Too long.

Excitement hummed in him.

The way she moved was almost like a dance, graceful and fluid. He couldn't wait to make her his next masterpiece, to bring out the beauty in her through his art.

But he had to wait.

It had to be perfect.

So he sat in the shadows and watched as she went about her mundane routine of preparing dinner for one. He knew everything about her, from her fear of the outside world to her obsession with true crime podcasts—including the one by Alexis Summers. That bitch who nearly ruined decades of work.

His blood boiled. He should've killed her when he had the chance, but—

Well, it didn't matter now.

Alexis didn't matter.

She wasn't perfect.

Not like his muse.

He looked back toward the small house, and panic sizzled over his nerve endings. She wasn't in the kitchen anymore. The window was dark.

Where was she?

Had she left?

No, he assured himself. Of course she was still in the house somewhere. His muse never left it.

But he had to make sure.

He slid toward the house and peered through the living room window. It was a risk, but he'd done it many times before.

There she was.

Sitting on her couch, her TV dinner uneaten on the coffee table, hugging a pillow to her chest. Her eyes were glued to the television, but she wasn't watching it.

He pressed his palms against the glass, feeling the coldness of the night on the window. She didn't notice him.

Poor thing. Lost in her own pretty head. He'd help her with that. He'd free her. Soon.

"Hello," he whispered, his breath fogging the glass. "Veronica."

The Redwood Coast Rescue adventure continues with Veronica's book, Searching for Shadows!

also by tonya burrows

Redwood Coast Rescue

Searching for Rescue

Searching for Risk

Searching for Justice

Searching for Shadows

Northern Rescue

Northern Escape

Northern Deception

Northern Salvation

HORNET

SEAL of Honor

Honor Reclaimed

Broken Honor

Code of Honor

Reckless Honor

Honor Avenged

HORNET: Class Alpha

Fragmented Loyalty

Wilde Security

Wilde Nights in Paradise

Wilde for Her

Wilde at Heart
Running Wilde
Too Wilde to Tame